Sharing

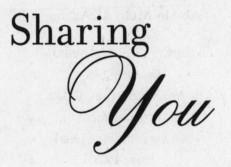

You

Also by Molly McAdams

Sharing
You

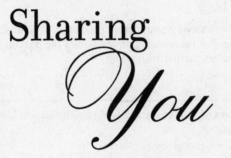

MOLLY
McADAMS

wm

WILLIAM MORROW
An Imprint of HarperCollins*Publishers*

HarperCollins books may be purchased for educational, business, or sales promotional use. For information please e-mail the Special Markets Department at SPsales@harpercollins.com.

FIRST EDITION

Library of Congress Cataloging-in-Publication Data

McAdams, Molly.
  Sharing you : a novel / Molly McAdams.
    pages cm
  Summary: "Sensational New York Times bestselling author Molly McAdams breaks bounds with this emotionally wrenching, heartbreakingly real New Adult novel of love, passion, guilt, honor, and infidelity. Twenty-three year old Kamryn Cunningham has left behind a privileged, turbulent past for the anonymity of small-town life. Busy with her new bakery, she isn't interested in hook-ups or fix-ups. Then she meets the very sexy, very married Brody. Though she can't deny the pull between them, Kamryn isn't a cheater and she's not good at sharing. Twenty-six year old Brody Saco may be married, but he isn't happy. When his girlfriend got pregnant six years ago, he did the right thing. and he's been paying for it ever since. Now, his marriage is nothing but a trap filled with hate, manipulation, and blame—the remnants of a tragedy that happened five years earlier. While he's never broken his vows, he can't stop the flood of emotion that meeting Kamryn unlocks. Brought together by an intense heat that is impossible to resist, Brody and Kamryn share stolen moments and nights that end too soon. But is their love strong enough to bear the weight of Kamryn's guilt? And is Brody strong enough to confront the pain of the past and finally break free of his conniving wife?"—Provided by publisher.
  ISBN 978-0-06-229940-6 (paperback)
  1. Man-woman relationship—Fiction. 2. Adultery—Fiction. I. Title.

  PS3613.C25S53 2014

  813'.6—dc23

                        2014008305

---

14 15 16 17 18   OV/RRD   10 9 8 7 6 5 4 3 2 1

For R & S, you know who you are.
Your story is beautiful, and your love is something of dreams. I'm so
happy y'all are finally able to live out the Happy Ever After you deserve.

Sharing
You

For the Readers

THIS IS OUR story. It's one many won't understand or accept, and some may even be offended by it . . . but this is the reality of our fight for each other and our struggle to be together.

In a perfect world, you have a soul mate, you'll search until you finally find each other, and you'll begin this perfect journey you've been planning out for years. As for us . . . well, there was nothing perfect about the way we had to do things.

Our connection was instant, and there was no doubting the pull we had for each other. But with everything in our lives forcing us to stay apart, our relationship was full of secrets, pain, guilt, sorrow, and the most beautiful love either of us has ever known.

And we wouldn't have had it any other way.

Prologue

Kamryn

September 2, 2014

THE SOUND OF three familiar, masculine laughs stopped my retreat to my room, and I quietly tiptoed back toward the study. *What are Charles and his dad doing here?* I peeked through the door they had left cracked and was thankful for the darkened hallway. I knew from experience they wouldn't see me unless they were actively searching, and since all of them were huddled around a far table with drinks in their hands, I figured I was fine.

I pulled my cell out of my pocket and glanced at the time before dimming the screen again. Charles wasn't supposed to pick me up for another four hours, and we'd *just* had brunch with his family. Couldn't he go away for a while?

Charles. Good God, what had he even changed into? He had brown loafers—no socks—khaki shorts, and a dark pink polo on. And yeah, the collar was popped. His dark blond hair had that "I just got out of bed" look, but I'd had the unfortunate pleasure of watching him spend twenty-five minutes to make it look that way that morning, so it had lost its appeal.

I'd been dating Charles York since our junior year of high school, and it was safe to say that over the last six years . . . I'd really come to loathe him. His clothes, his too-perfect bleached smile, his fake tan, his laugh that had to be louder than everyone else's in the room, the fact that he was the *third* Charles York, his signature silver BMW he upgraded for the newer version every two years like it was a cell phone or something. And this was probably the worst part of all—he was so close with my dad that he was having drinks with him on his own time.

I'm sure most girls dreamed of a man their parents would absolutely adore, but my parents hadn't exactly given me a choice when it came to Charles. I had to date him. It was a match made in "Kentucky Derby Heaven," as my mother liked to say. And no, I'm not joking. Both our families were from the Brighton Country Club neighborhood in Lexington, and every year for the last fifteen years either Charles's family or my family has had a horse win the Kentucky Derby. Our parents were always talking about combining our stables, and I was beginning to think I'd already been sold off to the York family to make this happen.

Why not just break up with him and tell my parents to shove it? Uh, yeah . . . not so easy in my family. I was a Cunningham; in the racing world, we were pretty much royalty. My parents

were Bruce and Charlotte, and as the only daughter of the perfect power couple, I was expected to be perfect as well. Perfect
hair, perfect clothes, and a perfectly planned life. That perfectly
planned life included marrying Charles someday. And breaking up with Charles didn't just mean ruining the plans both our
families had for us; it would be devastating to the racing world.
Mom's words, not mine—she's a little dramatic.

It hadn't always been awful with him. We'd grown up together, I'd crushed on him for as long as I could remember before
we actually started dating, and we'd been friends our entire lives.
When I say *entire,* I mean I'm praying I burned all the evidence of
our moms bathing us together when we were babies. Charles had
always been funny, incredibly smart, and attractive—probably
too attractive for his own good, because, unfortunately, he *knew*
how good he looked. It wasn't until after we began dating that
he started turning into the guy I couldn't stand to be around . . .
or maybe it was just that I began realizing how much I hated the
world I'd grown up in. That world was full of people with too
much money, a place where unfaithful and backstabbing relationships were the norm, where you couldn't have a conversation
unless you were gossiping or slandering someone, and where
friends and enemies were one and the same. Yeah . . . now that I
think back on it, Charles hadn't changed at all when we started
dating, it was just that it also happened about the same time I
decided I needed to get away from Kentucky . . . away from everything I'd ever known.

I started pulling away from him as much as my parents would
allow when he went away to college and thankfully I only had to
see him about two days out of the month, unless he was on break.
Once he graduated and came back home, I'd just had to stomach

it. Because doing anything that wasn't on my parents' planned-out path wasn't an option. I'd found that out the hard way one night when my mom overheard me mentioning my desire for a life without Charles . . . I can't imagine how she would have reacted if she'd known I'd planned to take a very different path from the one she'd made for me.

The only thing I'd ever done for myself was go to culinary and then pastry school, and that had been a huge to-do in our house. The only people who had supported me were our maid, Barbara, and, surprisingly, Charles. I'd been so taken aback and grateful—Charles's support had gotten my parents to finally agree to it—that it'd been the only time since we started dating that I'd ever called him by his preferred name, Chad. He hated the name Charles, and I think that is why I refused to call him anything else.

Charles said my name, and I leaned closer to the door in time to catch whatever his dad had begun saying.

"You're sure she'll say yes? I don't know what's going on with that girl of yours, Bruce, but she's seemed rather . . . hesitant lately."

Say yes to what?

"I'm sure of it, she knows her place. She knows how important this merger is."

"I don't know . . ." Chuck, Charles's father, began.

"Dad, stop. She'll marry me. Like Bruce said, she knows her place, and thank God for that. The sooner she gets off this pipe dream of owning a bakery the better."

Dad's eyebrows shot up. "That's surprising, seeing as you're the only one who encouraged Kamryn to go to those food schools."

Charles laughed and took a sip of his drink. "No offense to

your home and wife, Bruce, but I want a wife who knows her place in my home as well as by my side."

Chuck and Dad both snickered. I continued to stand there with my jaw on the floor.

"Don't get me wrong," Charles went on. "Charlotte's great for business and public outings, but that woman couldn't cook if her life depended on—"

Dad cut him off. "Which, of course, means Kamryn couldn't cook before she went to those schools."

Charles clucked his tongue and pointed his hand—the one holding his scotch glass—at Dad. "Precisely."

"Smart kid you've got there, Chuck." Dad laughed into his glass before taking another sip. "Damn smart kid."

"So you *aren't* letting her open up the bakery? Your mother and I have been worried about your judgment in letting her do this."

"Hell no." Charles laughed, shooting his dad a look like he was crazy. "There's a reason I haven't let her open one yet—I'm just trying to keep her happy until we're married."

"And you'll be proposing tonight?"

My eyes about popped out of my head at my dad's question.

"Yup, gonna push for that whole 'we've been together forever, there's no point in having a long engagement' thing. My guess, end of the year, we'll be married and we can stop dicking around with this merger."

"Sounds good," Dad said, and the men stood up to shake hands across the table.

I made sure to keep quiet as I quickly backed away from the door and took off for my room. Get married to him? Oh, hell no. I might have stayed with him to keep Mom and Dad happy and off my back for the last six years, but no way in hell was I going into a lifelong commitment with him. And I couldn't believe he would encourage me to go to the cooking schools just so he'd have a wife from the fucking fifties!

"Cook for you?" I hissed as I shut my bedroom door and hurried to the closet. "I'll cook for you." Grabbing a small suitcase, I threw it onto the bed and opened it up. "With rat poison."

I buzzed Barbara before grabbing only a few of my favorite clothes and shoes and tossing everything in there. I was throwing the necessities from my bathroom in a small bag when I heard Barb's voice in my room.

"What can I do for ya, baby girl . . . Kam, honey?"

"Barb!" I apparently still hadn't graduated from hissing. "He's proposing!"

Her eyes were wide as she looked at the too-full suitcase. "I thought we were already expecting that?"

"Tonight! And he just told Dad that we would be married by the end of the year. That's barely four months away!"

"Oh, my sweet girl." She smiled sadly and sat on my bed. "I knew this day was coming, but I'm not ready for it yet."

"Me neither, but, Barbara, I can't—I can't keep doing this. Six years with him, and twenty-two years of not being able to live. I *have* to go."

"I know."

"It was one thing to continue dating him while he was away at school and I was trying to save money for this, but it's an entirely different thing to be engaged to him. And you know Mom and Dad won't let me say no!"

"I know," she said again, and there were tears falling down her plump cheeks.

"Barb, don't cry, please don't cry!" God, now I was going to start crying. Barbara had been my parents' maid since before I was born, she'd taken care of me growing up, and she was the reason I'd wanted to go to culinary school. She was the reason all of this was about to be possible, and she was the only reason I'd followed my parents' path as long as I had. She had also been what my mom used against me to keep me with Charles.

I'd been telling Barb about a date with him I'd just come back from and how torturous it had been, and when I'd gone to my room a few minutes later Mom was in there waiting for me. After reminding me of how much my relationship with Charles meant to both our families, she'd asked, "You don't want to see anything happen to Barbara, now, do you?" The threat had been clear. And it had been enough to keep my mouth shut and keep me with Charles over the next few years as Barb and I began preparing for this night.

Dad refused to pay for the schools, not like I expected him to or would have allowed it. I'd gotten loans and simultaneously started asking Barb for her help. There was no way for Barb or me to bet on the races without word getting out that we were doing so, and Dad would have flipped if he'd known. I didn't want to use his money for anything, so I'd sold a few things Mom would never notice were missing from my room and used that money for Barb's brother to start placing bets for me. All the bets started off small, since I hadn't sold anything of much value, and over the last four years they'd multiplied like you wouldn't believe.

I'd paid off the loans first before replacing what I'd originally sold from my room, and then continued to place higher and higher bets. The last race I'd bet on—and won—I'd put down close to six figures. You get the right races, and the right pockets with horses competing, you can make a fortune. And that's just what I'd been doing.

Barbara and I had spent many nights planning this day, but like she'd said, we weren't expecting it to happen just yet.

"I'm sorry," she said, wiping away some tears. "I'm happy for you, baby girl, really I am. I'm just gonna miss you so much."

"I'll miss you too." I hugged her fiercely and let a few tears escape as she held me. She would be the only person from this entire state I would miss. "As soon as I get to Oregon and get settled, I'll get a phone and call you so you'll have my number."

She nodded and cleared her throat as her arms left my waist to grip my hands. "You can do this, Kamryn. I just know it. You have the money, you have the smarts, you have the talent, and you have the drive. Get away from here, baby girl, and don't come back to this life. This life is its own form of prison."

It was. God, it was.

"Do you have everything packed?"

"I do."

"All right." She cleared her throat and her lips quivered as she spoke. "I'm going to call my brother and have him come right over to take you to the train station. I just pulled some cookies out of the oven. You go take some and a glass of milk to your daddy. Your mother is at her tennis lesson and then going to a massage, so she won't be back for some time now. By the time you're done sweet-talking your daddy, Ray will be here and I'll have your suitcase and money waiting in his car."

I took a deep breath and stood when she did. "I'll miss you, Barbara. I love you."

"I love you too, baby girl. Go live."

1

Kamryn

May 4, 2015

"KC! GIRL, I am definitely going to need some chocolate to get through today."

"Kinlee, seriously?" I huffed as I came through the double doors with trays of cupcakes. "We aren't even opened yet. That key I gave you was for emergencies if I wasn't available."

"You're open—I flipped the board for you."

I rolled my eyes and smiled. I'd met Kinlee almost immediately after moving to Jeston, Oregon, and I thanked God every day for that. I'd never had a friend like her and didn't know how I would get through day-to-day life without her. "Only you, Lee, only you." I handed over a chocolate cupcake with peanut butter cream cheese frosting and started stocking my pastry case.

Within two weeks of getting to Jeston, I'd bought an SUV, found a condo, and leased a small space for what would be my bakery. Over the next two and a half months I was overseeing renovations for KC's Sweet Treats, and that's how I'd met Kinlee. She was two years older than me and shorter than short, had long black hair and a bubbly personality I'd die for. She and her mom had the boutique right next door to me, and she'd come by asking if I knew what was going to be put in next to her store. One thing led to another, and I was her new best friend because I could bake. Kinlee could be crude, she could be sweet, and she was loyal to those she cared for. And I absolutely adored every bit of her.

Barbara and I spoke at least once a week when Mom and Dad were both out of the house, and though I missed her like crazy, I didn't regret my decision. I did feel bad, though, for leaving her in that hell-storm. Apparently my parents and Charles's family had gone nuts when I left, but ultimately they saw my "disappearance" as a chance for more publicity: they twisted it, saying I'd been kidnapped, so they could wind up on a few news stations. I didn't know what the status with my "disappearance" was, because I really didn't care. Other than talking with Barbara, I didn't pay attention to anything that had to do with racing or Kentucky. My life was in Oregon now, and that was all I cared to focus on. If I worried about them looking for me, or having others look for me, it would just make me paranoid. I couldn't live like that.

And I loved it in Jeston. This city of roughly 15,000 people had an old-time small-town charm to it, and I wondered how it'd taken me twenty-two years to get here. There was no doubt in my mind that I belonged here.

The best part? No one had a clue who I was.

The minute I'd gotten to Jeston and checked into a hotel, I'd found a salon, chopped fourteen inches off my hair, and dyed my golden locks a rich brown. Even with the fourteen inches gone, my hair still brushed the tops of my shoulders. With the thick, black-framed glasses I bought at a drugstore, I looked like a new person. And I couldn't be happier.

"Oh, my God, heaven!" Kinlee groaned as she hopped onto the counter near the register. "Kace, tell me how you aren't fat yet?"

I snorted. "Probably the same way you aren't."

"You mean you're having wild animal sex twenty-four/seven? I was wondering why you wouldn't let us set you up with anyone! You've been holding out on me, haven't you?"

"Oh, God, okay, definitely not the same way as you. Ew, Kinlee, all I'm going to be able to think about when I see Jace is you two having wild sex."

"Say that again!"

I froze with my arm inside the pastry case. "Uh, all I'm going—"

"No, no. The last few words." She leaned close and stared at my mouth as I ran over everything I'd said.

"Having wild sex?"

"*Wald?* For real, where are you from?"

I blew out a heavy breath and shook my head as I smirked at my case. "Just not from here." I tried to tame my accent—which I didn't even know I had until I moved here—as much as possible around Kinlee. She and her husband, Jace, were always trying to figure out where I'd moved from, but if they found out they'd want to know why I was here at all. And I wasn't ready for that.

"One of these days, Kace, I will get it out of you." She took another bite of cupcake and moaned. "This is better than *wald* sex with Jace."

"Okay, your husband is hot and all, don't get me wrong, but I really don't want to be thinking about him like that."

"Just saying." She held her hands up. "You were the one who asked."

"Uh, no. No, I didn't. And back to your original question: I run most mornings. Not all of us can avoid getting fat by having crazy hot sex, especially when we're not having sex at all."

She shoved the last bit of cupcake into her mouth and spoke through the bite. "KC, I have been trying to set you up for the last seven months! It's not my fault you refuse to go on a date with anyone. You're twenty-three—time to go on a date, woman!"

"Can I remind you that the last guy you tried to set me up with was shorter than me?"

It's not like I'm an Amazon or anything, I'm five-seven, but I do love heels. Just another reason why I couldn't stand Charles: he was one inch taller than me, so heels were a no-go. Of course, I wore heels whenever he wasn't around, but he made me carry flats just in case he showed up anywhere I was. There are only so many flats you can wear before you want to find all the flats in the world and burn them.

"I only know so many single men!"

"This barbecue tomorrow, you aren't going to try . . ." I trailed off when I noticed her looking away. "Kinlee!"

"*I* didn't invite them! Swear to God, I didn't invite them this time. The guys on Jace's shift from the department are all gonna be there, and most of them are single, but that's not my fault."

Oh, Lord, single firemen.

"But it won't just be the guys from the department, there will be other people, some couples from the neighborhood, all people you've met before."

I nodded and shut the pastry case doors. "All right, well, you know I'll be there, not like I have anything else to do on a Sunday. Want me to bring something?" I don't know why I even bothered asking anymore, it's not like I'd show up without something anyway.

"Cookies, cupcakes, whatever you want." She leaned back and blew an air kiss before jumping off the counter. "Jeez, KC, I know you needed help taste-testing and all—what with your lovely faces you make—but you've really got to stop keeping me from opening my store. You're bad for my hips and business."

"My faces when I eat sweets are a secret, Lee! Only you and my employees know about them!"

With a wink and a saucy smile, she was gone.

Well, they were the only ones in Oregon who knew about them. I was teased relentlessly in pastry school for the faces I'd make whenever we tried our dishes, and Barb used to give a big belly laugh every time as well. Charles wouldn't let me eat sweets in public *because* of those expressions, but he sure seemed to like them when we were alone. I shivered thinking about Charles and was glad that for eight months now I hadn't had to pretend to not be swallowing back bile every time he kissed or touched me. I took a quick glance at the front of my bakery and smiled to myself before going to the back. For the first time in my life, I was exactly where I wanted to be.

Brody

May 4, 2015

"OLIVIA!" *WHAT THE fuck is all this?*

"Hmm?"

"Liv, come here."

"What?" she snapped when she got to the living room.

I took a deep, calming breath and planted a smile on my face. "What's all this?"

"It's called furniture, Brody." Her eyebrows rose. "You know, you sit on the couches, put drinks on the coffee table, put your feet up on the ottoman . . ."

"Cute, Liv, real cute. Where did it come from?"

"The furniture store," she said slowly, like she was talking to a child.

I huffed and gritted my teeth. "Olivia, where did you get the furniture and how much did it cost?"

"Do you not like it?"

"That's not what I said, please answer my question."

"These are the exact same couches the Cunninghams have in their house! They had a five-page spread in *Better Homes and Gardens* last month!"

You've got to be kidding me. I could only play this game with her so many times before I snapped. And I only had about another two minutes before I lost the calm tone I was working so hard to maintain. Liv and her parents were obsessed with some family they viewed as royalty, had been since before I'd met them. They were in the same social circles but had never met, considering a good portion of the United States separated them.

I didn't understand it. To be honest, I'd always found it weird how they tried to be exactly like the Cunningham family—and now it was one of the main reasons I freaked out on Olivia when I did. Because just as Liv wanted to make sure she was identical to the Cunninghams' only daughter, she also thought she needed to blow money the way they did. Money I wasn't earning fast enough.

"The Cunninghams," I said, an edge to my voice. "For the millionth time, Liv, you can't live as if you *are* them. You can't live like we have all the money in the world."

"How could you not like it?" Tears instantly fell to her cheeks, and I bit back a groan. "I bought them for you, it was only seven grand."

Seven—*seven* grand. *Only* seven grand. "Olivia, where did you get seven grand?" *Please, God, please say from your father.*

She sniffed and swiped at her eyes. "You had five thousand just sitting in the savings account, I had to do something with it!"

"Olivia! Are you—are you—damn it! You pulled this shit *again*?"

Her tears kept falling, but she stopped sniffling. "How dare you! I did this for you!"

"Every time, Liv, every time I start saving money you go and blow it on something we don't need, all because of some fucking famous family! And now this time you spent an extra two thousand? I have to pay the mortgage in a week."

"Regardless, it was *still* a gift. You could at least say thank you! Every time I buy something you get upset. At least I'm *giving* you something—all you've ever done is *take* from me."

With that, she turned and stormed down the hall to her bedroom, leaving me crushed, aching, and once again so damn tired of this. I rubbed my chest, where the constant dull ache was now stabbing, and fell into one of the kitchen chairs.

Not more than ten minutes later, she was back and bouncing through the kitchen. "Hey, babe! What do you want for dinner?"

I wasn't even surprised by this anymore; I'd just been waiting until she came back. "It's after midnight, Liv. I'm not really hungry."

"Did you already eat dinner? I'll heat some of this up." She murmured the last part to herself as she continued to pull takeout boxes from the fridge.

"Yeah, earlier tonight."

"Oh." She slammed the fridge door shut and turned to look at me. "All right, I get it. I can't have kids, so I'm not good enough to heat up food for you. Yeah, fine, Brody. Feed your damn self."

And here she goes again.

My wife hadn't always been like this—and despite how it seems, she's not crazy—and our relationship hadn't been like this either. We'd been high school sweethearts, and then I'd left for the Army right after we graduated and everything changed. I came back home to visit after a deployment, and though we had stayed together, Liv and I weren't close anymore. I knew why she'd stayed with me, but I hadn't cared either way. She was someone to come back to when I visited my family.

Her parents hated me, and they let me know it every time they saw me. I wasn't good enough for their daughter because I wasn't going to college and didn't come from money like they had. My family wasn't poor by any means—we'd grown up in a great house in a great neighborhood. But we weren't dripping with money, and we didn't belong to the country club that Liv's parents did. So apparently that meant we were trash. Olivia loved that her parents didn't accept me, and I knew that was the only reason we'd stayed together as long as we had. But like I said, I didn't mind.

I had a year left in the Army when my world changed. She called me crying, saying she was pregnant. I'd requested emergency leave as soon as we got off the phone and married her the minute I got home. Her parents were furious—hell, so were mine—but no way was I going to let her go through that alone. I couldn't take care of her like her parents did, but I'd take care of her the best I could.

It took a lot of people high up pulling strings, but I was able to get us a house on base for as soon as I got back. Only thing was, she refused to go back to the base with me. Basically said thanks for marrying her and she was going to stay with her parents until I decided I was done "playing Navy." Shit you not. And I wasn't even in the Navy.

I couldn't get leave often, but even when I did, she still didn't see me. Didn't even try. When I'd ask her, she'd say, "What's the point? We're already married."

Yeah. Married and I haven't seen you since two days after the fact.

The only thing she did include me in was the baby. After every appointment she sent pictures of the ultrasound, and she'd let me help her pick out a name. I'd gotten the message the minute she went into labor and received more pictures after he was delivered. The next time I got leave she still refused to see me and wouldn't let me see our son. Instead, I stood outside her parents' house and called her, only to find out that if I wanted to see either of them, I wouldn't reenlist and I'd move back to Jeston.

So that's what I did. When it came time to reenlist, I declined and moved back. Bought us a house—it wasn't much, and her dad let me know that all the time—but I'd bought it and that's all that mattered. Once I had it furnished, I called her, and she finally let me meet my son for the first time.

"Brody!" Olivia snapped, and I blinked away the best day of my life. She held out her hand momentarily to show she was on the phone before continuing. "Daddy said he'd pay you back for the couches, since obviously with your pay you can't afford what I need to be happy."

My eyes narrowed. It was almost 12:30 in the morning, and she was calling her dad to talk to him about the damn couches? I rubbed the sharp pain in my chest and pushed away from the table before standing up. "He can keep his money, I don't want it. Good night, Olivia."

"BABY, ARE YOU awake?"

I sat up in my bed less than an hour later and rubbed a hand over my face. "Uh, yeah. What's up, Liv?"

"I'm so sorry!" She burst into tears and crumpled to the floor.

Aw hell. I hopped out of my bed and went over to her. Sliding down until I was sitting up against the wall, I pulled her onto my lap. "It's okay, you just have to stop spending our money like that."

"B-but the c-couch we had w-was three years old! The Cunninghams never have couches three years old."

"I know, but ours was still a perfectly good couch," I crooned softly. "Just because your parents and the Cunninghams can refurnish their entire houses every few years doesn't mean we can, all right?"

She nodded vigorously. "I just—I just needed something to do."

I took a deep breath in and scrunched my face together as I prepared for what might happen next. I knew this could turn out bad again, but I had to try. "Maybe we should get a dog."

"A dog? A damn *dog*? No! You can't just give me a dog and make it all better, Brody!" She scrambled off my lap and sprinted down the hall, heading for her side of the house.

Yes, I said *her* side of the house. I normally don't even see her because she prefers to spend her days at her parents' house unless she's in a mood like the one tonight. It usually lasts a week, as this one has, and we go through every emotion possible about fifteen times a day. I try to be patient with her because I know I'm the reason she's like this, but after four and a half years of this constant happy-depressed-flirty-pissed-horny-sweet-flat-out-bitch roller coaster, I feel like I'm losing my damn mind. And what's worse? As soon as we're in public she's normal Liv—not the Liv I fell in love with in high school, but the one who's confident in herself and her parents' money, and the one who will eat you alive if you cross her.

Her door slammed shut, and I stood to stumble over to my bed, thankful again that I was able to buy a big enough house that we could have our own spaces. We'd been married for almost six years, and I could count on one hand the number of times we'd had sex in those years. We hadn't even slept in the same bed since a few months after I got back from the Army.

As I tried to get comfortable enough to go back to sleep, I rubbed at the ache in my chest and prayed the nightmares stayed away.

2

Kamryn

May 5, 2015

"KINLEE, YOUR HUSBAND thinks I'm a freak now."

"Did he not before?"

"Funny," I mumbled drily. "I just burst out laughing as soon as I saw him because I thought of y'all's crazy sex life."

Kinlee froze with the boxes of cupcakes still in her hands. "Did you just say *y'all's*? I'm adding that to *wald* and *shew*. Where'd you say you were from again?"

"East of here." I smirked. We were almost on the coastline of Oregon. Everything was east of here. To avoid her narrowed eyes, I took the boxes back from her and started arranging the cupcakes in the holders I'd brought with me.

Jace came into the kitchen talking on his phone and grinned at me curiously before kissing Kinlee's head and snatching a red velvet cupcake. "Sweet, I'm glad you'll be here. Yeah, man, see you soon."

"Who's coming, babe?" Kinlee took a piece of his cupcake and shoved it in her mouth before helping me arrange the rest of them.

"Brody. Guess the bitch is letting him out of the house without her for once."

"Oh, thank God. I thought you were about to say she was coming too."

Jace gave his wife a horrified look. "Uh, no. She's not allowed here, and she knows that."

Kinlee was shaking her head back and forth as she said in a softer tone, "Well, I'm glad he's coming. It'll be good for him to get out. We haven't seen him in a long time. Poor guy."

"Um, who is Brody?" I asked sheepishly. Not like it was my business, but Kinlee had sat in my lap to finish arranging the cupcakes, so it wasn't like I could leave the conversation.

"Jace's brother—"

"Jace, you have a brother? How did I not know this?"

"'Cause his wife's a bitch and doesn't let him do anything other than work," Jace said around the rest of the cupcake.

"That must be hard for him if y'all—*you guys*—don't get along with his wife."

Kinlee turned in my lap, her eyes wide. "No way. Honestly . . . *bitch* is practically a compliment for that woman. Brody doesn't even like her."

"Then why is he with her?"

"He—it's just been difficult for them," she said, eyeing Jace, and I saw him nod his head at her. "It's really sad. Brody's the nicest guy you'll ever meet, but he's just stuck in this marriage with her. And it's wearing on him—every time we see him he looks a little worse. Like she's just making everything that makes Brody *Brody* disappear."

"Shouldn't have married her," Jace said with a small shake of his head.

"Babe, he was just trying to—"

"He shouldn't have married her," Jace repeated, then walked toward the living room when there was a knock on the door.

Kinlee sighed and leaned her back against the table, still facing me. "Jace *hates* Olivia. Well, we all do, but I think he hates her more than anyone. Jace and Brody were inseparable growing up, probably because they're only a little over a year apart, but like I said, we almost never see him anymore. And it's all because of her."

I just nodded my head and kept my mouth shut. I knew from experience there could always be some underlying situation that kept a bad couple together. And Brody and Olivia were married—it wasn't like he could just break up with her . . . or disappear like I had. Obviously, whatever was going on with them, Jace and Kinlee knew all about it, but I doubted they realized how hard it must be for Brody to have his family so against his wife. Whether he liked her or not.

"Hey, KC, I've got someone I want you to meet," Jace said on his way back in.

I rolled my eyes and let Kinlee know that I was going to kill her as soon as this barbecue was over. I'd been in a relationship for six years before getting here, and then I was trying to start my business. I didn't have time for, or want, a relationship then or now. But Kinlee and Jace were set on setting me—oh, holy firemen buddies.

"Which one?"

Kinlee, still in my lap, leaned back to whisper, "The cute one."

"Right." I nodded. "Which one?"

She laughed and stood up to hug each of the guys as Jace started the introductions. "KC, these are some of the guys on my crew: Josh, Craig, and Aiden. Guys, this is Kinlee's friend KC." Before I could say anything, Jace whispered, "Aiden, this is the girl I was telling you about—"

"With the bakery, right," Aiden said with a bright smile. "It's great to finally meet you."

Finally? Really now? I glanced at Jace and shot him a glare as I stood up before turning to look at Aiden. "Nice to meet you too."

Aiden was even taller than Jace's six-one frame and had kind brown eyes and short buzzed hair that made his handsome face look rugged, and God it worked for him. He was wearing a loose gray V-neck shirt that seemed to add to his looks rather than make him look feminine, like it did Charles. And while he wasn't bulky, his muscled arms promised a hell of a lot to look at underneath that shirt.

A slow grin tugged at his lips, and I realized I was just standing there staring at him. Turning away quickly to hide my embarrassment as Jace left to answer the door again, I began gathering up the boxes to break down.

"So Jace said you just moved here?" Aiden grabbed the last two boxes off the table and followed me toward the kitchen counter.

I risked a glance at him as I nodded. "Yeah, about eight months ago."

"Where are you fr— Oh, KC. I thought your name was

Casey." He looked at the top of the cupcake carrier for another second before flattening the box and moving on to the last one.

"No, it's just my initials, but I've gone by KC forever." *If eight months could be counted as forever.*

Before he could ask another question about my name, one of the other guys spoke loudly. "Oh, hell. Aiden, you need to try these."

Aiden smiled and tilted his head back toward the kitchen table. "Which one do you recommend?"

My mouth popped open, then immediately shut. "The—" I worried my bottom lip as I looked over the four different cupcakes. "You really—" I started pointing toward the triple chocolate and quickly brought my arm back. "Well, this one—"

"That good, huh?" He chuckled and flashed that bright smile at me again.

"Well, I made all my favorites today. You can't ask me to choose between them."

"Then I won't." Grabbing one of each, he set them all out in a row in front of him and pulled another chair toward him. "All right, let's do this."

I laughed out loud and grabbed a knife before moving to take the seat next to him. "Trust me, you'd regret it if you ate all of them." My cupcakes weren't exactly small, and they were rich—he would go into a sugar coma in about half an hour if he finished those off. I grabbed the triple chocolate and cut it into fourths before handing him a piece and cleaning off the knife.

"Oh, damn," he said with a groan. He kept chewing until it was gone. "Was that—" He looked at the rest of the cupcake. "Is that pudding in the center?" I smiled and started cutting the chocolate peanut butter one. "You put pudding *in* a cupcake?"

"Yeah, my ma— Um, my aunt Barbara and I wanted something different than the normal crème or custard that usually goes in the center." I looked back into his brown eyes and shrugged. "It's messier, but it works for that one. And that's the only cupcake I do that with. All right, try this one. It doesn't have a filling."

He tasted the next two cupcakes, and after groaning or grunting his appreciation for each one, he kept pointing back to the "pudding cupcake," saying it was still his favorite. But the red velvet was next, and it was a customer favorite, so . . .

"I thought you were going to be eating these with me. If I'm picking my favorite out of the bunch, you need to pick your favorite too—or at least your favorite for today."

I laughed uneasily. "Uh, no, I'm good."

Aiden nudged my side and pointed at the banana nut cupcake he'd just tried. "You're this incredible baker and you don't even eat your own food?"

"Oh, no, she does," Kinlee spoke up for me. "She just doesn't when other people are around. Well, people other than me."

Aiden's face fell. "You're not one of those girls who won't eat in front of guys, are you?"

"She'll eat all right, just not sweets."

"I'm really critical of myself—" I began, but Kinlee cut me off.

"Pfft, no you're not. She just looks like she's having an orgasm every time she eats something sweet."

My breath came out in a huff and I couldn't help but laugh as my elbow hit the table and my forehead fell into my hand.

Jace, Craig, and Aiden all burst out laughing, and Aiden tried to speak through his hysterics. "Oh, God, I have to see this now."

"No, you really don't!" I leaned back in my chair, eyes wide.

Aiden was still laughing so hard he could barely keep his arm

up as he teased me. "I'll even feed it to you—we'll call it fore-
play."

A shot of desire hit my stomach hearing his deep voice say
that, but I was able to maintain my sanity for the time being
and dodged the piece of cake in his hands. "Kinlee! We are not
friends for the rest of the day and no free cupcakes all next week."

She gasped. "What? That is beyond rude! Jace, hold her arms
down!"

I slipped out of the chair, darted past Jace, and took off for the
living room. It was just like Kinlee to say something like that in
front of guys I'd just met—one of whom she was trying to set me
up with—but they didn't understand, it was *really* embarrassing
the way I reacted to my sweets. No way in hell I was gonna allow
them to feed me!

I'd just rounded the corner leading out of the living room when
I ran into a brick wall. The wall's hands shot out and grabbed
my upper arms to steady me at the same time I reached out and
grabbed broad shoulders in an attempt to keep myself upright
and looked up. I inhaled audibly, and his gray eyes widened as
his lips separated. My chest was rising and falling quicker than
normal, and it had absolutely nothing to do with running away
from Jace or running into the most incredible-looking man I'd
ever seen, but damn if it didn't have everything to do with the
man himself.

He was looking at me as if he'd just found what he'd been looking for—and the look was so open, so intense, it sent a shiver
running down my spine. It should have scared me, but it somehow felt like what I was looking at was a reflection of what I was
feeling.

And that just made no sense. I wasn't looking for anyone. But this man? Yeah, I'd found everything I'd never even known I'd been looking for . . . in him. I could feel it in the way I felt like I needed to be closer to him than I already was, the way the tips of my fingers were tingling with a need to explore his body, the way I was physically aching to know everything about him. And yet, I felt like I knew everything there was to know about him, and we still hadn't said a word. It felt like hours had passed before Jace's voice sounded behind me.

"Kace, sooner you eat a bite, sooner this is all over!"

Eat a bite . . . what? I couldn't remember why I'd even ended up in the entryway of Jace and Kinlee's house, let alone make sense of his words right now. All I knew was that Jace had brought me back to reality, that I felt like I was home, like I was where I was meant to be for the first time in my life . . . and it was in a stranger's arms. That thought—that realization—was scaring the ever-living hell out of me.

The stranger holding me blinked rapidly, and his hands tightened before he let go and took a step away from me. Even then, we still couldn't tear our eyes away from each other . . .

"KC, you can't hi— What the hell, you're not even trying to hide. Oh, hey, Brody!" Jace said loudly, stepping between us to hug him.

. . . until Jace's last word. I dropped my head to stare at the floor, my eyes wide with horror.

Brody? Oh, God, this is Brody? The married brother? I felt so stupid, I should have realized it the second I'd seen him. I didn't have to look back up to notice that he was practically the same height as Jace, with the same black hair, amazing smile, and tan skin from their Italian heritage. It was obvious they were brothers, but at the same time they looked nothing alike to me.

Of course, Jace was attractive, hell, he was more than attractive, but Brody was . . . you couldn't even begin to describe Brody as *attractive*. *Perfection* was a better word to start with. Though nothing about him was so perfect that he looked put together in the way Charles always did. His nose had a slight bump along the ridge, his white smile showed perfectly straight teeth, but was crooked . . . and I could look at that crooked smile all day long.

"Yeah, just walked in and I ran into . . ." I glanced up when he trailed off, noticing that his gray eyes were on mine, and his gravelly voice lowered even more. ". . . Uh, I ran into her."

"Oh, right. Brody, this is KC. Kace, this is my brother, Brody."

That crooked smile was back as he reached an arm out, only this time it was directed at me instead of his brother. And God it took everything in me to stay away from him when he directed it at me.

"It's a pleasure," he said quietly.

"Jace, it's not fair if only you see KC's O face," Kinlee called out. "She has to be in the kitchen for all of us to see!"

My breath rushed out in a huff, Brody's eyebrows lifted, and Jace started laughing along with Craig and Aiden as Kinlee came around the corner.

"Hey, Brody! I didn't know you were here already! Good to see you." Kinlee hugged his waist hard and looked up at him. "Glad you got to come out today. Can I get you anything?"

He smirked at her, and his eyes met mine again. "Well, apparently I'm here just in time to see KC's O face."

My shoulders slumped, and I dropped my head to look at the floor again. "Kinlee, swear to all that is holy no more free cupcakes, *ever.*"

"Oh, get over it, Kace." She bumped my shoulder and smiled sweetly at me. "It's funny and you know it is. Plus, we don't have to worry about an icebreaker now, everyone's having a good time." She squeezed my hand and began towing me back toward the living room, but I pulled my arm free.

"I'll be back." I tried to avoid Brody's eyes, but it was impossible as I turned and made a beeline for the bathroom to collect myself. I wasn't mad at Kinlee, it had been funny at first, but I was beyond freaked out by my reaction to meeting her brother-in-law.

Turning on the water in the sink, I realized my hands were shaking. I made quick work of taking off my glasses, splashing water on my face, and turning the water off before gripping the counter. What was happening to me? And what happened in the entryway with Brody? My heart was still beating fast, and I swear I could feel his hands on my arms. The way his gray eyes had captured mine and held them, making it feel like time stood still, was unlike anything I'd ever experienced. This was fairy-tale shit, this kind of thing didn't happen in real life.

Except, it just had.

And the man was married.

I groaned and shakily put my glasses back on as I stared at my reflection in the mirror. My blue eyes were too bright and my cheeks still too red. I looked excited. I *was* excited—I'd just found a man who changed everything I'd ever known. Taking a deep breath in, I held it for a few seconds before I blew it out as I realized that I'd found the one thing in life I would never be able to have. Why, after only two minutes of being near him, did that hurt so badly?

Brody

May 5, 2015

GLANCING BEHIND ME, I looked around for that Casey girl and came up empty. What the hell had just happened with her? She was beautiful, sure. Wide blue eyes, full lips that had been drawing me in, and the kind of body I'm sure a lot of women paid thousands for. But that wasn't what got me. There was something else in those eyes, and it had taken Jace blocking her from view before I could stop looking at her. God, what was it about her? I could still feel her pressed against my chest. Now I was forcing myself to stay where I was instead of finding her to ask what had just happened.

"Man, I was surprised as shit when you called to say you were coming over, it's been a long time. Too long."

I smiled and took the beer from my younger brother's hand, trying to be grateful for the distraction. "I know. It's been kinda intense lately. Shift change at the department has really screwed with me, I'm still not used to the time changing on me, and then Olivia . . . well . . . you know how that goes."

Jace grunted and Kinlee rubbed my arm as she passed me to go stand in Jace's arms. "What happened now?"

"She drained our accounts again," I mumbled. Looking around once more, I made sure no one was close enough to overhear our conversation. I took a long pull from my bottle and shrugged like it was nothing new—because with Liv, it wasn't.

"Shit, how much this time?"

"Seven thousand on couches. I didn't know couches could cost that much! And I only had five grand in savings before she bought it all, so you can imagine how that's blowing over."

"Jeez, Brody," Kinlee said with a shake of her head. "We'll help, how much do you need?"

I quickly swallowed my next gulp. "None, we'll be fine. I save some money that she doesn't know about for times like this, so the bills will all be paid. I'm not worried, I'm—God, I'm just tired of this shit, you know? And then she went and called her dad because I wasn't happy about it, and it was after midnight. It's just—I don't know. Just same ol' Liv."

"Brody, you're miserable. You can't keep doing this, you don't see Kinlee and me, you never see Mom and Dad . . . and you look like you're dead. No offense, but my brother's gone. She's bringing you down, and I have no idea why you're staying with her. I get it, divorce is bad, but there are exceptions, and Olivia is the damn exception! She's doing this to you on purpose. She's not struggling like you think she is. And I know you think you're stuck, but you're not."

"I don't think I'm stuck—"

"Yes, you do! And if you hadn't married her psycho ass, you wouldn't be stuck with her now that Tate's—"

"Jace!" Kinlee smacked his stomach, her eyes and mouth going wide.

All the air left my lungs in a rush, and I mashed my lips together as I nodded my head in order to not lash out at him—or break down in the middle of their kitchen. I drained my beer, tipped the bottle toward my brother, and slammed it on the counter. "Thanks for the invite, Kinlee. Good seeing you guys again." I took a few steps before grunting, "It's Tate's birthday, if you forgot."

"Brody . . ." they said at the same time, but I was still stalking toward the front door.

I rounded the corner at the same time Casey hit the end of the hall, and my steps actually faltered. Her wide eyes behind those fucking adorable glasses got even wider when she saw me, and one of her hands went up to the wall as if to keep herself up. Without realizing it, I'd changed direction and taken two steps toward her before I could stop myself. What *was* it about her? I'd never felt anything like this before, and I wasn't sure if I wanted the feeling to last forever or wanted to run far from it. Because no matter how addicting the feeling was quickly becoming, I knew I couldn't keep her.

I'm married, I kept repeating to myself. To a woman like Olivia or not, I shouldn't be thinking about another woman this way . . . and Tate—shit. I swallowed the lump in my throat and had to force my eyes shut before I could turn away from Casey and leave my brother's house.

3

Kamryn

May 9, 2015

"THINGS ARE GREAT, Barb, I swear."

She sighed. "If you say so, baby girl. You just sound off today."

I am off. And I know exactly why. I haven't slept since the barbecue at Jace and Kinlee's four days ago because all I can think about is a certain brother.

"You're sighing."

"I am?" I kept myself from sighing again and looked around the coffee shop to make sure I didn't know anyone there before hanging my head. "I met a guy, Barb."

"You did? Oh, baby girl! Then why do you seem so sad about this? Tell me all about him! Is he handsome?"

I smiled and felt my cheeks get warm. "Yeah, you could say that. But nothing's going to come of it."

She tsked at me, and I pictured her pointing whatever cooking utensil she was holding in the air like I was there next to her. "Kam. I don't know why you won't let yourself date any of these men Kinlee tries to set you up with. It's not like you got out of a long relationship that you were happy in. You were miserable with that preppy bastard. You deserve someone better, so let yourself be happy."

"That's not it, Barb. This isn't one of the guys Kinlee tried to set me up with, although she tried that this weekend again. And if I hadn't met this other guy, I actually think I would've really liked to get to know Aiden—"

"Oh, what a great name," she whispered.

I laughed. "But then I met Brody . . . he's Kinlee's brother-in-law." Even I could hear how pathetic I sounded now.

"There's nothing wrong with that, I'm sure Kinlee wouldn't mind—"

"Yeah, but I'd bet his wife would," I mumbled lamely.

"Oh, baby girl. Don't you go getting caught up in that. Nothing good can come from that, and I raised you to be above all that nonsense."

"I'm not, Barb. I told you, nothing's going to come of it. And besides, I only saw him for all of two minutes."

"So then why do you sound like your mother when I hide her Xanax?"

I laughed out loud and covered my face with my free hand when people around the coffee shop looked at me. "Oh, my God, Barb . . . you're the one who does that?" My mom didn't suffer from anxiety—she just liked the effect Xanax and vodka combined had on her. She was always accusing my dad of hiding the pills and would go into a faux-depressed state until they reappeared. Knowing Barbara was the one hiding them made me love her even more.

"Course I do. Now explain. Two minutes knowing a *married* man and you're acting like this?"

"I—I can't explain it without sounding crazy."

"Well, I've lived with Crazy One and Crazy Two for twenty-five years, I'm an expert on it."

"True," I huffed softly. "We just . . . had these moments. We couldn't look away from each other, couldn't speak to each other . . ."

"This is all my fault for letting you read trashy romance novels growing up," she mumbled, and I laughed.

"I'm being serious! I swear I distinctly remember the way he smelled, and I can still feel where his hands were." I looked down to see goose bumps spreading on my arms at the same time I heard the aforementioned cooking utensil hit the counter.

"He had his hands on you and he is married? He is bad news, Kamryn! You stay away from him!"

"No, Jesus, Barb! He caught me. I literally ran into him and almost fell over. He just caught and steadied me."

"Oh. Well. Still. You need to remember the man is married, and there are some lines you just don't cross. And don't you dare take the Lord's name in vain around me again, young lady."

"Yes, ma'am."

"Why don't you tell me more about this other guy . . . Aiden, right? Let's talk about him until Kinlee gets there. I'm assuming she's running late again?"

"Of course, she is." I sighed and rolled my eyes as I looked up at the door to see if it was her who just walked in. "Oh . . . my . . . word. He's a cop," I whispered.

"Who is?" she whispered back at me.

"Brody. He just walked into the coffee shop."

"Kamryn, don't you dare—"

"Barbara," I hissed as I forced my eyes away from Brody in his uniform and looked around to see if there was anything I could hide behind. There wasn't. "He's married!"

"Baby girl, you are not too big for me to give your behind a good swat! Don't you use that tone with me! I'll fly to Oregon just to remind you of your manners."

"Yes, ma'am, but I need to hide, and there's nothing to hide behind. Maybe he won't—"

"KC?"

Son of a bitch! "He found me," I whispered, before turning to look at Brody. "Hi," I said through gritted teeth. Oh, Christ, he looked better than I remembered . . . and with that uniform on, this was not about to go over well.

Brody gave me a strange glance before looking to the side and back to me. "You don't remember me, do you? I'm Brody—"

"No, of course, I do. You're Jace's brother." *How am I supposed to forget you? I can't sleep because of you!* "Barb, I have to go, call me later." She was spouting off warnings as I tapped the END button and laid my phone on the table.

"Sorry, I didn't realize you were on the phone. You didn't have to get off."

"It's fine." I wanted to ask how he was, or if he'd been able to get any sleep since this weekend. But we hadn't even said anything to each other at Kinlee's house. I wasn't some old friend who could ask how the family was. *Wife, Kamryn. He has a wife.*

Like a bucket of ice-cold water had been thrown on me, my mind cleared and I straightened in my chair. "So, police officer, huh?"

That crooked smile crossed his face, and his eyes bore into mine. "Yeah."

"Y'all's family is really covering all the bases. Jace is a fire-fighter, you're a cop. Do you have another sibling who's an EMT?"

He huffed softly, and I tried to focus on anything other than his face. "No, no other siblings, but my parents really should have thought about that one when they were having kids. Would have rounded it out well."

"Right?" I said with a laugh. His eyes were locked on mine, and I felt myself wanting to get lost in them. Clearing my throat, I broke the connection for a moment and shot him a grin. "So you left kinda quick the other day. Everything okay? Or do you just not like slumming it with the firefighters?" I instantly regretted teasing him when a wave of some indescribable emotion passed over his face. Whatever it was, it wasn't good.

"I'd just forgotten I had somewhere to be." He looked around the shop quickly before his eyes landed back on me, but that crooked smile was gone. *What did I say?* "Are you meeting someone here?"

"Um, just Kinlee, but she's—"

"Late? Figures." He shook his head, and that perfectly imperfect smile was back. "Well, I need to get back on patrol. Can I buy you a drink?"

"Oh, no, that's fine. You have a good night."

"I insist. I mean, it's the least I can do. I interrupted your phone call."

That had to be the *last* reason for needing to buy me coffee.

But that stupid crooked smirk was there, and his gaze was holding mine intently, and to be honest, I was starting to forget why I wasn't supposed to be attracted to this man. "Okay."

He stepped back and waited for me to stand before silently leading me over to the registers. After ordering a large coffee for himself and a caramel latte with whip for me, he walked over to the side with me to wait for my drink, and I tried to hide my smile.

"What do you do, KC?"

"I own a bakery." His eyes widened, and I stupidly pointed in the direction of the strip where my bakery was. "It's right next door to Kinlee's boutique."

"How old are you?"

"Um, twenty-three?" It came out sounding like a question, but I didn't understand why he was looking at me the way he was. "Why?"

"You're twenty-three and you *own* a bakery. That's just really impressive. Something like that obviously has to be something you love, and not many people get to say they do what they love for a living. To be that young, own your own business, and be doing what you love—like I said . . . it's impressive."

"Th-thank you. I guess? Um . . . huh." I turned back toward the counter and waited for my drink to appear. I could feel the heat in my cheeks and felt it get worse when I saw him watching me from the corner of my eye. I didn't know how to respond to what he said. *That was a compliment, right? You say "Thanks" to compliments . . . don't you?* My mind flashed through different instances with Charles and my parents, and I quickly shook my head to get rid of any thoughts of them. Those people wouldn't know how to give a compliment if their life depended on it.

"How long have you been in Oregon?"

My head snapped to the right, and Brody laughed softly at my question-mark expression.

"Well, it's obvious you're from the South."

I always went back to talking normal—well, normal for me—after a phone call with Barbara, and I hadn't even tried to hide it. I cursed silently and smiled as I reminded myself to talk as not-normal as possible. "About eight months."

"Where'd you move from?"

"Don't even try it, Bro. She won't give it up to me, she's not about to tell you."

Brody and I both jolted away from each other at the sound of Kinlee's voice, and I grabbed my latte as she kissed his cheek and grabbed me for an awkward hug. I hadn't even realized how close Brody and I had gotten to each other until then, and from the way he was looking in between his sister-in-law and me, he hadn't either.

"Sorry I'm late, there were people on the road, and they were in my way. You know how it goes."

I nodded and laughed. "Other drivers? Yeah, they do tend to get in the way sometimes, Lee."

"Whatever, they should've known I had somewhere to be. There're other roads they can be on." She turned toward Brody and grabbed his hand before whispering. "You okay? I'm sorry about Jace, don't let him . . ."

I quietly stepped back and walked over to the table where I'd been sitting. The way Brody's face instantly shut down when Kinlee asked if he was okay let me know I was not meant to be there for that conversation. I wanted to know what Jace had done, and I figured that must have been why Brody left their house so suddenly last weekend, but I kept my life private. I wasn't about to go snooping through theirs. The hair on the back of my neck stood up, and I looked up from my coffee cup to see Brody standing there looking down at me.

"Why won't you tell her where you're from?"

"It's a part of my life I'd rather forget about," I whispered before I could stop myself.

His brow furrowed and his mouth opened, but it snapped shut and he leaned away as his eyes got a faraway look. After a few seconds he grabbed the radio on his shoulder. "Unit four-eighteen, go ahead—unit four-eighteen, ten-four en route. I have to go," he stated, but he didn't move away, in fact he moved closer, his gray eyes pinning me to my seat.

My heart began racing impossibly faster as I once again felt something I'd never experienced with any other man but the one standing less than two feet from me. It felt like I was being pulled to him, and I wanted to give in so bad.

"Have a good night, KC," he said in a low voice, and I shivered from the warmth and roughness of it. "I enjoyed seeing you again."

"Be safe tonight."

One corner of his mouth pulled up, and he knocked his knuckles against the table twice before backing away with his eyes on me. When he got a few more feet away, he turned, called out a good-bye to Kinlee—who was tapping rapidly on her phone as she waited for her coffee—and walked out the door.

I tried not to, but I followed his movements as he jogged out to his patrol Tahoe and pulled open the driver's door. At the last second, he turned to look at the window where I was sitting, and I swear I could feel the heat from his gaze even from that distance.

"Okay!" Kinlee exclaimed, and I jumped. "I'm here. Sheesh, I really need to start driving with you so I won't be late anymore."

"That would just make both of us late."

"Exactly, but then technically we're both on time because we get here at the same time."

I shook my head and took a sip of my latte. "I don't understand how your mom trusts you to get the boutique open on time."

"Easy, she told me a long time ago that we open an hour before we really do. I know now that we don't actually open at eight. But I still get ready like we open at eight, so I usually make it there in time to open by nine."

"Huh, makes sense."

She pointed at the cup that was pressed to my lips again. "What *I* still don't understand is how you can drink something that's sweet and not be affected by it."

"Espresso and coffee have the perfect amount of bitterness. Putting something sweet in it is the only way it's drinkable, and the bitterness overrides my enjoyment of the sweetness."

"Uh-huh. Whatever." Her phone chimed, and she replied before looking back at me. "Did Brody say anything to you about last weekend?"

Just hearing his name had my heart rate increasing and my body warming. "No, he actually kinda changed the subject when I brought up him leaving so soon."

Kinlee groaned and sat back in her seat. One hand rubbed at her temple, and she grimaced. "Poor Brody. Jace was such a dick to him when he came over. I want Brody to leave his wife just as much as the rest of his family, but really, Jace crossed a line this weekend."

I waited to see if she'd add anything, but she just sat there worrying her bottom lip in between sips of coffee. "You really love Brody, don't you?"

Her eyes darted over to mine, and she smiled. "I grew up next door to those boys. Brody's like my older brother."

"Lee, I didn't know that." I crossed my arms over my chest and sat back. "So you married the boy next door, huh?"

She laughed. "I did. He told me when I was five years old that he was going to marry me, and he kissed me on the playground."

"What? How have I never heard about any of this? That is the sweetest thing I've ever heard!"

"Not at the time it wasn't! He was gross, and my older brothers told me all boys had cooties or something. I don't remember, but I punched him in the nose and got sent to the principal's office."

I forced down the sip I'd just taken and burst out laughing. "Oh, God. That's amazing, I'm bringing that up next time I'm over."

Kinlee's phone went off again, and I watched her smile grow even wider. "Aiden is asking if he can have your number."

"What? No."

"KC!"

"Kinlee." I mimicked her whiny three-year-old tone.

"Why not? What was wrong with Aiden?"

"Nothing, he just—" *Isn't Brody. Brody is married . . .* married, *Kamryn!* I thought about the way Aiden made me feel. It'd been more of a response than I'd ever had for even Charles. More than any guy, really. Why did I have to meet him on the same day I met Brody? Why did I have to meet Brody at all? Barbara's words from our call came back to me, and I uncrossed my legs and sat straight up. "You know what? Give it to him."

Kinlee's jaw dropped. "What?"

"Have Jace give him my number."

I've never seen Kinlee move that fast. She dropped her phone twice because she tried to pick up her phone and begin texting simultaneously. "Oh, my God, Kace! I'm so excited right now! I can't believe you're actually letting us give a guy your number. Does this mean you liked him? You looked like you were having a good time, but I didn't think—" She cut off and started cracking up before showing me her phone. "Jace doesn't believe me."

I glanced over the screen.

> *HUBBY:*
> *Aiden's asking about KC, he wants her number*

> *You know she won't let you give it to him. But I'll ask.*

> *HUBBY:*
> *Thx baby*

> *HOLY SHIT SHE SAID GIVE IT TO HIM!!!!!*

> *HUBBY:*
> *Ha. Fuckin hilarious babe. You actually had me for a sec*

I smiled and grabbed my phone.

> *Seriously. Give Aiden my number.*

> *JACE:*
> *No fucking way! I feel like a proud older brother or something. My lil KC is growin up n gon' get her a boyfran.*

Whoa buddy. I said give him my number. Let's start there.
And stop making fun of my accent over text. Ass.

"There, all taken care of. Now will y'all stop trying to set me up with every single man you know?"

Kinlee happy-clapped and took a long sip of her drink. "As long as things work out with Aiden!"

I groaned and let my face fall into my hand.

4

Kamryn

May 10, 2015

"Where is Aiden taking you tomorrow?"

I stopped going through different tops and turned to look at her. "I thought you were supposed to find that out, Lee!"

"You know Jace doesn't know these things. And besides, they've been busy this last shift. I haven't talked to him much."

"Well then, why am I here looking for an outfit if I don't even know how to dress?"

Kinlee stopped pulling boxes of shoes out of a shipment that had been delivered and walked over to where I was standing. "Well, Aiden's just Aiden. He's kind of a 'what you see is what you get' guy. He won't try to impress you with fancy restaurants or something just to get you to like him." She turned quickly and pointed at me. "That doesn't mean he won't treat you well and show you a good time. It just means he's not going to shell out for some crazy expensive dinner on the first date to get you to think he's loaded."

"Thank God." I'd had enough of people who were loaded to last me a damn lifetime.

"So don't be too fancy, but don't go in yoga pants, and you should be fine."

I made a face. "Because that really narrows it down. That's basically your entire store and 90 percent of my wardrobe."

"Make sure the shirt is blue, or has blue in it. Or dark gray or black! We need your eyes to pop."

"Yes, Mom," I mumbled and walked around more when she went back to putting the shipment away.

Aiden hadn't wasted time, that's for sure. By the time Kinlee and I left the coffee shop the night before, he'd already texted me to see if Jace had given him a fake number, and after talking for a while when I got home, we'd set up a date that Saturday.

"How's this?" I held up an electric-blue see-through top.

"Perfect. I just got in these black shorts, where did they go? Anyway, they'll look great with that and your legs."

"Yay," I said unenthusiastically.

"Well, don't try to sound excited or anything."

"I am excited." Wasn't I?

Broad shoulders, gray eyes, and a crooked smile filled my mind. No, I was so not excited.

THE NEXT NIGHT with Aiden was going much better than I'd thought it would. We had the same humor and had spent practically all of dinner laughing to the point where I'd started crying. But everything about the date and Aiden screamed friendship to me. Those few flashes of attraction the weekend before at the barbecue had been it for me when it came to him.

All I could see was Brody. And I hated it.

I was still barely sleeping, and the few hours I did sleep he starred in every dream. If that wasn't enough, I spent all my waking hours going over every detail about him while simultaneously trying to get him out of my mind.

When Aiden gave me a smile and I wished for it to be crooked, I realized it obviously wasn't working. And this wasn't fair to Aiden.

We were walking to a little coffee shop around the corner from the restaurant when he grabbed my hand in his, and my mind instantly went to Brody.

"Aiden," I began, pulling my hand back.

"I'm sorry. Too fast?"

I stopped walking and shut my eyes tightly before looking up at him. "No, it's not . . . it's just—"

Understanding and disappointment came over his face, and I wished I could give him something more. "I pushed you into this, I know," he said. "I'm sorry."

"I belong to someone else," I blurted out, and no matter how impossible that seemed, the moment the words were out of my mouth I knew it was true. I belonged to a man who I didn't know and who would never belong to me. Aiden was the kind of guy I needed—deep down I knew that, but I just wasn't into it.

"You're seeing someone? Jace swore you were single."

"I am single." His eyebrows drew together, and I shook my head. "I'm not seeing him, but right now, I belong to him. And it wouldn't be fair to lead you on when he's all I can think about."

"Huh. I, uh—well, I guess I have to be thankful for that kind of honesty." Aiden rocked back on his heels and looked around embarrassed. "Does he know?"

"What?"

"This guy. Does he know that you feel this way?"

"Oh, God, I hope not."

Surprise and confusion flashed through his eyes before he smiled widely at me. "Then I'll wait."

"For wh— Why?"

"Well, you were kinda obvious that you don't want him knowing about your feelings, and you said you belong to him *for now*. So I'll wait my turn."

"Aiden," I whispered and scratched at my forehead. "That's not . . . I don't want you to do that. I don't want to lead you on."

"And you're not." His smile somehow seemed to get wider as he draped an arm over my shoulders and began walking toward the little coffee shop again. "You told me how you feel, and I'll respect that. To be honest, I don't have a lot of time for dating, as I'm sure you can see with Jace's schedule. Last weekend and tonight with you were some of the best times I've had in the last year. So we'll stay friends, if nothing else. Just know that if you ever change your mind, I'll be waiting."

I sighed, but was hopeful that he was serious about staying friends. I had as much fun with Aiden as I did with Kinlee and Jace. "If you say—" I cut off on a gasp. *Oh, mother of all that is holy.*

My body went rigid, and if it hadn't been for Aiden's arm guiding me, I'm sure I would have stopped walking. Barely ten feet from us, frozen with a coffee cup halfway to his lips and his wide eyes on us, was the man haunting every second of my life.

"Hey, Brody! Where'd you go last week?"

My pulse jumped when Aiden said his name, and though I tried to keep my eyes anywhere else—the street, the cars, the shops, my feet—they kept pulling back to Brody. My eyes quickly traveled over the tight-fitting Henley shirt and perfectly worn jeans on his body, and I wished he'd been on patrol so he would've been in his uniform instead. A flash of Brody in his uniform went through my mind and I realized that actually would have made it harder to tear my gaze from him. Someone needed to put the man in a cardboard box. No, he just needed to leave and I needed to never see him again.

"Um, I just—I had somewhere I needed to be." His eyes barely held Aiden's for more than a few seconds before darting over to me, and over to where Aiden's hand rested on my shoulder. He blinked a couple times and seemed to clear whatever he'd been thinking about. "What are the two of you up to?"

I couldn't respond to him even if I'd wanted to tell him what I was doing here with Aiden. My mouth had gone dry, and I had to keep my hands clasped so I wouldn't reach out toward him. I had a soul-deep yearning to be closer to him, and I knew the second I stepped into his arms I would feel like I was exactly where I was meant to be again. I'd been craving that feeling ever since we'd separated in Kinlee's entryway, and being this close to him for the second time since then was making it practically impossible to stay away.

"We grabbed some dinner, and now we're going over to get coffee before I take her home."

Which means date. Brody knows I'm on a date with Aiden. Obviously, as if seeing us out like this wasn't enough of a hint. But I hated that he knew, and I hated that I hated that. Brody's eyes narrowed for a fraction of a second as he stared at Aiden, and his forehead tightened when his eyes met mine again. I would have given anything to know what he was thinking about in that moment. Because I needed him to crush the hope I had that he didn't look happy about the fact that I was standing here with Aiden's arm around me. I knew he couldn't care, but I was making myself believe that he did. And that wasn't going to help in getting me to stop thinking about him.

"Well, uh, I'll let you get back to that. It was good seeing you again, KC. Aiden," he grunted by way of closing the conversation. And with one last look from Aiden to me, he took off toward a dark Expedition parked at the sidewalk.

My body automatically took a step in the same direction, but Aiden started walking us toward the coffee shop again. I exhaled roughly when the sense of loss hit me.

It's official. There's something wrong with me. These are not normal feelings to have for someone I don't even know. It's not normal to crave and obsess over a man I've only had a five-minute conversation with. Aiden removed his arm when we got to the door of the shop, and I turned to look at the dark SUV just sitting there. The need to catch another glimpse of him, or at least hear his voice again, was so strong that I could feel this energy working its way from my chest to my arms, as if calling me to him.

"KC?"

"Huh?" My head snapped back to look at Aiden and his patient smile. I tried to feel something, anything, for the man standing in front of me. But there was nothing. My entire body was now buzzing, and somehow I knew Brody's eyes were on me, and that knowledge sent a welcome shiver up my spine.

Aiden's smile faltered when he noticed how distracted I was.

"Did you still want coffee or did you want me to take you home now?"

"Of course, I do," I assured him. "Let's go in."

When I stole a glance at the street, the Expedition was gone.

Brody

May 13, 2015

WHAT ARE YOU doing? What the fuck are you doing? I tapped my thumbs on the steering wheel of the Expedition and looked out the windshield toward the shop. It was early Monday morning, it had been two days that felt like a damn week since I'd seen her, and I felt like I was going crazy.

Casey—or KC, as I'd found out—had consumed my every thought over the last week, waking and sleeping. I knew I should forget about her and the weird moments we shared, but I couldn't. And now here I was sitting in front of her bakery. I'd reminded myself thousands of times over the last week that I was married, that I couldn't think of her the way I had been . . . but then I saw her on Thursday, and again on Saturday, and Saturday was what broke me. I wanted to rip Aiden's arm off her. An unwelcome amount of jealousy and pain surged through me when I saw them walking together, and I knew then that my attempts to forget about her were futile.

The fact that it pained me at all to see her with someone else irritated me to no end as I went over everything a dozen times yesterday. But as the day wore on, I realized that what I felt for

KC, as strange as it might be, was something I'd never known and something I knew I'd never experience again.

I was prepared to live with that knowledge and never act on it. I don't know if it was the fact that Tate would have been five last week, or that Olivia came home trashed from her parents' last night telling me that because I *only* make fifty thousand a year I'm a worthless piece of shit she keeps around for laughs, but I decided then that I couldn't keep living my miserable life when there was a woman who made me feel more alive than I had in the last five years with just one look. And before I knew what I was doing, I found myself in front of her store this morning.

I shifted down in my seat as my sister-in-law came bouncing out of the bakery and over to the shop she owned with her mom, unlocked the door, and went inside. My eyes shot back over to the bakery, and even though I knew I shouldn't, there was no talking myself out of what I was about to do.

A little bell chimed overhead when the door to the bakery opened and shut, and I heard her voice from the back of the shop. Her accent wasn't as heavy as I remembered it, but God the sound still pinned me to the floor. "What'd you forget, Lee?"

"Uh . . . not Kinlee," a thin guy standing behind the pastry case called out before eyeing me curiously.

KC came through a swinging door with a black apron on, covered with smudges of what I assumed was flour and cake batter. Her dark hair was pulled back, and a few loose strands had fallen in her face. She looked more incredible every time I saw her.

"Brody," she whispered and set down a tray of cookies and puffs.

That was the first time I'd heard her say my name, and a million different things flashed through my mind. I wanted her to say it again, I wanted to hear her moan it as I had her body underneath mine, and I wanted to have her whisper it in the dark as we got to know each other on every other level, not just the intimate one.

"Well, hello, Brody," the guy said, and KC made a face before waving him toward the door she'd just come through.

"I have this, Andy."

Andy and KC seemed to have a short, silent conversation before Andy rolled his eyes and walked to the back. KC stared at the swinging door for a second before turning around. Her body was facing me, but her eyes darted around the bakery—looking anywhere but at me.

I didn't know how to start this conversation. I hadn't planned this out. I'd just known I needed to talk to her about what was happening between us. I needed confirmation that I wasn't the only one who was slowly going insane over this—this—whatever this was. "I need to know what this is," I finally blurted out.

No "Hi," no "How are you." I just went past all the small talk . . . went past everything a normal man and woman would talk about . . . and threw out the issue I'd probably been deluding myself into thinking both of us had been plagued by the past week.

Her eyes widened and met mine momentarily before touching everything else in the bakery again. She cleared her throat twice before stuttering, "What—what *what* is?"

I managed to close as much of the distance between us as the counter would allow and waited until she finally glanced at me again. "*This.*" I used my index finger to indicate the two of us. "You have to know what I'm talking about." *God, please know what I'm talking about.*

She exhaled deeply and shook her head. Her eyes flickered to the front door, and then to the tray of cookies she'd just brought out, where they stayed. "Brody, you're married," she said softly, and the statement sounded so pained I had to grip the countertop when my hand began reaching out toward her. "I can't—I don't—you're *married.*" Her blue eyes finally met and held mine, and I knew then that this had been tormenting her as much as it had me.

"I know. But I've been going out of my mind since I first saw you last Sunday, and I—I don't know, I know this is insane, KC." Looking to each side of the counter, I found the space to get behind it and walked over to her as I said, "One thing I've learned in my life and my line of work is that life is short, and I know that I don't know you yet . . . but I know I wouldn't be able to live with myself knowing I walked away from the only person who's made me feel alive in years, the only person who's made me feel—whatever the hell this is—*ever.* Tell me I'm not alone in this," I pleaded.

She looked around the store and shut her eyes tightly as she shook her head. I wanted to beg her to open them again, but words left me when she spoke. "You're not. Brody, I swear the world stops when I look at you."

My entire body relaxed, and my already quick heartbeat took off.

"But that doesn't change the fact that you have a wife. So what's all this for, Brody?" she asked, her pained voice now laced with venom, and the relief I'd felt disappeared. "Just to make yourself feel better knowing that someone else wants you? Or are you just wanting an affair because you're tired of your spouse? Because if that's what you want, I suggest you go find someone else who's looking for the same." Her blue eyes narrowed and she spoke through gritted teeth. "Do you know that for the last eight days all I could think about was a married man who stirred up emotions in me I didn't even know I could possess? And it's been killing me, Brody!"

"No, KC . . . God, no. This is a weird situation, trust me, I know. I've been at war with myself with what I know is right, and what I don't think I can live without. I do not want an *affair*. I don't know what something between us could be called, but that word doesn't do what's happening between us justice. But I know that my marriage is over, I know I want you more than I want my next breath, and I know I would be insane to walk out that door and away from you."

Her eyes fluttered shut, and a sound that was something between a whimper and a cry left her lips before she could cover her mouth with her hand. Everything in me wanted to pull her close, but I forced my hands to stay on my hips as I waited for her response. I didn't know if she wanted me to touch her, and honestly, I didn't know if I was ready for what would happen if I had her in my arms.

KC looked back up at me and blew out a shaky breath. "I didn't know I could feel this for someone else, but, Brody, I can't be the reason your marriage ends."

"It's been over," I said, the truth in my words clear. "We were over before we ever got married."

"Is that why you don't wear a wedding ring? Or did you take it off because you were coming to talk to me?"

I glanced down to my left hand and shrugged lamely. "Um, no. Olivia wouldn't buy one for me when we got married, and never did afterwards. But if she had, I doubt I'd still wear it."

She nodded, seeming to accept my answer, and then shook her

head quickly. "But this is crazy. Whether your marriage is over or not, you're still married. This . . . it's wrong."

"I know," I murmured. "But I can't imagine walking away from you now, and from the look in your eyes, you don't want me to walk away either."

KC worried her bottom lip for a few moments as she studied me, before admitting softly, "I've thought of nothing but you since Jace's house. Why do you have to be married?" She whispered the last part to herself and huffed a sad laugh. Her eyes slowly met mine as she rubbed at her chest. "I feel like I'm losing my mind. It physically hurts to think about not being with you, and I don't even know you."

When I saw her blue eyes fill with tears, I took the last steps toward her and pulled her into my arms. She let out a shaky breath, and her eyes stayed glued to her hands resting on my chest.

We stood there silently for a few minutes before she tilted her head up and looked into my eyes. "What are we going to do?"

I couldn't help the smile that spread across my face when I responded. "I'm not sure, but we'll take it slow and we'll figure it out."

5

Kamryn

May 16, 2015

BRODY LEFT TWENTY minutes later when my first customer came in, but not before getting my phone number and promising to call. It didn't make sense to be swapping phone numbers given what we'd just confessed—we knew that. But we also knew that in those first seconds after I'd run into him and he'd caught me, we were both already completely lost in each other. And though there were red flags flying up all over the place, this feeling that was drawing us together was strong enough that we were both knowingly, and willingly, ignoring every one of them.

Brody and I knew we wouldn't be able to talk often, and I had been prepared for that. But I'd had no idea how hard it would be to wait for his call. It was Thursday night, Kinlee and I were out for coffee again, and I hadn't heard from him once.

"What is going on with you today?"

My head snapped up to look at Kinlee. "What do you mean?"

"You haven't said more than two words, you just keep checking your phone. Do you have somewhere you need to be?"

"No, no, I'm fine. I'm sorry, I'm just so distracted. I haven't talked to Barbara in a while, and I get antsy when I don't." Part of that was true. I hadn't talked to Barb in exactly one week. But that wasn't why I couldn't stop checking my phone.

I'd put it on silent, not even wanting to risk it vibrating while I was out with Kinlee, and yet I still couldn't stop checking it. I was ready to take off running out of the coffee shop if he called. Half terrified that Brody would call while I was with her, half wishing he would just call already . . . it was safe to say I was going a little crazy.

"She'll call, she always does. Are you worried about her or something? The way you're acting is starting to make me anxious, and I don't even know her."

I started to say no but stopped myself. "Uh, yeah, I kinda am. Like I said, I haven't heard from her in a while, and she's not in the best situation back home. But I'm sure she's fine, she's the sweetest woman you'll ever meet, but she's tough as nails."

Kinlee fidgeted in her chair as she studied me before shooting me a smile. "Then cheer up, friend!"

I tried to smile as I glanced at my phone again.

"Hey, why don't you go back and visit, or have her come visit you?"

"You know I can't, I barely have enough free time as it is with two helpers in the bakery, and I'm not making enough to hire someone else on yet. And she definitely can't come here, she, uh, she works for some assholes. They'd never give her time off to come see me."

"That sucks." Kinlee tsked. "Why don't you ever talk about your parents? What happened to them?"

"Just never had a good relationship with them, you know? Barb's the only one I talk to from back home."

"And let me guess, home is someplace far, far away . . . out east . . . not here . . . somewhere you don't want to think of again?" she teased as her phone on the table started to chime and she picked it up.

I laughed softly, thankful to her for taking my mind off the call I still hadn't gotten. "Pretty much."

"Now, you know I think it's good for everyone to have their secrets, but I've got to know: Where you're from, was it really that bad, or do you just think I'll judge you?"

Both. Definitely both. "It's just someplace I'd like to forget."

"All right, all right, I hear ya." She gasped and brought her phone even closer to her face. "You told Aiden you didn't want a relationship right now?!"

"Uh, yeah." Not exactly in those words, but same meaning.

"What was wrong with him? He's freakin' hot and super sweet!"

"You're right, he is. But I felt about him the same way I feel about Jace. He's just friend material."

"Okay, there *has* to be something I'm missing!" Her hand flailed out in my direction and started counting off. "It's been at least eight months since you've been with someone. Jace and I have introduced you to tons of guys—all of whom you haven't liked. Aiden is crazy hot, you can still wear your heels with him, *and* he's the first guy you haven't had something bad to say about. Those are five things that are confusing the hell out of me. Unless you're gay—then this would all finally make sense and I could stop wondering what's stopping you."

I laughed lightly. "I'm not gay."

"Then what the hell is stopping you? You're twenty-three, you are by far the most gorgeous person I've seen in real life, I would *kill* to look like you, you're sweet, and you're really funny when you open up to people. So tell me."

I'm falling for your brother-in-law harder than I have for anyone in my entire life. And I can't even tell you about it. "I was in a relationship for six years before I moved here, one that I didn't want to be in. This is the first time I've been alone in my adult life, and I'm enjoying it. Besides, it's not like I'm a hermit. I own a bakery that I'm at for ten to sixteen hours a day, depending on the day, and I have you and Jace. I'm too busy for a relationship."

"Six years? And you didn't even want to be in it? Why were you with— Oh, God, was it like a Brody situation? Were you married to him? Oh, wait, no, that's not right, you would have been what . . . sixteen, seventeen?"

My heart fluttered at the mention of Brody. Another glance at my phone confirmed that he still hadn't called. "Yeah, no, not married. I didn't have a choice in dating him, though."

One dark brow shot up.

"Bad relationship with my parents," I said by way of an explanation.

"Jeez, what did they do? Sell you off to his family or something?"

Laughing—because she wasn't too far off—I emptied my caramel latte. "Something like that."

Kinlee studied me for a few moments before asking, "You're being serious, aren't you?"

"Told you. Home's a place I'd like to forget."

ONCE I WAS back at the condo and in a pair of sleep shorts and a stretchy tank top, I walked into the kitchen and stared in the fridge and then the pantry for a few minutes before just grabbing the box of granola. It wasn't like I didn't have tons of things I could make, but my mind was just so all over the place that I could barely figure out how to put the granola and milk in the bowl without spilling it onto the counter.

By the time I finished and cleaned the bowl it was half past eight and I was too keyed up to even attempt to sleep. I tried watching TV, but nothing was holding my attention. I grabbed my Kindle, but realized ten minutes later that I didn't even know what book I was reading. With a frustrated sigh, I set the Kindle down and walked back into the kitchen. Planting both hands on the kitchen island, I stared down at my phone and willed it to ring. With a miserable-sounding laugh, I let my head fall onto one arm and chastised myself for being like a middle schooler with a crush. What was happening to me? Obviously, whatever was happening between Brody and me was unlike anything I'd ever experienced, but I couldn't believe I'd been reduced to a ridiculous girl glaring at her phone and not being able to do or think of anything else because of him.

I'd just let myself start believing I was going to go another night without hearing from him when my phone rang, causing me to jump back from the counter and reach for it without looking at the screen.

"Hello?" I asked breathlessly.

"Hey, baby girl!"

I hung my head and rubbed at the back of my neck. "I was wondering when I'd hear from you again, Barb."

"Aw, have you been missing me?"

"Of course."

She laughed and sighed. "I miss you every day, Kam. But I'm glad you're out of here. And before you go telling me you're sorry for leaving me again, you might as well pick up where we left off last week when you hung up on me. I want to hear more about this Aiden boy."

"Ah, Aiden. Yeah, I'm not so sure about that one, Barb."

MY HAND FLOPPED around on my nightstand later that night until I hit the offending device and brought it to my ear. "Mmm, 'lo?"

"God, I woke you up. I'm so sorry, go back to sleep."

I shot up in my bed and looked over at the clock. It was after midnight. "Brody?"

He sighed softly. "Hey, KC, I'm sorry it took so long to call. Honestly, I didn't think I was even going to be able to tonight, we're never this busy. But go to sleep, I'll call you tomorrow."

"No, no. It's fine. How are you?"

"At the risk of sounding cliché?" he asked, laughing huskily. "I'm better now that I'm talking to you."

I smiled widely in my dark bedroom and rested my forehead in my hand, my elbow on my knee. I'd talked to Barb for thirty minutes and finally forced myself to bed at ten, coming to terms with the fact that I'd been played by Brody, and baffled that it hurt so bad. I tried to tell myself it didn't matter, that I really didn't care. I would just go on with my life as I had been and try to push the thought of Brody away. Not that I could. I hardly knew him, but I knew no one would ever come close to making me feel the way I did with Brody. But even knowing and feeling what I did, it didn't stop the insecurities from creeping in. The fact that I hadn't heard from him since the day we'd put all our feelings out there had been slowly pushing the thought forward that all this had been a game to him. The long wait made me second-guess everything. The way I felt when he was near or looked at me, the way it felt when he held me, the sincerity in his voice that morning in my bakery. All of it was slowly replaced with doubt and fear that I'd thought everything up. I'd never been insecure in anything, and being insecure in this—about him—was terrifying me beyond reason. By the time I'd fallen asleep, I'd been rubbing at my aching chest and telling myself over and over again that if he did ever call, I wouldn't bother answering or playing this game with him.

But then I heard his voice, and all of that went away. The insecurities seemed redundant, the torture of waiting for his call seemed like nothing, and I knew in a heartbeat I'd do it all again.

"Me too," I replied honestly. "What was so busy about tonight?"

"We had a five-car wreck on the highway right after I got on, a family assault not ten minutes after that finished up, a seven-year-old boy went missing and ended up being under his bed, and my favorite was at Mr. and Mrs. Andrew's."

He'd ended the last on a laugh, and my eyebrows rose. "Oh, really? And what happened with them?"

"Tonight it was throwing hot tea on his, uh, manhood because she didn't feel like having sex."

"Lord! Seriously? Poor Mr. Andrew. You said *tonight,* do you deal with them often?" What *was* it about this man? We hadn't talked in days and now were talking about his job—and yet, I couldn't remember being happier than I was in that moment.

"Oh, yeah, they're my favorites. He's eighty-six, she's eighty-three, and they've been together since she was fifteen. Absolutely madly in love, have a great family, lots of kids, tons of grandkids, but they like keeping it interesting. I think they get lonely now that it's just them, so whenever they do something to each other, they call the cops and make it dramatic. Like last week, she called because he wanted some kind of vegetable and she didn't feel like cooking it. So she threw the can of corn she'd been planning on cooking at him; it missed him and ended up breaking a window and she wanted him arrested."

I laughed out loud. "Oh, my God, they sound great."

Brody was silent for a moment. "I really like your laugh."

My cheeks warmed and my smile softened as I admitted, "I was afraid you wouldn't call."

"Shit, KC, I'm sorry. Nights are never this busy in Jeston. The Andrews' house is one thing, but all of that on one night is rare, and I literally just finished all the reports when I called you. I've been dying to call you, and almost did yesterday, but Olivia didn't leave home once because she was getting ready for this trip she left for tonight with her parents."

"It's fine. I mean, it's what we have to do, right? It's not like I have the right to talk to you whenever I want."

"I wish that wasn't the case," he said softly, and didn't talk again for a long moment. "Can I see you again soon?"

"Please?" I laughed lightly. "When?"

"Now." I laughed again, and he added quickly, "I'm sorry, I forgot what time it is. Um, how about—"

"No, I want to see you," I practically blurted, and held my breath for the few seconds it took for my heart to calm down enough so I could speak again. "Do you . . . did you want to come over?"

"Yeah," he breathed. "Yeah, KC, I do."

After giving him directions to my house and telling him I'd leave the garage open so he could park his patrol car in there—just in case I had any nosy neighbors—I jumped out of bed and tried to get ready for him to come over. Fortunately for him, and unfortunately for me, he had to pass by my neighborhood on his way home and he was already less than five minutes away.

Not having time for much of anything, I put on a bra, pulled my hair back in a ponytail, and did the essentials before heading into the kitchen. I was about to get a glass of water when I heard an engine in the garage and went to open the door that led from the garage to the laundry room. His big black-and-white patrol Tahoe pulled in next to my forest-green SUV, and I had to admit, I liked seeing them next to each other.

As soon as his car was off, I pressed the button for the garage door and watched him exit the Tahoe. The second he rounded the back of it and looked up at me, that crooked smile crossed his face and I'm pretty sure I melted into the door frame.

Brody's smile broadened when he got closer to me. I'm pretty sure he knew what he was doing to me just by being near me. "Hi, KC."

"Hi." I smiled like an idiot and finally stepped back when I realized we were just standing there staring at each other. "Uh, come on in. Can I get you anything to eat or drink?"

"I'm good."

His gray eyes didn't leave mine as we walked into the kitchen, and we fell back into a silence. Neither of us knew what to say or do now that we were near each other again. I drummed my fingers on the island and forced myself to stay on the side opposite him rather than going to him like my body was craving.

"How've you been?" he asked at the same time I said, "Can you stay for a while?"

"Do you want me to?" When I nodded shyly, he smiled again. "I'll stay as long as you want me to. Liv and her parents are in Washington until Monday morning."

Throughout most of the years I'd dated Charles, I couldn't wait for him to leave or drop me off back home. So why, after having been around this man for only about an hour total, was I already wishing he would never have to leave?

"You can make yourself comfortable. If you want to take off your gear, you can put it on the table." I nodded over to the large rectangular kitchen table behind him. "Or you can stay in it, it's totally up to you. I just figured, since I'm in my pajamas and you look like you're about to arrest me, I'd give you the option. I don't know why I said that—you know what, I'm just going to shut up." *Oh, my God, Kamryn! Shut up!*

Brody's warm laugh filled my kitchen, and I dropped my head into my hands after planting my elbows on the island. Biting back my embarrassed groan, I peeked through my fingers when I heard movement and let my hands fall from my face as Brody began taking off his gear. His gray eyes met and held mine as he unbuttoned his uniform shirt and slowly removed it. It felt like I was getting the best striptease of my life, and he was still fully dressed underneath.

His already gravelly voice was even huskier as he reached for the Velcro straps on the sides of his bulletproof vest. "If we're going to take this slow, you really need to stop looking at me like that."

My teeth released the lip I hadn't realized I was biting down on, and heat instantly crawled up my neck and cheeks. I spun around so my back was facing him, silently cursing myself for how awkward I'd made tonight already, and pushed away from the island to grab a glass from the cupboard. As I was filling it up with water from the tap, I felt Brody come closer and turned to find him occupying the space against the counter where I'd just been.

It felt like I was fighting going to him, and it was draining me to stay away from him. The heavy silence filled the space between us, and for the life of me I couldn't think of anything to say to him that seemed appropriate for us at this early stage of our . . . *us*-ness. I wanted him to hold me, I wanted to feel his full lips pressing against mine. I wanted to know what he wanted out of life—and yet, we still needed to get to know each other. We needed to figure out what exactly we were going to do. We needed to talk about everything we'd left unsaid the other morning in the bakery. None of this was making sense. It felt like we were way beyond this stage. Beyond having to take things slow and forcing ourselves to not go to each other. But we weren't there yet. He was married. We weren't technically anything. We just *were*.

I simply didn't know how to start from the beginning when I already knew how we both felt about each other.

"This is ridiculous," he finally said. "KC, I need you in my arms. Pulling you to me feels like the most natural and needed action right now. And to be keeping myself from doing that is taking every ounce of energy I've got and all my concentration.

We'll take this slow, I swear to you we will. But I need to be able to touch you again."

I'd barely set the glass down on the counter before launching myself at him. My arms went around his neck and his hands crushed me to his body. I felt the rumble build in his chest and his lips went to my ear.

"I'll take that as a confirmation that I wasn't the only one having trouble staying away?"

Leaning back enough so I could look in his stormy gray eyes, I couldn't even be embarrassed about my assault on him. He was still gripping me to him tight enough to let me know he needed me close, but not so hard that it was painful.

"I think we're gonna find out real soon that neither of us is the only one feeling a certain way about the other," I whispered, and a smile pulled at my lips. "I felt like I didn't know what to talk to you about. I kept thinking how was I supposed to start a conversation with you when I can't find the happy medium between getting to know you and already knowing that I need you."

His lips tilted up into a soft smile, and one of his hands left my waist to brush loose hair from my face. "You need me." It wasn't a question, but I nodded my head anyway. "This is what I've been needing. You, exactly where you are now, reassuring me I'm not crazy for what I feel for you and what we're about to go through."

My hands slid from his neck down to the black undershirt covering the lean muscles of his chest. "If you're crazy, then I'm right there with you . . . but I think we need to figure out what exactly it is we're about to go through." His smile fell, but acceptance settled over his features as I continued. "Because I don't know what we are, what we're going to be, what we're doing—and I need to. Despite my feelings for you, Brody, this whole situation is terrifying for me. And with how hard it already is to stay away from you . . . well, I can't go into this blindly. I can't just know that we want each other and be okay with it—we need to talk about what that means for us."

"I agree," he mumbled as he twisted more of my hair away. "But first, there's something that's been bothering me. What's your name?"

My eyebrows pinched together, and I automatically answered, "KC."

"But those are just initials."

"Yeah, but that's what everyone calls me." It felt like I was going to throw up once I knew what he was asking, and though I knew how stupid that was, I couldn't shake that sinking feeling. No one in Oregon knew my name. *But Brody's different,* I kept telling myself.

"I don't want to call you what everyone else calls you. Not when I've already admitted things I probably never should have said out loud. Not when I'm about to ask you for so much more and hope like hell that you don't think I'm crazy for wanting something I shouldn't be allowed to have. So, *please,* what's your name?"

"Kamryn," I whispered, then cleared my throat to say, louder, "My name's Kamryn."

"Thank you." That crooked smile crossed his face as he pushed me back toward the opposite counter near the sink and placed his hands on the counter on either side of me, caging me in. Dipping his head, his gray eyes looked directly into mine as his soft voice filled the space between us. "I have been thinking about my life, my situation, and you ever since I ran into you at my brother's house. No matter how you think about this, it seems wrong, and I know it won't be easy for us—and if you'll go through this with me, I'm so sorry for putting you through this in advance. But I need you to know some things before I even ask you *to* do this."

"Okay," I said warily, waiting for him to continue.

"Kamryn, I need you to know that I don't do this. I'm not this guy. I've been faithful to my wife even though we've had a shitty marriage. I need you to know that I haven't slept in the same bed as her for almost five years, we've been married for almost six, and the first year of our marriage I was away in the Army. Even still, I have always been faithful to her and never even given another woman a second glance . . . until you."

"I don't . . ." I trailed off, shaking my head quickly. "I don't understand why you're married to her then. Jace and Kinlee said she was horrible, and with what you just said, I just don't . . . it doesn't make sense."

"Olivia and I have been together since high school. When I left for the Army after we graduated, we stayed together for two completely different reasons. For me, it was convenient to have someone when I visited home. For her, she liked dating someone her parents hated. But it was just a title, and someone to fool around with when I was here, nothing more. Then she got pregnant, and I figured if I was man enough to get her pregnant, I was man enough to marry her."

My stomach clenched and dread filled me. I couldn't do this to a child, I couldn't break up a kid's parents.

"I wasn't going to let her go through that alone. But that entire first year after we got married she wouldn't even see me, and she wouldn't let me see our son until I left the military and bought a house for us. Once that happened, we shared a bed for a few months, but we still didn't *share* a bed most of that time. After those first few months of living together, we went to separate rooms, and it's been that way since."

"You have a kid?" I breathed.

A dark look fell over Brody's face, and he slowly shook his head back and forth. "No, I don't."

The pain and hardness in his voice had my body tightening, and I knew it was a sensitive subject for him. Whatever had happened, it was clear that Brody wasn't ready to tell me. "Then if you don't have any kids, why are you still with her?"

"Because I married her, and there's been a lot of hard times for us. I couldn't just leave her."

A harsh breath left me, and my eyebrows slammed down. "Then once again, Brody, what is the point of all this? If you've stayed married to someone like her, and just admitted to me you couldn't leave her before, why are you here? Why are we doing this—whatever *this* is? I don't know what I was expecting from you, but from what you said the other day, it wasn't this. I'm sorry, but I'm not okay with being someone's mistress!"

"Kamryn, no! You're not getting it. Yes, I stayed with her even though my life has been hell over the last five years since I've been back in Oregon, but I thought it was my punishment, and it was a punishment I would have gladly paid for the rest of my life if I'd never met you. But I did."

"Punishment?" I whispered, my voice barely audible.

Brody continued as if I hadn't spoken. "Kamryn, if—if I'm not the only one feeling this, *needing* this, then I'll leave Olivia to be with you, and not once for the rest of my life will I regret my decision in doing that. But it's going to take time. Olivia has some issues, and there are things I have to work through with her first to make sure she'll be okay when I do leave. She spends most of her time with her parents anyway, but I just need to make sure she'll go to them rather than do something stupid. Her family is vicious, so we'll need to be quiet until I can file for divorce. I know this is asking a lot of you—to be patient with me before we can be completely together. If you can't do that and you want to wait until I'm already divorced, then we'll wait. But if not, I told you on Monday, this isn't going to be an affair, for me this is all or nothing."

My mouth opened, but no words came out as I stared into his sincere gray eyes. I believed he wasn't the type of guy to normally do this, and if he said he was all in, then there wasn't a part of me that worried he was lying to me about leaving Olivia. I still didn't want to be the person who broke up someone's marriage, but I had to agree wholeheartedly with what he'd said earlier this week . . . I would be insane to walk away from this.

The old Kamryn would have run in the opposite direction as fast as she could, and I knew Barbara and Kinlee would never approve, but I also knew that going through life and never again feeling the way he made me feel would be the opposite of living. No matter how happy I'd been here in Jeston before I met him, I could never go back to the way I'd been.

"I can't believe I'm about to say this," I whispered and lowered his head so his forehead was pressed against mine. "If it's with you, Brody, then I want it all. I agree we need to be quiet about it. I don't want to be seen as the girl who ruined your marriage to anyone. Your family, friends, Olivia, her family . . . I don't want to be that person."

"You're not, and you won't. I wouldn't do that to you, and I'll protect you from any fallout from leaving her, all right?"

"This is crazy," I breathed.

"I'll be right there with you through all the crazy."

I worried my bottom lip, and it felt like we both stopped breathing in those few seconds before I nodded my head and said, "Okay, Brody."

His eyebrows shot up, and his grip on my waist tightened. "Okay?"

"Okay."

He pressed his lips against my forehead, then moved back to look me in the eye. "That word has never sounded so good."

WE STAYED LIKE that before eventually making our way to the couch, where we talked for hours into the morning. Now that we knew what we were doing, we were trying to make up for all the getting-to-know-each-other time we had lost. He told me all about his childhood and time in the Army, and I shared stories of Barb and what made me want to open the bakery. Not once did our hands leave some part of each other, and never once did we go past that. And when I rested my head on the back of the couch and rubbed my eyes under my glasses, he stood up and pulled me up with him.

"I've kept you up way too long, I'll let you get some sleep."

I grunted my dislike for that idea. "No, it's all right. I'm not ready for you to go."

He pulled me into his arms, and I felt more than heard his

chuckle. "Your accent gets thicker the more tired you get." When my body stiffened, he ran his hand over my back and leaned away to look at me. "Why is that a bad thing? I love it, you have no idea how sexy your drawl is."

"Because it's a part of home," I answered after a while. "And I don't like or want anything from there."

Brody's eyebrows pinched together, but he nodded instead of prying. "Maybe one day you'll tell me why?"

A yawn interrupted my answer, and I was thankful for its timing. I buried my head in his chest, and he rubbed at my back.

"Come on, you need sleep." Following him over to the table in the kitchen, I watched as he put the rest of his uniform back on, then walked with him to the garage. "Can I come see you tomorrow night?"

"I was hoping you would."

He smiled and pulled me back into his arms, one hand going up to cup my neck, his thumb brushing along my jaw. "Then I'll be here after work. Thank you for tonight."

His breath washed over my mouth, and my lips parted in anticipation. I watched his eyes darken as the movement caught his eye. His chest rose and fell heavily as the air thickened around us, and I was close to begging him to kiss me. The hand at the small of my back pushed me closer to his body and the thumb at my jaw stopped moving—and I swear I stopped breathing until his eyes snapped back up to mine and realization hit them.

"Sweet dreams, Kamryn."

I suppressed my whimper when his arms released me and told myself that we needed to keep this slow.

Offering him a small smile, I leaned up against the doorjamb as I watched him walk to his Tahoe. "Drive safe, Brody. I'll see you later tonight."

It shouldn't have been that hard to watch him walk away. It shouldn't have felt that wrong for him to leave at the end of the night. But it did, and I just had to hold out until I saw him again later. Already the hours separating our time together felt like they'd never pass.

6

Brody

May 19, 2015

RAKING MY HANDS over my face, I groaned and tried to focus on the cars passing in front of me. I was running radar at a little speed trap for the last thirty minutes of my shift since it had been quiet for the past few hours, but I wasn't seeing the cars driving by me. I was seeing Kamryn. Flashes of the past three nights had been torturing me all day, but God, I didn't want the torture to stop.

Her full lips parting in anticipation, my mouth claiming hers, her heated eyes locked on my own as we tried to stay away from each other, the way her body felt pressed against mine, that sound she made when I bit down on the soft skin of her neck—all of it played over and over again in my mind. The memories had me straining against my pants, and I hoped like hell I didn't have to pull anyone over because, if I did, it was gonna be fucking awkward.

The second night I'd gone to her house, we hadn't been able to keep ourselves from kissing each other. But even through the agonizing hours of trying to keep ourselves away from each other, we'd managed to only kiss when we were away from any surface either of us could've been pushed down on or up against. And even though we'd both kept repeating that was as far as we would let it go, last night had been a different story.

With only two minutes left of my shift, I pulled out of the spot where I'd been running radar and started in the direction of my house. Images of her chest rising and falling harshly as she pinned herself to the opposite side of the couch last night hit me, and I welcomed them. I'd lost count of how many times we'd already broken apart, repeating the words "slow . . . we're going slow." And I remembered that, as I sat there taking in her erratic breathing and heated stare, I couldn't think of why we'd even agreed to that. Because slow when it came to Kamryn was painful. Not just sexually. Everything about taking our relationship slow was killing me.

But then I'd remembered—I'd remembered why. Because I was married to a broken woman who needed me to get her help.

Never once in the last five years had I thought about *actually* leaving Olivia. Through all the bullshit, heartache, and grief, I'd remained faithful to a wife whom I no longer loved . . . and who had probably never even loved me . . . because I felt like I owed it to her. But the second I saw Kamryn everything in my life changed. To find someone who could change me so completely before I even heard her speak was a gift that I would have been blind to not accept.

Finding someone who made me feel alive, who had me willing to actually leave Olivia and ready to change my entire life just so I could spend the rest of it with her—that was what made it impossible to remember to go slow. Physically. Emotionally. Mentally. I wanted all of her, and I wanted to give all of myself to her.

I don't know who had reached for the other again first, but she'd moved toward me at the same time I'd gripped her waist and pulled her onto my lap. She'd quickly pulled my shirt off before bringing our mouths back together, and I hadn't been able to stop myself from pressing her harder against my erection as her fingers trailed over my shoulders and chest.

When we'd pulled away from each other minutes later, she hadn't gone back to the other side of the couch like she already had so many times that night. She'd stood up and backed away from me, and it was clear that she was fighting against the urge to continue or trying to go slow—like we'd said we would. Making it easier for both of us, I'd left, not knowing when I would see her again. Olivia was coming back into town sometime the next day, and neither of us thought we could see each other a fourth night in a row and continue to stop ourselves from what we both wanted.

But like I was being pulled to her, I turned to head toward her place instead of mine. She was *my* gift, and I wasn't going to pass up on our already rare, stolen moments.

Kamryn

May 19, 2015

MY PHONE STARTED ringing as I stepped out of the shower, and I hurried to dry off before running to the nightstand. A wide smile crossed my face when I saw his name on the screen.

"Hey! I didn't think you were going to call." Even though I hated not knowing when we would get to see or talk to each other again, the surprise of hearing from him almost made it worth it.

"Can I come over?" he asked hurriedly.

I frowned and glanced at my phone quickly before bringing it back to my ear. "Of course. Are you okay?"

"I am, I just need to see you."

My smile came back, and I took off for the door leading to the garage. "Okay, I'll have the garage door opened, and the other one unlocked. Just come in."

"Be there soon."

Running back to my bathroom, I threw the towel on the floor and started brushing my teeth, cutting it short when I heard the door shut.

"Kam?" his deep voice called from the front of my condo.

"Shit!" I hissed and rinsed out my mouth before running to my room. "Be out in a sec!" Throwing on the first tank top and shorts I could find, I took a few seconds to settle my breathing before walking calmly out to meet him.

He already had his shirt and vest off, and the way his dark eyes raked over my body had my stomach heating. There was a determined look on his face as he took long steps to meet me, and just before we got to each other, he shook his head and said, "I can't do 'slow' anymore."

His arms went around me, and he brought his mouth down to mine. The minute our lips touched, something in me ignited, and a small groan came from Brody when I opened my mouth to him and his tongue met mine. His large hands slid down my sides, his thumbs barely grazing the sides of my breasts before continuing down to rest on my hips, pulling me closer to him. I let the tips of my fingers trail down his chest until I hit the bottom of his undershirt and lifted it—letting him finish taking it off and drop it on the floor.

"If you want to stop, you need to say it now."

"I'm not saying anything," I whispered against his lips.

I couldn't. We'd agreed to go slow, but nothing about what we were doing was normal. Even though we'd kept the last three nights pretty chaste, the charge between us had been growing steadily, and we'd been in some sort of unspoken agreement that it was getting too hard to stay away from each other. We'd been silently moving away from each other when the electricity between us grew, both pulling away breathlessly from kisses that had our resolve quickly slipping.

Just before his mouth slammed down on mine, he mumbled, "Thank God."

The force of his kiss surprised me, and a high-pitched moan slipped from my chest. Brody laughed softly as one of his hands left my hip and went to my back and under my shirt, his hand leaving a trail of fire on my skin.

Turning us so the backs of his legs were hitting the couch, I pushed back and followed him down, planting myself on his lap and stifling another moan when our new position had his erection pressing against me. Brody brought our mouths back together, and when I rocked against his hard length, he took my bottom lip between his teeth and tugged gently. When he released me, I sat up straighter so my chest was directly in front of his face and went back to rolling my hips against him.

With a growl, he leaned forward and pulled the stretchy material of my tank top down to free my breasts and sucked one nipple into his mouth. I whimpered when he bit down before resuming his torturous licking; when my eyes were finally able to flutter open again, I looked down to see him looking up from under his dark eyelashes, and goose bumps covered my body at the sight. It was strangely erotic, and I couldn't stop watching him tease my nipple now that I'd started. The hand that wasn't caressing my breast was gripping my hip and I reached down to slide his fingers under the thin material of my shorts.

He released my breast with a soft pop and brought my face to his, staring intently in my eyes. "You sure you're okay with this?"

I sat up on my knees, giving him better access, and leaned in to whisper, "I was stupid to think we could take it slow." I pressed my lips softly to his once, but didn't move away. "Don't leave tonight, Brody, please. Stay with me."

His response was to kiss me deeply while his fingers moved to stroke along my soft folds. "Christ, Kamryn," he groaned, and slid one long finger deep inside me as his thumb rubbed against my clit, and I couldn't stop the whimper that bubbled from my lips from having him touch me like this.

I ground my hips against his hand as he continued to move his fingers in a way I'd never experienced with Charles—not that Charles and I hadn't done numerous sexual activities, but he was always pushing for the ones that benefited him, and sex with him didn't last long. More often than not, I ended up frustrated or excusing myself to go to the bathroom to finish myself. The muscles low in my stomach tightened, and my entire body was warming. I was close to begging him not to stop when he slipped a second finger inside and my body exploded. Hard. My head fell back as a breathy cry left me, and I rode out wave after wave of the most intense orgasm I'd ever had.

His fingers didn't still, but softened and slowed as he pressed his lips against my throat. "You're so beautiful."

Bringing my head back down, I rested my forehead against his as I fumbled with the zipper and button on his uniform pants. My hands were shaking so much from the aftereffects of my orgasm that it took two tries just to pull the zipper down, but the moment I finally succeeded Brody's hand left my shorts and his large fingers curled around my wrists.

"I don't have condoms." He looked to the side and blinked a few times, his brow furrowed. "God, I can't even remember the last time I bought any."

Brody's hands preventing me from continuing only made me want this more. I flexed my fingers and knew that this stop was a good thing, something we should probably take advantage of. But I didn't care. "Are you clean?" I asked softly.

"Yes. Are you?"

I nodded. "And I'm on the pill."

I'd barely finished my sentence before Brody had both of us off the couch, my legs around his hips, and was walking away. "Room, Kamryn, where is it?"

"Down the hall, last door on the right."

His mouth captured mine again as he turned toward the hall

and began taking long strides. Not two feet from the bedroom door his pants fell the rest of the way down and he tripped, sending us crashing into the wall. Our kisses never faltered, even through our laughing, but I unwrapped my legs from his hips as he hurriedly stepped out of his boots and pants. When he kicked them to the side, he grabbed the backs of my thighs and pressed his hard-on against me as I wrapped my legs back around him.

"Bed . . . bed," I pleaded around his lips, and once again he was walking us toward my room.

Making it the rest of the way without incident, we fell onto the bed in a mess of searching hands and tearing clothes. My tank top was somehow on the floor before I was fully on my back, and I reached up to crush our lips together as his hands pulled my shorts off at the same time I reached for the waistband of his dark boxer-briefs.

His erection sprang free, and I didn't even try to continue pulling his briefs down the rest of the way as I took his length in both of my hands. Brody groaned and his head fell to my shoulder as I watched both my hands make their way up him. Letting one of my hands leave to edge the waistband down his hips, I slowly pumped from base to head with the other. I couldn't take my eyes off him. Everything about him was incredible and perfect.

"Babe—I haven't been with anyone in years, so this already isn't going to last long, but if you keep doing that it's gonna be over before it can begin."

I bit back a smile at his confession and leaned my head back when he started leaving openmouthed kisses on my neck and guided him to me. We both stilled for a few seconds, a harsh breath leaving him when he pushed into me, and I wanted to cry in frustration when his body left mine before he was slamming back into me. His name left my lips in a breathless whisper when he began moving inside me, and my fingers curled into his back as his pace quickened.

I could feel the muscles in his back tightening, and the pull in my lower stomach grew as I got closer to my climax.

"Come on," his gruff voice whispered in my ear. "Give me one more."

Bringing his hand between us, he rolled his fingers against my clit, and I whimpered incoherent words as the mix of him moving inside me and his hands on me sent me over the edge. It felt like my body was suspended in air for long seconds before it came crashing down, and Brody's body shuddered beneath my fingertips as he followed me into his own orgasm.

He lazily kissed up my throat until he reached my lips, and somehow I figured out how to release my death grip on his back to pull my hands through his dark hair as I returned the slow kiss.

"God, Kamryn. I don't think I'll ever be able to get enough of you. Not after that."

I smiled against his lips, and feeling his hard length still inside me, pushed him back and rolled us over until I was on top of him. He groaned when I moved my hips, his hands flying back to grab them. I'd been afraid he was about to stop me, but his fingers flexed against my skin before pressing me harder against him. Sitting up, I let him lead our movements, and my head fell back from the feel of the new position. This time was slow and controlled as we took our time getting to know each other's body, but the heat and passion only seemed to grow.

My body curled over his, and I pressed my forehead into his chest when it was over. Every part of me felt like it was floating, and at the same time I couldn't find the strength to move from where I was lying on him.

"Come here," he said as he pulled his body from mine and wrapped his arms around me.

Pressing a kiss to my lips, he tucked my head under his chin and tugged on the comforter until he could pull it over us.

"You'll stay?" I asked as I pressed closer to him.

"I need you in my arms right now," he said simply. And just before sleep claimed me, I heard him say, "I'm not going anywhere."

MY BODY JERKED awake, and I lay still as I listened for whatever had woken me. Brody was now behind me with his body curled around mine, and the sound of his soft snores was all that met my ears for a few moments. Closing my eyes, I relaxed into the pillow again when I heard the ringing. Moving from Brody's arms, I glanced around for my phone but didn't see it. Then I remembered I'd left it in the bathroom—this ring was coming from outside my room. Grabbing for the pants that were on the floor in the hallway, I searched the pockets until I found Brody's phone. My body turned to ice when I saw the screen.

Olivia.

"Brody," I said as I climbed back on the bed and shook his shoulder. "Brody, wake up."

His eyes shot open and moved quickly to the phone I was holding out to him. "What—"

"Olivia is calling you."

"Fuck," he whispered and pinched the bridge of his nose as he turned to his back. Taking the phone from my hand, he cleared his throat a couple times and answered. "Hello?"

"Where the hell are you? Do you know what time it is?"

I didn't need to be sitting directly next to him to hear her. I'm positive I would've been able to hear her shrill voice if I'd been back in the hall.

Glancing at his phone for a second, his aggravated expression never changed as he brought the phone back to his ear. "Yeah, Liv, I got caught up at work."

"And you couldn't call to tell me?"

"You said you'd be staying with your parents if you got back from Washington tonight. I didn't know it would matter to you if I was late or—shit, Liv. Why . . . fuck, why are you crying?"

"Well, *obviously* I'm not at my parents', Brody! I thought something had happened to you. You know, I'm trying to be a good wife here. And you are hours late and don't even think to—" She cut off on a sob.

Brody's hand fell over his face, and his head gently shook back and forth. "All right, I'm sorry. You're right, I should have called you."

"Come home, please. Please, come home."

My body locked up when I heard her desperate plea, and I watched as Brody's hand moved and he turned his head to look at me. Even in the dark I could see the war he was fighting as he listened to his wife cry on the phone and watched my every move.

Olivia said something that was now too low and mumbled for me to hear, but Brody's expression suddenly looked like he was in pain.

"I'm finishing up a report, I'll be back soon." Without waiting for her to respond, he ended the call and reached out for me, but I stopped his hand.

"Stay. Please."

His jaw clenched shut, and he shook his head once. From the way his eyes studied my face, as if trying to memorize it, I knew he wouldn't. Twisting away, I got off the bed. I needed to get away from him before I lost it.

"Kamryn, don't do this, I'm sorry. But you know I—"

"I know. You have to leave, Brody, it's fine." I quickly grabbed up my clothes on the floor and dashed into the bathroom.

"Kamryn!"

Once I'd dressed, I pressed my hands to the marble counter as I bit down on the inside of my cheeks to keep from crying. I'd gone into our relationship knowing we wouldn't be able to have this—nights together with nothing standing in the way—but after the night we'd just shared I'd let myself hope.

Olivia's call had been like a slap to the face. I couldn't do this, I couldn't be this person. But as Brody came up behind me and eased his arms around me to press our bodies together, I knew that for this man, I would. I would go through anything if it meant he was mine in the end.

"I'm so sorry," he said softly before pressing his lips to the sensitive spot behind my ear. "Please don't be mad. I couldn't handle it if you were."

I kept my eyes trained on my hands gripping the countertop and nodded, not trusting my voice anymore.

"One day . . . one day we won't have to do this anymore. I'll come home to *you,* and get in *our* bed, and never leave. I swear."

My vision went blurry, and I closed my eyes tightly against the tears.

How was it possible that I was already falling so hard for this man that the thought of him anywhere but beside me had me feeling like I was drowning and unable to pull in the air my body needed to live? I was quickly becoming addicted to him and the way he made me feel with the smallest of touches. We were dangerous together, but I knew I couldn't live without him.

"Forgive me," he pleaded, and suddenly his body and warmth were gone. As much as my mind and body screamed at me to follow him, to beg him not to leave, I was rooted in place for long minutes until I heard the door shut and his car start up in the garage.

Taking shaky steps back until I hit a wall, I slid down until I was seated on the cool floor, and the tears I'd been holding back fell mercilessly as desperate sobs racked my chest.

Brody

May 20, 2015

THE SECOND OLIVIA'S car pulled out of our driveway, I was rushing to pull on clothes and running out the door. I needed to go to Kamryn. I needed to try to fix what I'd probably destroyed the night before.

Waking up to Kamryn telling me Olivia was calling me—being pulled out of my perfect moment with Kamryn to have the truth of our situation thrown in my face—had been agony. There was no other word for it. We'd decided when we began that we would go slow, and Kamryn knew there would be days at a time when I wouldn't be able to see her or even talk to her. But that had changed last night.

It had killed me to see the look on her face as I talked with Liv, and everything in me had been yelling at me to stay with

Kamryn, to take care of *her*. Then Liv brought up Tate, and I remembered why Kamryn and I had agreed to keep this quiet: I needed to make sure Olivia was going to be okay first. So I'd given in.

Olivia was asleep in her own bed by the time I got home, though, and had woken me before the sun rose this morning to the sounds of her screaming and throwing dishes across the kitchen. I'd wrapped my arms around her to stop her from grabbing for more. She responded by screaming at me not to touch her because I was a baby killer.

Olivia needed help, and I needed Kamryn.

I pulled into Kamryn's driveway, frowning when I found her garage door open from the night before and the door leading to her house still unlocked. Shutting the garage door, I let myself in and jogged through her house, calling her name.

The sound of bare feet on hardwood met me before I saw her quickly turn the corner in the hall.

"Brody, what are you doing here? How did you get—"

Closing the distance between us, I pulled her into my arms and kissed her firmly before burying my face at the base of her neck. "I'm sorry. God you have no idea how sorry I am," I whispered and ran my nose up her smooth skin. "Please forgive me. I know I fucked up, I just . . . I don't know the right way to do this. I know what I want and need, and I know what I have to do. And I'm so fucking torn between getting her the help she needs and staying with you that I feel like there is no right way to go about it."

Kamryn's body was shaking, and it felt like someone had punched me in the gut when I tilted her head back and saw her wet cheeks.

"I can't do this to you. I can't ask you to do this."

"What?" she asked breathlessly, her expression dropping.

"It's not fair to you."

Her blue eyes widened and searched my face before more tears fell. "What are you saying?"

"I won't make you do this. You shouldn't have to be in a relationship where it's kept a secret, and—"

"Brody, stop!" Her hands came to rest on my arms, and she looked around like she couldn't figure out the right words to say. "Last night was hard. God, it was so hard. I want to promise you that if that happens again I'll deal with it better, but I can't, because there's no easy way to deal with something like that. We put ourselves in this position, though, and if that's what we have to go through to be together in the end, then I'll do it. But you can't ask me to just give up on us because it's not 'fair to me.' This situation isn't fair to anyone, but we knew that going into this." Kamryn's eyes searched mine, and she squeezed my forearms. "Right?"

"Right," I said softly, my lips tilting up in a smile as I looked at this amazing woman. I didn't know what I'd done to deserve her.

"If what you said last night was the truth, if you can promise me that one day we'll be together, then I'll go through hell for you."

Leaning in, I pressed my mouth to hers and spoke against her lips. "I promise. One day we're going to have our forever. Nothing will stop us."

The kiss started off slow, but built quickly when she pulled me closer, her full breasts pressing against my chest. My hands slid from her neck to the top of her jeans, and I pushed her back against the wall as I unbuttoned them and slid the zipper down.

"Brody," she whimpered when my fingers trailed against her heat.

"Tell me what you want."

"You. Just give me you."

Removing my hand from the confined space in her jeans, I moved her away from the wall and walked her backward into her room until we hit the bed. "Jeans. Off," I ordered and stepped back to watch as she slowly pushed them and her underwear off and stepped away from them. "Now lie down."

She sat on the bed and scooted back before lowering herself onto it, her blue eyes dark and hooded as she watched me push apart her legs and kneel between them. Letting my fingers trail against her wet folds, I pressed two fingers inside her, and a surge of need built up in me seeing her head fall back onto the bed as her eyes shut.

I needed this girl. I needed to make her mine. Only mine.

I opened her legs wider, baring her to me, and leaned forward to taste her.

"Oh, God!" she cried, and her hands clenched the comforter in her hands. "Brody, please."

Smiling against her, I ran my tongue up her once more before sucking her clit into my mouth. I hadn't realized Kamryn's heavy breaths had suddenly stopped until I heard the voice.

"I'm actually on time today, so you better be ready!"

The sound of keys falling to the counter could be heard as Kamryn sat up and I jumped off the bed, her horrified expression making my heart race.

"Kinlee," she whispered, and my blood ran cold.

"KC," Kinlee drew out her name in a singsong voice.

"Shit. Fuck. You need to hide!" Kamryn hissed as she scrambled into her underwear and grabbed her jeans. "Go to the closet!"

I couldn't believe I was actually going to hide in a closet like I was about to be caught in my girlfriend's room by her parents, but I knew Kinlee couldn't find out about us, not this way. Grabbing the back of Kamryn's head, I pulled her in and kissed her roughly before quietly making my way toward the closet.

"Brat! Why aren't you answering?" Kinlee's voice was close.

"Sorry, Lee! I was . . . talking to Barb. Let me go to the bathroom and I'll be out." Kamryn bit down on her bottom lip, her worried eyes glued to me as she waited for Kinlee to walk into the room.

" 'Kay, 'kay! I'm going to make some coffee to go."

Kamryn exhaled, and her eyes shut in relief as Kinlee's voice slipped deeper into the condo. After buttoning her pants, she walked quickly to where I was standing in the doorway to her closet and threw her arms around me. "I forgot she was picking me up today, I'm sorry, I have to go."

"I know, have a good day, I'll call you when I can."

Pain covered her worried expression, and her hands slid around to press on my chest. "When do you think that will be?"

"I don't know," I admitted, and an unsettling feeling unfurled in my stomach. "Just know that every moment I'm not with you, I'm counting down the minutes until I can see you again. You're all I think about, Kamryn, and I'll do anything so I can see you again."

She bit down on her lip and nodded resolutely, but it didn't mask the sadness in her eyes. "Okay." Taking a deep breath in, she started to leave, but turned back to kiss me soundly. "Until then."

"Jesus Christ, how long does it take you to pee now?" Kinlee's voice was back, and Kamryn stilled against me.

"There's an extra clicker for the garage door in a drawer in the kitchen. Take it."

I nodded and slipped into her closet as she walked toward her bedroom door, bending down to grab her Converses as she left.

"Shit, I thought I was going to have to send a search-and-rescue team to get you out of the toilet."

Kamryn laughed. "You're early, you can't expect me to be ready for you when you're not running an hour late."

"Whatever." Kinlee snorted. "Don't judge me."

I released the breath I'd been holding when their voices faded, and then waited for a handful of minutes after I heard the door shut before moving from my spot. Going into the kitchen, I searched the drawers until I found one full of random stuff and pulled out the garage door opener. But after what had just happened, I didn't know how often I would be using it. That had been too close. Kamryn and I needed to find a place where something like this couldn't happen.

7

Brody

May 29, 2015

DRUMMING MY HANDS on the steering wheel, I took a few breaths in and out before shutting off my SUV and stepping out. This time of year was always bittersweet for me. With Tate's birthday came sorrow, guilt, and wonder at what *could* have been. Knowing that I was struggling with the grief worse than I did the rest of the year, my two closest friends from the Army were never far behind. No matter what was happening in their own lives and with their families, both Coen Steele and Keegan Hudson came here from Colorado to remember Tate. Well, and I'm sure they were making sure I wouldn't do anything stupid.

I'd never asked them to come. They both just showed up on

what would have been his first birthday and had come back every year since—either on or near the day. I couldn't begin to explain how much their yearly visit meant to me. It was something to look forward to rather than focus on the fact that Tate was gone and not living his life.

But in the last few weeks since his birthday, I'd been terrified about them coming. These two knew me better than anyone— even better than Jace—and I couldn't lie to them if my life depended on it. Not only that, I didn't want to lie to them. We'd been through a lot together in the Army, and there had been times when we were all each other had. Lying to them was never an option. I just didn't know how they would react to what was going on between Kamryn and me. I had no doubt they would find out something was up, and I wouldn't deny what it was when they did. We had to keep our relationship hidden from everyone for numerous reasons, one of them being that Kamryn didn't want to be seen a certain way. So the fact that two of my friends would soon know had me on edge.

Walking into the restaurant, I looked around until I spotted them and began walking toward them.

"Saco!" they yelled in unison, and stood to greet me.

"You both look ancient," I said as we all sat down.

"Fuck you, man," Hudson snorted and signaled the waitress.

I shrugged and flipped open the menu. "I'm just saying. And are you getting fat, Hudson?"

Hudson grinned and ran a hand over his stomach. The guy practically lived in a gym—he couldn't get fat if he tried. "Aw, don't get jealous now."

"How've you been?" Steele asked as he hit my arm with his menu.

"Good. Work, avoid Olivia, watch as she spends all my money. What else is new?" I shrugged.

Steele eyed me curiously before nodding. The three of us had all been close, but he'd been my roommate, and the one I'd called the day Tate died. To be honest, I think he was always waiting for me to go off the deep end. I almost laughed. If he wanted to see someone going off the deep end from Tate's death, he should have come to my house for one of Liv's fits.

"What about the two of you?" I asked after we ordered food and beers. "What's going on with the families?"

"Well, this fucker can't figure out how to put on a condom apparently," Steele said with a laugh.

Looking to my left, I watched as Hudson fought a grin as he stared at the table. "Seriously? Again?"

"Yep! Number four's on the way." He looked up, and his smile was wide before a familiar, haunted look crossed his face—and suddenly all emotion left him.

Fuck. Not yet. I just sat down. Kicking Steele's foot under the table, I nodded my head at him. "What about you and Reagan?"

"Uh . . ." He cleared his throat and looked away for a second. "We're great. No more kids, we're good with two. Studio and business are doing great, I've been slammed with photo shoots and weddings now that spring and summer are here. Reagan's amazing, but I won't go into that since I don't feel like getting punched by *someone* again."

"She's my fucking sister, Steele! You can't expect me to be okay with you talking about that shit in front of me." Hudson looked like he was going to throw up, and I just laughed.

"Five years we've been together. Five. Years. You gotta get over it at some point."

Hudson shook his head. "Nope. I don't have to get over shit. So, Saco, talk to us."

"Work is steady. Obviously there's not a lot of crime going on in Jeston." I shrugged.

"Man, just tell us how you are. You know we're worried about you, and it's stupid that we have to dance around the real reason we're here."

"Jesus. Are you for real?" Steele glared at Hudson before sighing heavily and turning to me. "You seem better than last year, and I'm not just saying that to bullshit you. I think I've seen you smile more in the last five minutes than I have in the past four years combined."

"Yeah," Hudson agreed. "It's been good to see."

"And we're sorry we weren't here on his birthday. This was the first weekend I had free."

I just sat there waiting for when they would stop. Every time they asked how I was doing, they never actually gave me an opportunity to answer.

"Feel like shit that we couldn't be here on the day," he continued.

"Yeah, but we thought about him, all my kids wore something with monkeys on it that day," Hudson added.

"Did you put a monkey on his grave?" Steele asked, and I waited a few more moments to see if one of them was going to continue.

Olivia had dressed Tate in a jacket with monkeys on it the day of the accident, and for some reason I was never able to get that jacket out of my mind. Some people remember what their child's favorite toy or blanket was. Me? I remembered those damn monkeys. So every year on his birthday I put a new monkey on his grave. Olivia didn't understand why I did it and told me it was morbid, but then again, she never went and visited his grave. So I couldn't care less if she didn't like it.

Nodding my head, a sad smile pulled at my lips as I looked at the guys. "Yeah, I did. And don't worry about not being here, the fact that you came at all means a lot. So just—yeah . . . thank you. You both know I appreciate it."

They were silent for a few seconds before Hudson said, "Well, you know we're here for you. We want to be here for this, we know it's a hard time of the year for you."

"And you and Olivia?" Steele asked, filling the silence that had settled between us. "You said you're still avoiding her, but I would have asked if things were getting better with what I'm seeing from you."

I huffed and shook my head. "No, Liv and I are just as bad as we've always been . . . if not worse."

"O-kay . . . ?" they both said, drawing out the word as if they were waiting for me to continue.

"I, uh . . . I don't really know how to . . ." I drifted off and shrugged helplessly when the waitress brought our plates. No one moved to touch their food.

"Are you finally leaving her?" Steele asked.

I wanted to laugh at the word *finally*. Did *anyone* like Olivia? Well, other than her family and herself. With a deep breath in, I shrugged again. "Yeah, that's the plan."

Hudson smacked his hand on the table, and Steele smiled widely at me. "Really, man?" he asked. "Gah, fucking finally. I'm happy for you, Saco. What are you gonna do? You want to move back to Colorado? Maybe a change of pace will be good for you, will help you with the grieving to get away from everythi—"

"Oh, you should," Hudson said, cutting him off. "We can help you look for a place to live there, and a job. Can you just transfer departments like that?"

Steele pointed at me. "Check into that."

"Guys, I'm not leaving."

"What? Dude, why not? I know your family is here, but this could be good for you."

"Because I'm not leaving Olivia just to leave her, Steele. You think I would go through almost six years of being married to a woman I didn't love, and then four and a half of her being psychotic, just to one day decide that I was done? I was *done* before I married her."

Hudson and Steele looked at each other for a few seconds before looking back at me. "Wait, what?" Hudson asked. "We've just been waiting for you to realize you deserved a life, man. If that's not what this is . . . why are you leaving her?"

"Oh, man, no shit," Steele said on a breath.

I caught his stare for just a second, but there was no doubting he knew.

"What the fuck am I missing?"

"Hudson," Steele said and smacked his hand on the table. "Focus, you fuck. Saco's smiling again. He's leaving his wife. And he wants to stay in this little town that holds nothing but bad memories and his soon-to-be-ex psycho bitch wife."

Hudson just shook his head and let his hands fall to the table. "Yeah, I'm still lost."

Steele smirked at me. "If she means enough that you're finally going to leave Olivia, then I bet I approve."

I eyed him and leaned closer so I wouldn't have to talk loud. "You're not going to judge me at all about this?"

His smirk faltered. "If you're already with her, I'm going to tell you to think about what you're doing. You're still married, Saco. You should divorce Olivia before you start anything with this girl."

"What the fuck, are you serious?" Hudson hissed. "You're cheating on Olivia?"

"But seeing how you're planning on leaving your wife for another woman, I'm betting it's already started," Steele continued as if Hudson hadn't spoken. "Am I right?"

I nodded and ground my jaw.

"I love you, man. You know that, and I know Hudson will agree that we just want to see you happy for once. If she's what makes you happy, then that's what we want for you. But don't do it this way. Leave Olivia, and then continue it. And I'm not saying that for Olivia, because you don't owe that bitch a damn thing. I'm saying this for whoever this girl is, she deserves to have you go about this the right way."

"I know she does," I groaned and rubbed my hands over my face.

"Unless she's just trash, then we need to have an intervention. But knowing you, I doubt that's the case."

I leveled a glare at Hudson. "She's not. I'm pretty sure she's killing herself over this, she hates what we're doing . . . and I hate that she feels like that. But it's hard, there's stuff I have to take care of with Olivia first. And we tried staying away from each other—swear to God we tried—but there was no way to. I know this is going to sound so fucking weird, but I knew within days of meeting her that I needed her to live."

Both guys just stared at me blankly for a few seconds. "Huh. Well, damn. What's her name?" Steele finally asked.

"Kamryn."

"Wh—um . . . this *is* a girl, right?"

I barked out a laugh. "Yes, her name is Kamryn." I spelled it out for them, and they both laughed.

"Shit, I was worried there for a second," Hudson said, and I shot him a droll look.

"Really, though, you would both like her. Brown hair, blue eyes, amazing smile and body. She wears these hipster glasses that I swear to Christ I would hate on anyone else. She has this southern drawl she tries so hard to hide, owns a bakery . . . I don't know. Just—everything about her."

"Well, come on, picture." Hudson grabbed for my phone resting on the table, and I shook my head.

"You won't find one. I delete our texts too. She's terrified of anyone finding out, and I don't want Liv to find out about her because I don't know what she'd do to her."

"How'd you meet her?" Steele asked.

I laughed hard once and scratched at the back of my neck. "Well, she's my sister-in-law's best friend. Kamryn's bakery is right next to the boutique Kinlee and her mom run, and I guess Kamryn is always at their house. I went over for a barbecue, and it just escalated from there."

"Well, I'm glad you found someone who will make you happy. It really is good to see you smiling again. But, like I said, think about what you're doing. She sounds nice, don't make her go through this. Finish whatever it is you have to with Olivia, and then be done with her . . . you don't want to be one of those guys who cheats on his wife, and if people find out, you don't want her to be seen as one of those girls."

"I know." I sighed. Everything he said I already knew and

thought about on a daily basis. I hated that I was making Kamryn go through this with me. I hated that I couldn't have been single when I met her. But I'd tried to stay away, and after feeling dead for so long . . . after finally getting a glimmer of being alive again . . . there had been no way for either of us to wait for me to be divorced. I just hoped I could figure out a way to get some help for Olivia soon.

8

Kamryn

June 5, 2015

CALLING OUT A good-bye to my employees, Grace and Andy, I rested my elbows on the counter near the pastry case and groaned into my hands. My days seemed to drag lately, and it had nothing to do with work. Business was steady, I still loved baking every day, and Kinlee made sure my days were never dull. But I missed Brody. I physically ached from having gone so long without him, sleep was practically nonexistent now, and I'm pretty sure people were beginning to get suspicious with my constant "Mondays suck" theme in the bakery.

If the day didn't start off well, making it feel like a Monday, we blasted music all day and put out a sign letting customers know that they could throw the old cupcakes against one of our walls to get frustrations out. And I'd been doing it almost every other day.

It had only been a little over two weeks since I'd seen him . . . but an hour without him was torture. Weeks without his touch? It felt like I was constantly suffocating, fighting for air.

I wasn't this girl who relied on men to survive, never had been. I'd been with Charles out of obligation, but was happy and free when I was away from him. And I'd been more than content being alone when I'd moved to Oregon. Now my world revolved around one man. I had turned into one of those love-struck teenagers whose dramatic fits would sound something like "I can't live without him." I knew how ridiculous I sounded, but my need for him was unlike anything I'd ever known.

I'd never believed in soul mates, because no one I'd grown up around had been happy with their spouse. But something in me called to Brody. I never felt as whole as I did when I was with him, and the time we spent apart felt as if my soul had been torn in two. I couldn't tell you if this empty, hollow feeling was how I'd always been, and it was just more pronounced now that I'd had glimpses of what being whole was like, or if it was all in my head. But I knew if there was such a thing as soul mates, Brody Saco was mine.

And he was still married to another woman.

Straightening up and turning to go into the kitchen to finish up the dishes, I rubbed at the pain in my chest and tried to force the bitter thoughts about Olivia from my mind. I didn't have the right to hate her. And still, I did. I hated her for being with the man I loved. I hated that she took him from me during the few stolen moments we were able to have. And I hated that *I* was the one who should be hated by *her*. I was taking her husband; he was being unfaithful to her because of me. I was ruining a marriage.

As I had done so many times since Brody and I had decided to be together, I felt sick over what we were doing. But even through the guilt, I couldn't stop my mind from going back to thoughts of Olivia. I wondered what it was about her that had kept Brody this long. I wondered why Brody still wasn't leaving her.

With a frustrated cry, I threw the dishes I'd been carrying into the sink and gripped the edge with both hands as I forced myself to stay standing.

"I'm not this girl. I'm not this girl," I chanted to the empty kitchen. *But I am.*

And it was slowly driving me insane. When we were apart, I second-guessed our decision to start the relationship before he could get a divorce from Olivia. I wondered why I felt bad at all if he was so miserable in his marriage. I hated his wife. I hated myself. A jealousy unlike anything I've ever felt made itself known more than once a day. Guilt spread through my body and threatened to cripple me. And my need to be with him again grew stronger with each passing hour.

All of this . . . all of these conflicted emotions . . . were like a broken record in me. I would go through all of them only to start at the beginning again.

So many nights, as I lay in bed unable to sleep, I would mentally scream that I couldn't do this anymore. That I couldn't handle the guilt anymore. But then I would talk to him, and even through the heartache of knowing he was going home to his wife instead of me, I knew I would go through this emotional torture again and again for Brody.

I just hated that I didn't know when I would see or talk to him.

We were supposed to be able to talk—if not see each other—every night he worked. He worked four days on, then had four days off, and in the beginning I'd lived for those four days on. But lately we'd been reduced to working around Olivia and her schedule since Brody had been worried that Olivia was getting suspicious of something. Which meant I hadn't seen him in two and a half weeks and had talked to him only three times.

Why was he worried about Olivia getting suspicious when he was supposedly leaving her? I didn't know. *Because you're stupid for thinking he'll leave his wife for you.* I gritted my teeth and pushed that thought aside. *He will leave her. He will.*

My phone rang, jolting me from my conflicted inner ramblings. Fumbling to get my phone out of my pocket, my heart skipped a beat before taking off when I saw Brody's name on the screen. He hadn't called in almost a week, and I hadn't been expecting anything for some time to come since today was day one of his four off.

Sliding my finger across the screen to answer, I put the phone to my ear and held my breath after I asked, "Hello?" My biggest fear was Olivia getting ahold of his phone and calling me, and me answering in a way that would easily give away that I was in a relationship with her husband.

"Fuck, Kamryn, you have no idea what just hearing your voice does to me."

My knees weakened, and I released a shaky breath as I used the sink to support my weight again. "Bro—" My voice gave out, and I tried to swallow past the lump in my throat.

"Ah, baby. I'm sorry. I'm so goddamn sorry I haven't called."

I nodded even though he couldn't see me. I still wasn't able to speak yet.

"This has been killing me, I need you to know that." No one could mistake the sincerity or pain in his voice. "Work has been crazy, and the minute I get off Liv has been calling me and won't let me get off the phone until I get home. She hasn't left the house at all, I didn't know what to do, I'm sorry."

"I know you are," I choked out.

"I need to see you."

"But y-you're off. How?"

"Liv just left for her parents'," he said, and his next statement sounded unsure. "I don't think she'll be back tonight, but I'm willing to risk it even if she does come back. I need you."

"Okay, okay, I'm on my way home right now." Screw the dishes. They could wait.

"No! Not after what happened with Kinlee showing up, it's too risky now."

I stopped halfway to my purse, and my shoulders sagged. "Then where, Brody? Obviously I can't come to your place."

"I've been looking up hotels outside the city. There's one about forty-five minutes from here. Can you meet me there? I'm already on my way."

I would drive for days if it meant seeing him. "I'll be there, just tell me where to go."

I shut everything off in the bakery and locked up as he told me the name of the hotel, and the exit to take to get off the freeway.

"I'll text you the room number when I get in there, okay?"

"Okay. I'm in my car now. I'll see you soon."

"Kamryn." His voice stopped me from ending the call, and I smiled as his deep voice came through the phone. "Drive safe please. I need you whole so I can show you how much I've missed you."

"I'll be with you soon," I promised and pressed END as I headed toward the freeway.

Twenty-five minutes later I got a text from Brody that said "1431" and nothing more. My stomach heated and curled in a delicious way as my car ate up mile after mile. My body felt hyper-aware of every touch, and goose bumps covered my arms . . . and I wasn't even with him yet. Just knowing I would be soon was enough to replace the crippling ache I'd been dealing with the last two and a half weeks with an ache much lower. An ache I knew would be relieved soon.

After parking, I didn't even bother trying to look civilized as I ran through the hotel and found the elevators. I'm sure I had flour, icing, and batter all over me. I had no doubt my hair was a hot mess. And I wouldn't even have put it past the staff to call the cops because some insane woman was running through their hotel. But I didn't care. As I punched the button for the four-teenth floor, nothing else mattered other than seeing Brody.

Looking at the signs to direct me which way to go, I ran down the hall and knocked quickly on room 1431 as I tried to catch my breath. Within seconds, the door was opening and Brody was hauling my body inside the room.

"Babe," he moaned into my mouth as he let the door slam shut and pressed my back against it. "I missed you."

My breathing was even more ragged as he moved his full lips across my jaw and down my throat in soft kisses. "Brody, *please*, I need you," I pleaded as I reached for the bottom of his shirt and pulled it over his head.

His hands found the tie at the small of my back and pulled, loosening it so he could pull my apron off my body and toss it to the side. I shivered when his fingers barely grazed my skin as he lifted the shirt off my body.

Whole. Finally after weeks without him, I felt whole again. My body burned for him, and everywhere his lips and hands touched me felt like he was branding me. God, how I loved it. My stomach was tightening and the ache for him was growing more intense, and he was still undressing me.

Grabbing for his jeans, I undid the button and pulled down the zipper at the same time he attacked my pants, shoving them and my underwear down my thighs until they fell to my ankles. Kicking off my shoes and pushing my pants aside, I moaned loudly as my head fell back to the door and his fingers slowly ran over my clit before he was pressing two inside me. I freed his erection and took it in my hands just as he removed his fingers only to roll them around my aching bud, and my back arched away from the door as I came apart.

Brody's mouth slammed down onto mine to quiet my pleasured cries, and he continued working me through my orgasm until my body settled back against the door. He removed my hands from where they were moving up and down his length, then let go of my wrists and grabbed the back of one thigh to hitch my leg around his waist.

"Hold on to me," he demanded.

The second my arms were wrapped around him, he pushed roughly inside me, and my fingers curled into the muscles in his back. My body moved against the door as he pumped in and out of me, and it was all I could do to keep myself standing. I couldn't feel my legs, and the one still keeping me upright gave out when his hand, which had been keeping our faces pressed together, released me and he ran his thumb over my sensitive bud again.

"I need you to finish with me."

My head shook back and forth. At the moment, I wasn't sure I could again, but I couldn't form actual words. I felt everything, and somehow at the same time wasn't sure what I was feeling anymore. I'd never come down from my first climax and didn't know how I could have another one when my body was still on such a high from his touch, from having him inside me.

"Kamryn," Brody growled as he thrust harder and harder into me.

I tried to tell him I couldn't when his thumb and index finger pinched down on my clit, and my mouth opened on a soundless moan as my world shattered. My body felt hot and cold all at once, my eyes rolled back, and I'm pretty sure I stopped breathing.

My fingers dug into Brody's back, and his teeth biting down on my shoulder to mute his groan had me quickly sucking in air again to relieve my straining lungs. I dropped my head and rested my cheek against the side of his neck as I tried to pull myself back together.

The blissful light-headedness slowly faded as my breathing steadied, and my shaking legs regained their strength as Brody covered the spot where he'd bitten down with soft kisses.

"Hey," he whispered against my shoulder, and I laughed.

"Hi."

"We went about tonight backwards."

"We go about everything backwards," I countered.

"True." Kissing my lips, he pulled us away from the door and walked us through the living area until we got to the bed. "How've you been, Kamryn?"

There was no way I could tell him the truth. That I couldn't sleep since I was always fighting off a deep ache and grief not being near him. That I couldn't eat because if I wasn't losing myself in my work, or throwing everything I had into the times when I was with Kinlee so she wouldn't suspect anything, I was killing myself thinking of a hundred different things that Olivia could be doing and saying to keep him . . . and then I would feel too sick to even think about putting food in my stomach.

No, I couldn't tell him that.

He would see how much I relied on him. He would think I wasn't secure enough in myself to be alone, or that I wasn't secure in our relationship. I would look exactly like how I was acting. Young. Naive. Dependent. Needy. Weak.

I hated that I'd found a man whom I would give anything to be with, and now I was reduced to this seemingly insecure person.

Looking in his gray eyes, I simply shrugged and let my fingers slowly trail through his dark hair. "I've been okay."

From the look in his eyes, I could see that he and I both knew that *okay* was an exaggeration of the last couple weeks.

"I'm sorry you have to go—"

"Don't," I pleaded and placed two fingers over his lips. "We knew it would be hard. Stop apologizing."

"Kamryn . . ."

"Tell me something else. Anything else as long as you aren't apologizing."

"Okay." A ghost of my favorite crooked smile crossed his face as he looked down at me. "Thank you for driving all the way up here to be with me."

"Of course, Brody." I grabbed the hand that was lightly brushing at my jaw and kissed his palm before intertwining our fingers. "But this hotel doesn't exactly look like the kind of place you can pay cash for a room. Aren't you worried Olivia will find out? I think my condo is safer than this."

"I have a credit card Liv doesn't know about, and I don't receive the statements in the mail. I've had it for years to help us when she blows all our money. She's never found out about it."

My eyebrows pinched together. "Blows all your money? Does she do that a lot?"

"About twice a year."

"Brody—"

"Babe." He cut me off. "I finally have you again, I don't want to talk about Liv. I want to order some room service and feed you because you look like you've lost weight since I last saw you. I want to make love to you slowly after. I want to spend time just talking to you. Then I want to have you coming again and again until you're begging me to stop. I want to take a shower with you when we're almost too weak to stand, and then finally fall asleep with you in my arms. But no Olivia, all right?"

I'd started to worry when he mentioned eating, afraid he'd somehow known what I'd been thinking only a couple minutes before. But as he laid out his plans for us for the rest of the night my worries left and a smile tugged at my lips. " 'Kay."

Brody

June 5, 2015

"BRODY, WAKE UP! She's calling, wake up," Kamryn said, leaning over my body.

My hands moved to her bare hips, and I pulled her down so her heat was pressed against my hardening cock.

"Brody, she's calling."

My eyes snapped open when the agonized tone of Kamryn's voice finally registered in my mind, and I grabbed at my phone in her hand when I realized what she'd been saying. Kamryn scrambled off my lap and the bed, and as much as it killed me to have her body move away from mine, I was grateful. I couldn't handle feeling her, touching her, and looking at the hurt in her eyes when I was talking to Olivia.

Clearing my throat, I checked the time before answering the call and hoped like hell I didn't sound like I'd just been asleep. "Hello?" I answered.

"Where the fuck are you?" Liv hissed through the phone.

I panicked for a few seconds as I tried to think. It was one thing to say I was at Jace's when I could easily get there, or when I knew for sure Liv was at home. But even though she was supposed to be at her parents', she could be anywhere. She could have already driven past my brother's house. "My buddies from the Army are in Portland for a couple days, I drove up here to have some beers with them and catch up." I held my breath as I waited for her to respond, then let it out in a silent rush when she seemed to buy it.

"You think I care if those dumbasses want to see you? You're supposed to be here! You're supposed to be home, Brody!"

"I thought you were staying at your parents' tonight."

She paused for a few seconds before screaming, "What is that supposed to mean?! Do you just wait for me to leave, Brody? Is that what you want? For me to leave so you can go do whatever you want? You're such a selfish bastard, Brody Saco!"

"Fuck, Olivia, stop yelling. I was just saying I don't know why you always expect me to be home since you're not there half the time."

Suddenly, Liv's anger was gone and was replaced by loud sobs. "I can't do this anymore, Brody. I—I just can't!"

A huge wave of relief and guilt for turning her into this person washed over me. *I can't keep doing this either. This is it. I just need to say the words.* As I opened my mouth to tell her I wanted a divorce, she stunned me into silence.

"I need to be with Tate. I can't keep living without him. I can't keep living in the same house as a murderer. I need to be with him," she mumbled the last sentence. "It's time for me to go. Good-bye, Brody."

"What? Olivia, no! No!" Before I even realized I was moving, I was off the bed and fumbling for my clothes.

"It'll be better this way. I can be with my son, and I won't have to live in fear of the day you kill me too."

"Olivia!" I shouted, but my voice was strained. *How can she say something like that to me? How can she put that on me like this? God, what the fuck have I done to make her into this depressed, paranoid, and suicidal woman?* "Olivia, don't! I'm on my way home. Don't do anything, I'll be there as soon as I can."

There was no response, and I looked down at my phone to see she'd ended the call.

"Fuck!" I roared into the room as I pulled my shirt over my head. Grabbing my keys off the desk, I ran toward the door, and skidded to a stop when I heard a muffled sob. Turning, I saw Kamryn standing a dozen feet away from me. One hand clutching at her bare chest, the other covering her mouth. Shit, I'd forgotten why I was even away from my house.

"Don't go," she pleaded.

"I have to, Kamryn, I'm sorry!" I took long steps back to her and reached for her, but she pressed a hand to my chest to stop me from pulling her in.

"You don't have to. We don't have to do this, Brody!" Fat tears rolled quickly down her cheeks, and my heart broke at seeing her like this again. "Whatever she said to you, you don't have to go back to her. If you're so miserable, then stay with me. Don't go to her."

I squeezed my eyes shut tightly. Fuck, she hadn't even heard what Olivia had been saying. Of course, she didn't understand, but I couldn't explain Tate to Kamryn right now. Not when Olivia was about to commit suicide. I needed to leave. I might not have loved Olivia, but I couldn't let her kill herself. "I do, you don't understand, but I *have* to go. I'm so fucking sorry. I hate that I've said that so much tonight, but I'm more sorry than you know. One day we won't be doing this anymore. I swear one day it will only be you and me. We'll be past all this and we'll have our forever, but right now, I have to leave." Kissing her quickly, I turned and bolted from the room and ran to the elevators.

I raced down the freeway and cursed the storm that had started sometime that night. The road was slick, and rain pelted down relentlessly as I wove in and out of cars on my way back to Jeston. I tried Olivia's phone over and over again, but each time it went straight to voice mail.

Slamming on the brake in the driveway, I didn't even shut the SUV off or close the door as I raced into the house, thankful the front door was unlocked.

"Olivia!" I yelled as I ran toward her side of the house. "Olivia!"

She didn't respond, and I searched wildly through her bedroom and bathroom before backtracking. Her car had been out front. I knew she was here.

"Olivia! Answer me!"

I tore through the living room and grabbed the wall just as I entered the hallway to slow myself to a stop. With careful, slow steps back toward the kitchen, I turned and eyed Olivia sitting at the bar talking quietly on the house phone.

"Liv."

She didn't move or acknowledge me in any way.

"Olivia, look at me!"

Slowly lifting her head, with eyes wide, she pointed at the phone. "Can't you see I'm on the phone, Brody? Jesus!"

"Get off the phone and fucking talk to me!"

"Daddy, do you hear him? He's crazy. I don't feel safe being in the house with him, all he does is yell at me. If I stay here I'll end up in the hospital or worse. Can I come stay with you?"

My jaw dropped as I listened to her. "I'm crazy? *I'm* crazy? Olivia, you just told me you were about to kill yourself!"

She gave me a look like I was some ridiculous child. "Now he's trying to make me believe I'm suicidal. I swear this house is bad for my health. Tell Mom I'll be there as soon as I pack a bag. If I'm not there or you don't hear from me within twenty minutes, call the cops. Brody's a loose cannon these days."

"Olivia, tell him! Tell him what you were just telling me."

Rolling her eyes, she sighed dramatically and pinned me with a look. "My dad wants to know if you have the money to buy me a new phone."

My head jerked back. "What happened to yours?"

"Oh, my God. Now he's acting like he doesn't know," she

whispered into the phone. Looking back at me, she spoke slowly. "Because you shattered my phone, Brody."

"I—what? You just called me from your cell phone less than an hour ago. I just got home. My goddamn car is still running!"

"Ugh. Whatever, I'll just pay for the new phone, Dad. Don't worry about it. I'll see you soon." Sliding off the bar stool, she walked past me and toward her part of the house. "I know, I'm scared to be here with him, but I'll be out of here soon. Love you too. Bye."

Dropping the phone on the couch, she kept walking and didn't stop until I slammed my hand down on the bar and yelled, "What the fuck are you doing, Olivia? You *know* I've been gone! You fucking called me because I wasn't home. I don't know what the fuck you did to your phone, but I still have it on mine that you called."

She shrugged. "I wanted a new phone."

"You—you wanted—you wanted a new phone?! That's what all this was about? Olivia! What the fuck is wrong with you? You told me you were going to kill yourself. You said you wanted to be with Tate, and I come home to find you telling your goddamn dad that I'm crazy, and scaring you, and you think I'm going to beat you?"

"Well, you were yelling, what was I supposed to think?" she screeched back.

"When have I ever laid a hand on you, Olivia? When?" She didn't respond and my voice got louder. "Answer me!"

"You haven't. Yet! But you're always yelling, you're always mad at me. It's only going to escalate. This is how abusive relationships begin—with the man treating the woman this way."

I huffed harshly a few times and paced the short distance between the bar and kitchen table before sitting down in a chair and grabbing at my hair. "You have got to be kidding me! You expect me not to yell when you pulled the shit you just did? When you drain our bank accounts? When you shatter practically every dish in our kitchen? And then you go back to acting like nothing happened at all? Or you break your own phone and then call your dad and place some weird blame for it on me? Who wouldn't yell at you about that shit after almost five *fucking* years?!"

"Yeah, Brody. Five years. Five! Five years of coping with the fact that my distant and hateful husband *murdered* my baby!"

The air left my lungs in a hard rush, and I gripped at the table when I started falling forward. When I was able to speak again, my voice was low and dark. "I did not murder Tate. How dare you even suggest that. You aren't the only one who's been struggling. I struggle through what happened every day, and there are days when I feel like I can't even get myself out of bed because the grief is too much. But you don't see me lying about committing suicide. You don't see me trying to place blame somewhere else."

"Because there *is* nowhere else to place the blame. It's all on you. Always has been, always will be. You've taken everything from me. Never forget that." She took a few steps and stopped before the hallway. "I'm going to my parents', as you obviously heard. Unless you've deluded yourself into thinking I'm going to commit suicide again," she sneered. "I want a new iPhone waiting for me when I get home tomorrow."

"You're sick, Liv," I whispered to the empty kitchen after I'd heard her bedroom door slam shut. "And you need help. God, you need so much help."

9

Brody

June 9, 2015

ONCE I WAS done explaining everything to my chief, I sat there silently as I waited for him to respond. He'd remained quiet and emotionless as I told him about the changes in Olivia since Tate's death, and how they'd been progressing quickly over the last couple weeks.

It'd been four days since she told me she was going to kill herself, and even though she'd spent most of that time at her parents' house, I'd refused to leave ours just in case.

And no, I hadn't bought her a new phone.

"Saco, I know it's been difficult for you ever since Tate passed," he finally said, "and I know things at home have been, well . . .

rocky. I respect that you want to get help for your wife, really I do. But you should maybe think about letting her family handle this."

My head jerked back and I scrambled for the right words. "What—how could—what does that—what are you—what?!"

"Sometimes, as men, we need to know when—"

"Are you kidding? Did you not hear all I just told you? She's with her family most of the time and she's only getting worse. She's telling them that she's scared of me, and knowing the kind of people they are, they'll believe that I'm actually beating her or something."

"They do, Saco."

I kept talking over him. "I need to get her help, I need to get doctors to see her. She won't willingly go, when I suggest something she—"

"Brody!" he snapped. "They do believe you're beating her."

My chest heaved up and down quickly as I stared at him. "What?"

Chief sighed heavily and sank into his chair. "I didn't want to have to tell you about this."

When he didn't expand on what "this" was, I slapped my hand down on his desk. "Tell me what?"

"The department received a formal complaint on you a few days ago. It was from Olivia's parents. Stated instances where Olivia has called them, scared of you, where you could be heard yelling in the background, and times when she's been able to escape you and come to their house, she's been claiming you had hit her."

I felt the blood quickly drain from my cheeks, and my head felt light. "Chief. No, you know I wouldn't."

He held up a hand to stop me, and I looked around the office for a trash can. "I know that. Which is why I hadn't planned on telling you about it and hadn't planned on taking any action against you. Besides, they even said they had no evidence other than hearing you yelling while she was talking to them."

"She's almost never home!" I defended myself unnecessarily as my eyes kept looking for something I could throw up in.

"I know. Saco, you need to breathe. Okay? Can is behind you if you need to hurl. Just breathe and listen to me."

I nodded my head and gripped the arms of the chair I was sitting in.

"The complaint came in a few mornings ago. From what you were telling me, it was the morning after her latest episode. Now, you said you were out when she called, correct?"

My mind flashed to the hotel with Kamryn, and my eyes slowly met Chief's. "Yes."

"And that person will testify to that if needed?"

I nodded again, even as I knew I couldn't put Kamryn in that situation.

"Because I know you wouldn't do this to anyone, Olivia included. But if her family decides to send a letter like this to a judge or someone else who doesn't know you like I do, then you'll need to be able to fight your side. You understand?"

"Yes, sir."

"That is why I said you might want to leave this to her family. Because even though she has threatened suicide to you, to others she's saying you're making it up. She hasn't done anything suicidal yet, and until then, you can't force her to be seen by a doctor. It has to be her decision. And if she's retaliating against you this way when you are suggesting she get help, I don't see this ending well for you, if you know what I mean."

I ran my hands agitatedly through my hair and leaned back in the chair. "But I'm the one who caused this. This is all on me. I owe it to her to get her help."

Chief was silent for a long time as he thought about how to respond. "I get it, Saco, I do. I just hate to see you doing this to yourself, and I hate to see her family trying to destroy you and your career even more. This is going to sound heartless and is to be kept between you and me, but just know that helping her now may hurt you more in the end. Like I said, it may be worth it to let her family deal with it."

I thought about my relationship with Kamryn, but pushed that to the back of my mind for now. "I appreciate the advice, Chief. But I need to keep trying." I stood to leave, then turned to face him as I reached the door and asked my original question again. "So there's nothing I can do that you know of?"

"No, sorry. Unless she does something suicidal, or something we can arrest her for, it ultimately has to be her decision to get help. I'm here if you need anything, Saco."

"Thank you. I'll be back before my shift tonight, there's something I have to do." I didn't wait for him to respond, I just turned and made my way out of the police department.

I drove to the familiar lot and parked in the same spot I always do. With a deep breath in, I got out of my Expedition and walked the too-familiar path until I was standing in front of the piece of marble with Tate's name and dates on it. Squatting down, I moved the stuffed monkey I'd placed there for his fifth birthday and traced the letters and numbers as I apologized again to my son.

After he died, my family and friends had all said that one day the pain would slowly start lessening, that one day it would get easier and I'd start moving on with my life. They were wrong. I still hated myself, the guilt still ate at me just as much as it had the day it happened, and my grief was as strong as ever. Kamryn was bringing me back to life, but with Tate gone, and with Olivia constantly throwing his death in my face, I didn't know how to even begin to deal and move on from the sorrow that was always waiting in the background.

Placing the monkey back in front of the headstone, I pressed my fingers to my lips before touching the cool stone.

"I love you, little man. I'm so sorry."

Kamryn

June 9, 2015

DROPPING THE TAKEOUT on the island in my kitchen, I took off for my bedroom and rushed to get into my pajamas. Just as I was slipping the shirt over my head, the doorbell rang, and I ran back through my condo to answer the door.

"Did you get the food?" Kinlee asked excitedly.

"Just got home from picking it up. Did you get the stuff for the drinks?"

She held up a large brown paper bag. "Pfft. Duh!" Turning to look at Jace, she made a shoo-ing motion with her hand. "You can go now, slave."

He rolled his eyes, but smiled as he looked at me. "Call me if she gets too trashed. Otherwise I'll be back at eleven."

"See you then!"

After kissing my cheek, he grabbed Kinlee's cheeks in his

hands and kissed her hard. "Call me 'slave' again and see who doesn't get that thing she likes tonight."

Kinlee whined, "Babe! That's not fair, you promised!"

"I think I just threw up," I whispered.

"You gonna call me 'slave' again?"

"No," she said and pouted.

"Then start counting down the hours until I—"

"I'm still standing here!" I yelled, cutting Jace off. "Still losing my appetite rapidly. Please leave."

He laughed loudly and with another quick kiss to Kinlee's forehead, turned and headed toward his truck.

"Y'all disgust me," I said when he left.

Kinlee looked at me with a mischievous gleam in her eyes. "Well, he sure doesn't disgust me."

"Oh, my God! We're done talking about this. Mexican food. Margaritas. Movie. No more thinking about you and Jace."

She shrugged as we walked toward the kitchen. "You could always join us."

I stopped walking and my jaw dropped. "Kinlee!"

"Oh, my God, you need to see your face!" she somehow managed to say between hard laughs. "Aw, Kace, you know I'm joking. But that was too perfect an opportunity to pass up—I had to say it. And your expression just shows me it was so worth it."

I gagged and thought about anything other than Kinlee and Jace's sex life. "Just make the freaking margaritas."

Hours later, we had eaten way too much, were already well into being drunk, had finished one movie, and for whatever reason had thought it would be amazing to make our own choreography to songs.

"I need to sit! I need water, and I need to sit." When I realized I was already on the couch, I laughed. "Okay, maybe just water."

Kinlee flopped onto the couch and laid her head on my lap. "We're amazing at that, don't you think? I think we're amazing. No one can dance like we can. We're amazing."

"Say 'amazing' again."

"Amazing!" she yelled and attempted what I think was the running man . . . while lying down.

"I can't move! I have never in my life been so tired."

Kinlee quickly rolled onto her stomach and then up on her knees. "Kace! Where in the mother effing world are you from?"

I laughed and fell back into the cushions. "Why?"

She flipped her hair back and grabbed the glasses off my face before putting them on her own. "I have naverrrr, in mah lahfe . . . been so tard."

Grabbing my glasses, I put them back on my face. "I don't sound like that!"

"Yes, you do!" she yelled out, still trying to give herself a southern drawl. "I've known you almost a year—it's about time you tell me."

My laughter slowly died down as I took in Kinlee's expectant expression, her eyes the most sober I'd seen them since our first margarita that night. I wanted to tell her, I wanted to tell her everything. Who I was, about Brody and me . . . all of it. But I couldn't yet. Sitting back up, I grabbed on to her arm and looked her in the eye. "Lee, what if I told you I'm not ready for people to know about my life before I moved here?"

She pouted, but not because she wasn't getting her way. "Was it really that bad, KC?"

"It might not have been as bad as you're thinking it was. But it was something I hated, something I wanted so badly to get far away from. And now that I am away from it, I'm so happy. Happy to not have to be that girl or think about her anymore, if that makes sense. And I guess I'm not ready yet for anyone to even get a glimpse of who I was. I'm sorry if that hurts you, I want to tell you, Kinlee. I really do. I swear, when I'm ready to think about that girl again, you'll be the first to know."

A slow smile crossed her face, and she nodded hard once. "Now *that* is something I can deal with. As long as I know that someday I'll know, then I'll stop bugging you to tell me. But I'm never gonna stop bugging you about the way you talk."

All expression left my face. "I really don't talk weird."

"Oh, yes, yes you do!" She stood, then had to steady herself for a few seconds. "Come on! One more margarita, and then I want to dance until Jace picks me up!" The bell rang, and she glared at the door. "No! Go home!"

"It's open!" I yelled and waved at Jace when he walked into the living room.

"Hide me!" Kinlee whispered as she pushed me back and lay down on top of me.

"That is the exact opposite of hiding," I said back to her and patted her back.

"Come on, drunkie. Time to go." Jace lifted her off me and cradled her in his arms. "Looks like the two of you had fun tonight," he said to me.

"Always."

Kinlee smiled widely at me and waved as Jace carried her away. "Don't forget, KC, you can always join in on the fun with Jace and me!"

Jace raised an eyebrow, and a horrified expression crossed my face. "Kinlee, go home and go to bed!"

"Do I want to know?" Jace asked.

"No. No, you don't," I assured him as I opened the front door.

With a nod, he turned and walked out the door with Kinlee still grinning in his arms.

Shutting the door, I went to the kitchen and began cleaning everything up from our girls' night in, and just as I was finishing my phone chimed. I ran to get it, hope building in my chest as I pulled up the text.

> *B:*
> *I can't call tonight. I'm sorry. I miss you.*

The hope that had been building quickly faded, and in its place was a feeling I felt myself drowning in, as I had so many nights before. *One day, Kamryn,* I chanted to myself. *One day.*

10

Kamryn

June 15, 2015

A LOW MOAN sounded in the back of my throat, and my head tilted back so it was resting against Brody's shoulder as his lips and teeth tortured the sensitive spots on my neck. Pushing my bottom against him, my body heated as I felt his erection pressing against me.

"You need to go," I said halfheartedly. It'd been a week and a half since we'd seen each other at the hotel. Now that I finally had him near me, I didn't want him going anywhere. "What if Kinlee comes in and catches you?"

"She won't." He spoke against my neck. Goose bumps covered my arms as his lips softly brushed against my skin.

"You can't know that. What if she sees your car?"

"Black Expeditions are everywhere. She isn't going to see one and automatically think it's mine."

I started to speak again, but was quickly spun around, and then Brody's mouth was on mine, effectively silencing me.

He parted my mouth, and I wrapped my arms around his neck when his tongue met mine. Never breaking the kiss, he searched blindly behind me until he hit the bowls I'd set down to wash and pushed them back before lifting me so I was on the counter. One of his hands stayed at the small of my back, the other traveled up and brushed against my breast.

"Brody." I whimpered his name like a plea. What I was asking for, I still wasn't sure of. He needed to leave before someone caught us. But I didn't want him to stop.

"You should let your employees leave early more often."

"They left because I closed up since I'm supposed to be finishing the cupcakes for Kinlee's party." Smiling against his mouth, I nipped at his bottom lip and kissed it softly as I pushed him back, only to grab his shirt so I could pull him back to me. "You're going to make me late and cupcake-less."

"And you're not about to hear me apologize."

"We can't both show up late," I said and pushed him away again.

"Okay, you're right." With a sigh, he nodded and grabbed a piece of the cupcake he'd been picking at earlier and popped it into his mouth. He grunted and went to pick another piece off. "Damn, these are good. Is this the kind you made for tonight?"

I didn't think twice when he put the piece in front of my mouth. I was already in such an intoxicated state from his kisses after over a week of not seeing him that I just opened my mouth and let him place the sugary cake in there. My eyes fluttered shut, and I moaned my appreciation for the sweetness—too late realizing my slipup. I swallowed quickly, breaking off the noises I was making, and looked up to see him standing in front of me with an obvious hunger in his eyes.

"Oh, God. I—"

Brody quickly closed the distance between us and crushed his mouth to mine. His tongue invaded my mouth relentlessly, and I clung to him as he pulled me closer to the edge of the counter.

"We're going to be late. I don't give a fuck what anyone says," he growled against my throat as he moved down to my collarbone. Moving my shirt to the side, he bit down gently and spoke again. "You can't make noises like that and then expect me to just leave, Kamryn."

With the way his mouth and hands were attacking me, I was forgetting the reasons to not let him take me right there. My hands pushed up under his shirt, and I lightly ran my nails over the muscles of his torso, causing him to shiver.

Simultaneously, the door chimed, Brody and I broke apart, and Kinlee's voice filled the front of my shop. "KC," she sang out.

Jumping off the counter, I straightened my shirt and apron and ran to the swinging doors. "Hey!" I said too brightly when I saw her.

Her eyebrows drew together, and I swear to God I stopped breathing. "Are you feeling okay? You're really red. Do you have a fever?" She moved toward me and went to touch my forehead, but I caught her hand and laughed it off.

"I'm fine, honestly. I'm just trying to get your cupcakes done so I can go home and change before going to your house." I hated lying to her, and yet it was all I seemed to do.

"Really? Ooh, can I see?" Her eyes brightened, and my stomach dropped.

"No, ma'am! You never accept anything I try to give you, so this is the only kind of gift I can make you take. Let me act like it's a present until later."

She pouted and crossed her arms under her chest. "But that's not fair! You won't let me buy you presents either."

"Get over it. You can't see them yet."

Kinlee looked like she was going to make a run for the kitchen, but thankfully, she huffed and turned back toward the shop. "Fine, fine." Turning her head to look at me, she winked. "I figured this was going to happen, so I won't count your cupcakes as a gift if you won't count *this* as a gift." Bending down, she picked up a bag from her boutique from the other side of the counter and set it down.

"Kinlee! No. Besides, it's not my birthday, so try the 'nongift' thing when it is."

"But Aiden is going to be there tonight, you need to look hot for him, and we just got this in! It will look amazing on you."

Oh, shit. There was no way Brody hadn't heard that. The acoustics in my shop were insane. "Kinlee—"

"I don't want to hear it," she called behind her as she jogged to the door. "Just know you will break my heart and ruin my birthday if you don't wear this tonight!" With a sly grin, she slipped outside and ran to her car.

She didn't play fair.

With a deep breath in and out, I turned and went back into the kitchen. I didn't even need to see Brody, the thick air in there was unmistakable. Chancing a glance at him, I cringed when I saw the angry expression on his handsome face.

"Brody . . ." I trailed off, not knowing what to say.

The muscles in his jaw worked a few times before he finally turned to look at me. "Do you know how much I hate that I couldn't walk out there and tell her that you belong to me? That my sister-in-law and brother still think something might happen with you and Aiden Donnelly?"

Oh, I'm pretty sure I had an idea. He hated that they wanted me to date someone? I hated that he was married. My body temperature started rising, and it had nothing to do with the way Brody and I hadn't been able to get enough of each other not even five minutes before. I was back to hating this situation, hating that I couldn't claim him as mine, hating that I had to share him with another woman.

I blinked hard against the sudden tears that pooled in my eyes and moved to the cupcakes that were waiting to be filled and frosted. "I really need to finish these and go home to change into whatever outfit Kinlee picked out for me."

A few tense moments passed before Brody let out a huff, then moved so he was behind me again. With a soft kiss to my cheek, he wrapped his strong arms around me and pinned my body to his. "I need to warn you now. If I see him touch you, then everyone will be finding out about us tonight. I won't be able to hold myself back, Kamryn."

Part of me wanted to lash out at him, and my body froze when I realized I felt that way. I'd never wanted to use our situation, or Brody's marriage, against him . . . and now that I was, I wasn't sure how I felt about that. As I fought with myself over my feelings Brody whispered in my ear . . . and the agony in his three words broke me.

"I *hate* this." His voice broke in the middle, and the tears that had flooded my eyes earlier rolled down my cheeks.

Three words we'd both used plenty of times over the last month and a half. But his tone, mixed with the way his grip tightened and his body trembled against mine, was breaking me. My anger faded immediately, and I turned in his arms to drop my forehead to his chest.

"I do too."

Brody held me in his arms for a few minutes before kissing the top of my head. "One day everyone will know. One day it will just be you and me. One day this will all be behind us."

When no words left my lips, I simply nodded against his chest as I replayed the words he'd already promised me so many times.

"I'll be waiting for you at their house, Kamryn. Don't be too long."

I felt empty as soon as he released me, and the second I heard the chime from the door as he left I let loose the pained sobs that had been building up in my chest. I continued to tell myself that he was right, that we would be together soon. But a small part of me was beginning to doubt my ability to keep this going. I didn't know how much longer I could handle all the guilt, secrets, and days alone wishing for things to be different.

A LITTLE OVER an hour later I was pulling up to Jace and Kinlee's house, my pulse drumming quickly. I parked behind Brody's SUV and sat there for a few minutes, just staring at it and telling myself that I could get through tonight. I could get through a night of being so close to him and, at the same time, so far away from him.

I'm meeting his parents tonight. I'm meeting his parents and will have to look them in the eye knowing I'm having an affair with their son. I can't do this, I can't do this! I quickly reached for the keys still in the ignition and started to turn them when a truck pulled up behind me. With a defeated sigh, I let my hand drop for a few seconds before pulling the keys out of the ignition. Reaching for the door handle, I jumped back and a startled scream tore from my chest when someone knocked on the window.

Aiden jumped away from the car and held his arms up like he was surrendering, and I sent him a shaky smile as I shook my head.

"You trying to give a girl a heart attack?" I asked as I opened the door.

He laughed and stepped toward me with a hand stretched out. "Hardly. I just pulled up and saw you sitting in here. Jace said you were bringing cupcakes, so I thought I'd ask if you needed help."

I took his hand and let him help me from my car and wrapped my arms around his waist when he pulled me in for a hug. Leaning back, he looked down at me with a soft grin, and it suddenly felt like I was too close to him.

"How've you been?" he asked, his voice low and barely audible.

Putting one hand to his chest, I pushed back until he released me. "Good. Busy, but good. How about you?"

The slight tilt to his lips fell, and he looked away as he realized I was distancing myself. Nodding twice, he glanced back at me and tried to smile again, but it fell flat. His words sounded rough but full of understanding when he stated, "You still belong to someone else."

It hadn't been a question, but I responded anyway. "I do."

With another nod, he shot me a smile, this one genuine. "Well, it's still great to see you, KC, and you look beautiful." Before another awkward silence could come between us, he shut my door and walked to the back. "What do you say we get the dessert taken in?"

"Aiden," I whispered. He stopped walking, but didn't look back at me. "I don't want you to waste time waiting for me. You should find someone who can be with you."

Turning, he shrugged. "If I find someone, then I find someone. But until then, I'd rather spend the time I have away from work waiting for you to realize you're in love with me," he said teasingly.

Whether he actually meant those words or not, I was glad the heaviness between us had been lifted, and I laughed as I opened the back of my car. Using the same teasing tone, I leaned forward to grab a couple of the boxes. "And what if I told you it was never going to happen? Would you stop then?"

"Ugh." He stumbled back from the car and gripped at his chest. "You're wounding my ego, KC."

"Oh, I'm sure that was a big blow to it."

"The worst." He sighed dramatically, but shot me a wink. "I'm not sure if I can go on after that kind of dismissal."

I laughed and pushed him away when he draped a heavy arm over my shoulders. "Toughen up, Donnelly. I need help taking these boxes in, and I doubt a firefighter turned princess is up for the job."

"Princess, huh?"

Turning my head to look at him, I eyed him and sucked air between my teeth before mouthing, *Princess*.

He laughed loudly and grabbed most of the boxes. "Better watch yourself, KC, I'll force-feed you one of the cupcakes in front of everyone."

I gasped and shifted the boxes to one arm so I could close up and lock my SUV. "You wouldn't dare."

"I don't know . . . in the last three minutes you crushed what little ego I had, and then called me a princess. I think that calls for a show of you eating your cupcakes."

Groaning, I followed him up the walkway to the house. "I hate Kinlee for telling y'all that."

"I sure as hell don't. It's now my mission in life to watch you eat something sweet."

"Not gonna happen."

"We'll see." He smiled widely and laughed when I rolled my eyes. Opening the door, he stepped back to let me in first, and I wished he hadn't.

Brody was standing just inside the living room with Jace and a few other guys I didn't know. Since Aiden wasn't blocking my view of him, I watched as his eyes lit up when he saw me . . . then saw all expression leave his face when he noticed the man behind me.

I heard Jace say my name and Aiden begin talking with the guys standing there, but I wasn't able to focus on anything else as I stared at Brody. He wasn't even looking at me anymore. His eyes were pinned to Aiden, and the jealousy there was apparent.

I knew if I stood there waiting for him to acknowledge me again, someone was bound to notice, so I straightened myself and walked into the kitchen so I could put the boxes down. Aiden was there setting the rest on the counter when I turned, and I thanked him before opening them up and putting them out on the platters Kinlee had waiting.

My head jerked up as I heard Brody's name being called, and I watched as he walked over to someone I assumed was his mother.

Kinlee came up behind me and wrapped her arms around me. "Don't you look hot!"

I laughed and looked back at her. "Thanks for the outfit, Lee."

"I saw Aiden helping you inside . . ." She drifted off, her voice full of meaning.

"Nothing happened, and nothing is going to happen. I told you, he's just not it for me." Kinlee scoffed, but before she could say anything I jerked my head toward Jace, Brody, and the two women they were standing with. "What's going on over there?" *And why does Brody look pissed?*

"Oh, that's my mother-in-law. Every time she sees Brody, she tries to get him to leave Olivia by setting him up with someone else. I guess Julia is the poor soul she's set her sights on this time."

I was going to throw up. Or yank Julia away from Brody. I hadn't decided yet. Forcing myself to unclench my jaw, I tried to sound like I didn't care either way. "Why do you say 'poor soul'?"

"Because every time his mom tries to set him up with someone else, the girl gets excited at the thought of being with Brody, only to be turned down. We all want Brody away from Olivia, we would love to see him with anyone else. But no matter how much he hates that woman, he's never going to leave her."

Throwing up. Definitely throwing up. My heart was currently residing in my stomach, and my stomach was churning. It wasn't a good feeling, and throughout all of it I had to retain my unaffected facade.

Brody looked over at me for a few seconds, before looking back to his mom, who was animatedly talking about Julia's successes. But in those few seconds I saw everything I was feeling reflected back at me.

Swallowing down my anger, I turned and grabbed Kinlee's shoulder as I gave her a kiss on the cheek. "I forgot something in my car, I'll be back. Happy birthday, Lee."

"Do you want Aiden to help you?" she asked too loudly.

I cringed and turned to see both Aiden and Brody looking at me. Aiden's expression was expectant, while Brody's was livid.

"No, I'm fine. It's just my purse." I waved Aiden and Kinlee off and tried not to look at Brody again as I turned and walked quickly across the kitchen, through the dark dining room, and to the entryway. As soon as I was outside I let out an angry huff and balled my hands into fists before pressing them against my churning stomach.

Putting a hand to the passenger side of my car for a couple minutes, I held myself up and dropped my head as I took deep breaths in and out. As if it wasn't enough what Brody and I were already doing . . . what we were already going through . . . now I had to watch his mom try to push other women on him?

My biggest worry for tonight had been keeping myself away from him when he would be so close to me. It hadn't occurred to me that I'd be silently fighting for him.

Straightening up, I mentally shook myself and opened the door to grab my purse sitting on the floorboard before shutting the door and locking my car again. I couldn't let this rule my night. Tonight was about Kinlee. Letting my situation with Brody get in the way of her birthday wasn't fair to her.

As soon as I walked back into the house a warm hand clamped

down on my wrist and pulled me into the darkened dining room. His full lips pressed against mine, and for a few seconds I let myself get lost in that kiss. But then I remembered where we were, and who was with us.

"What are you doing?" I hissed when I broke off the kiss.

"Why did you come with Donnelly?"

"Are you kidding me, Brody? He pulled in behind me and helped me in. Nothing more."

His eyes roamed my face for a few seconds. "Jace said Aiden—"

"I don't care what Jace said!" I cut him off. "Why didn't you tell me your mother is trying to set you up with other women? Why didn't you warn me that would be happening tonight?"

Brody sighed and pressed his body closer to mine. "I don't know, I wasn't thinking about it. To be honest, all I could think about was that Aiden would be here tonight and my sister-in-law and brother want you with him."

"Well, it looks like we're even tonight then. You don't like that they want me with him, and I don't like that I have to watch your mom push another girl on you."

Despite my anger, he smirked and brushed back some of my bangs. "Who knows? Maybe one day she'll push you on me."

Putting my hands on his chest, I tried to shove him away, but he didn't move. "That's not funny, Brody, and you know it," I said through gritted teeth.

"Kam, it was a joke."

"I don't want to be this person. I don't want to be seen as the girl who breaks up a marriage, you know that. So don't make light of something that you *know* is killing me."

"Babe. You're not breaking up a marriage. You're making me

feel alive for the first time in years. I'm sorry for joking, but if we can't joke about it, it's going to keep driving us crazy and put more strain on our relationship until we can be together."

I cleared my throat and shook my head as a sad smile pulled at my lips. "There is *nothing* about us, or our situation, that can possibly be found funny."

"Kamryn," he whispered. "I—"

"I need to get back to Kinlee," I said suddenly, and this time when I pushed, he let me go and stumbled back.

I didn't want to hash out everything with Brody right now. If we did, I would undoubtedly end up crying, and that would raise questions. I needed to focus on my best friend. Yes . . . I needed to focus on her and for a few hours try to forget about the pain, heartache, jealousy, and guilt that were slowly unfurling in my stomach—even with Brody here.

Brody

June 15, 2015

AFTER SHUTTING AND locking the front door, I trudged into the kitchen and dropped the box of cupcakes on the island. Tonight had been a disaster. I'd been so on edge watching Kamryn and Aiden, ready to rip him away from her if he touched her, that I'd been shaking for the better part of the night. But whenever Kamryn's eyes would meet mine, the adrenaline would quickly fade from my body and a deep ache would fill my chest as those blue eyes reminded me how much I'd fucked up earlier.

I hated that she'd seen my mom try to set me up with Julia, a girl I'd grown up with. I hated that I'd made it worse by joking about it. I hated that the woman I loved had to go through so much pain because of me. And I hated that I still hadn't told her I loved her.

We both knew. If we weren't in love with each other, we wouldn't be doing what we were doing. We showed it in touches, kisses, and looks. But realizing I hadn't told her as she walked away from me tonight had made it nearly impossible to go the next three hours without grabbing her and telling her in front of everyone.

Rubbing my hands over my face, I walked back to my room and stripped my clothes off before taking a hot shower. The entire time my body and mind were willing me to get back in the car and go to her.

But Olivia was home, and even though I hadn't seen her, she'd probably heard me. If I left again at eleven at night, I had no doubt she'd be calling me screaming within minutes.

As soon as I was done with my shower I dried off and pulled a pair of shorts on before going back to the kitchen. I stopped midstep and my blood ran cold when I saw Liv sitting on the counter in nothing but a bra and underwear. She was holding one of the cupcakes and sensually licking the frosting off her finger as her eyes bore into mine.

"I've missed you, Brody," she whined, and her lips formed a pout.

"What are you doing, Liv?"

She spread her legs, but I never looked away from her face. "I thought we could have some fun with the cupcakes you brought back for me."

I didn't even bother telling her they weren't for her. That would just make her start screaming sooner.

"Mmm, God, these are so good."

My stomach turned at her over-the-top moans, and I forced myself to take calming breaths so I wouldn't get sick.

"You haven't eaten food off me in a while, baby."

One of my eyebrows rose at her statement, but before I could say anything she was talking again.

"Is that what these are for?" She placed the cupcake down and reached behind her to unhook her bra before letting it fall to the floor. Grabbing the cupcake back up, she licked at the frosting and then licked her lips.

God, she was about to ruin Kamryn's cupcakes for me forever. "I'm not sure what you're talking about, Liv. I've never eaten food off you."

Her blue eyes widened, and her screech was the only warning I had before she was launching the cupcake at me. I ducked, and the cupcake slammed into the wall behind me.

"What the hell, Olivia?" I shouted and was hit in the chest with another one when I straightened. "Stop throwing shit!" Taking large steps forward, I grabbed the box from next to her and yanked it away before tossing it back on the island where I'd left it.

"Why won't you?"

"What?"

"Why won't you eat food off me anymore? Is it because I'm not good enough for you? Is it because of Tate? Because you can't stand to look at me now?" Each question was shriller than the last, and I fought the urge to cover my ears against the noise.

"I don't know what the fuck you're talking about! I've never eaten food off you. You're obviously mistaking me for someone else!"

"How could you, Brody?" she screamed and got off the counter. "How dare you tell your own wife that she's no longer good enough for you?!"

I stood there with my mouth hanging open as she stormed past me and ran down the hall, slamming her bedroom door shut.

What in the fuck just happened?

It took a couple minutes to gather myself enough to grab a wet towel to clean up the cupcake on the wall and floor, and as I stood back up from cleaning the last smudges and pieces I felt a naked body press to my back.

"I'm sorry, I love you."

"Olivia, stop." I moved away from her and over to the sink to rinse off the towel. When I turned back around, she launched herself at me, pressing her lips to my chest, which was still covered in chocolate frosting. "Olivia, *stop*!"

"Let me make it better, Brody. I love you. I'll make it better," she said as I grabbed her shoulders and held her back. Her hands reached out for my shorts, and I put more distance between us. "Please!"

"We need to talk, and you need to put some clothes on."

Her blue eyes flashed up to mine, and I instantly recognized the heat in them. "We can talk after. Come on, baby, I want to make you feel good." She grabbed my wrists and tried to move my hands from her shoulders, but I didn't let them budge.

"Liv, you need help. Let me get you help."

The coy smile instantly vanished, and the heat in her eyes was replaced with the anger I was so used to. "Help? Help?! You want to get me help? For what, Brody?!" Her voice was already back to the same octave it had been at before she'd left the kitchen, and it made me grit my teeth.

Keeping my voice calm, I released her shoulders and took another step back. "For your depression, to start. Olivia, you're bipolar, you need help. Do you not realize you went from trying to seduce me to screaming at me to seducing me again, all within ten minutes?"

"You think I'm depressed? Is that what you want? Maybe I should be! Maybe I will ask Daddy to pay for a goddamn shrink since you can't afford one! I'll tell him all about my feelings and about how I'm forced to live with my husband even though he murdered my son!"

"Olivia!" I barked.

"I'll tell him all about how you've been abusing me. How you tell me I'm not good enough for you!"

"Abusing you? Are you fucking kidding me? You're gonna start with this shit again? Again, Liv, when have I ever touched you?"

She threw her arms out and screamed, "Good question! When was the last time you touched me, Brody?"

I was so confused. I wasn't sure I even knew what she was talking about anymore.

"So maybe I had it wrong. Maybe you brought these home so I would get fat so you would have a reason not to touch me!" Taking a step back to the island, she grabbed one of the last two cupcakes and shoved it in her face. "Is this what you want?" she screamed and smashed it in her face again before throwing it on the counter. "You want me fat and ugly, Brody?"

"Jesus Christ, Olivia! This is what I'm talking about. You. Need. Help. Please, let me get you help!"

"I don't need *anything,* you selfish bastard!" she yelled, her face and teeth covered in chocolate frosting and cake pieces.

"I can get you—"

"Help!" she screamed louder than before. "Help me! Someone, please! He's trying to kill me!"

My eyes widened and I grabbed for her shoulders. "Olivia!"

"He has a knife, someone help me, *please!*"

Taking large strides, I propelled her back until she was pressed against the wall and covered her mouth with my hand. "Olivia, what are you doing? Stop!" I hissed.

She tried yelling against my hand, but the noise didn't travel far.

"Are you trying to get me arrested? What the hell is wrong with you?"

Her eyes watered before tears were rolling down her cheeks and over my hand, and her body stopped trying to get away from the wall and me. Releasing her mouth, I instantly wished I hadn't when she opened it. "That's what you deserve! That's what *murderers* deserve! You didn't have to pay for what you did to Tate! You didn't care!"

"You think—you think I don't fucking *care*? You think I'm not paying for what happened on a daily basis? I feel like I'm dying because of what happened to Tate. I will pay for it, and grieve for him, every day of my life. But you saying this, you using what happened against me, has got to stop, Liv! You are killing me more every time you blame me. I blame myself enough!"

"Until you're dead too, it will never be enough!" she sobbed. "I wish it'd been you instead of him!"

My arms dropped like deadweight, and she moved away from me seconds before I stumbled back and slid down the wall opposite where I'd had her.

I wish it'd been me too.

My eyes glazed over, and a strangled cry worked its way up my throat. Pulling my knees up, I rested my elbows on them and covered my face as I once again wished for my son to still be here. To be able to hold him one more time.

I was still sitting there sometime later, my head back on the wall, my legs sprawled out on the floor, when Olivia was suddenly sitting on my lap.

"Get. Off. Me."

"Let me take it all away, Brody. I'll make it better."

I grabbed her bare shoulders and pushed her back and to the side until she was off my lap. "All I want that has to do with you is to get you help. You are sick. There is something wrong with you. Let me get you the help you need."

"I know what will help me." Her hand snaked out toward my lap, but I stopped her advance.

"You need doctors," I growled and looked over at her. I was surprised to see her face cleared of the cupcake, not surprised she was still naked. "A shit ton of them. You have to know that, and you have to realize I'm trying to help you."

"I don't need help," she said with a confident voice.

"You do." I stood up and took a couple steps toward my room before looking back at her. "And I'm not stopping until I get it for you."

11

Brody

June 16, 2015

RESTING MY ELBOWS on the counter, I let my head fall into my hands as I waited for the coffee to finish brewing the next morning. I'd barely gotten any sleep as thoughts of Olivia's behavior went through my mind over and over again. Something wasn't adding up, and a part of me was getting ready to just give up on trying to get her help.

Her mood swings were off the charts. I had never thought too much about the fact that she'd always gone back to being her normal self when we were out in public until the night she'd threatened to kill herself. Coming home to find her perfectly fine and telling her father that she was afraid of me was what had me looking deeper into every encounter with her.

No bipolar or depression case was the same, I knew that. But whatever Olivia had been suffering from over the last several years couldn't be defined as any one thing. What was going on with her was both everything and, at the same time, nothing. Unfortunately, I'd overlooked this paradox until now. And now I was beginning to notice the weird patterns in Olivia's brand of crazy.

I'd wanted to get her help when I thought her reaction to Tate's death was the same as any normal mother would have, but now it had changed into something else entirely. With the inconsistencies in her behavior, and the brief flashes of the scheming girl I'd known so well in high school, suddenly I was no longer so sure I wanted to get her help. Had she just been playing a game with me to see how far she could push me? And had it taken me this long to catch on to what she was up to? She was constantly telling me she didn't need help, and I was beginning to wonder whether that was true. Was Liv just being Liv, someone who didn't need a goddamn thing from anyone other than her dad's money? If she was still the old Olivia I'd fallen for in high school, she was just putting on an act and then sitting back and enjoying the show.

I straightened and breathed out heavily when those thoughts went through my head again. *She can't be playing a game. She can't be faking grief over Tate's death*, I told myself for the hundredth time since last night.

I was so confused, so torn . . . and such a fucking dick. I wanted to be with Kamryn so bad that I was now making up excuses for Liv's behavior so I could justify leaving her without getting her help first.

The house phone rang, jolting me from the inner scolding, and

I turned to grab it from the counter. I ground my teeth when the name I'd briefly seen on the caller ID registered, but I'd already pushed TALK.

"Hello?"

"Where's my daughter?"

"How are you today, Mr. Reynolds?" I asked as I turned to walk out of the kitchen and toward Liv's side of the house.

There was a pause before he huffed. "We don't do small talk, Brody. Put my daughter on the phone and tell me why she wasn't answering her cell."

I rolled my eyes and suppressed a huff of my own. "I'm not sure, you can ask her when you talk to her. Liv," I called out as I walked down the hallway.

Letting my arm drop so I wouldn't have to play nice with my father-in-law anymore, I called out her name two more times as I let myself into her room and looked around for her. Rounding the corner into her bathroom, I froze for two seconds before I ran to where she was lying on the floor.

"Olivia!" I shouted and grabbed her limp body. "Liv!"

Pressing two fingers to the inside of her wrist, I grabbed the phone I'd dropped near her body, hung up on her dad, and called 911.

"Jeston Police Department, do you need fire, medical, or police?"

"I need an ambulance to 9709 Tuscany Way. Twenty-six-year-old female unconscious, I just found her with an empty pill bottle next to her. Breathing is very shallow, her body is still warm, though."

The line beeped as Olivia's dad continued calling me back, but he'd have to wait.

"Is this Brody?" the dispatcher asked cautiously.

"Yes. It's Olivia . . . my wife."

The dispatcher cursed softly. "Okay. What kind of pill bottle?"

I grabbed for it and read random things off the label. "Uh . . . duloxetine. It's for thirty pills, the prescription was filled . . . four days ago." I said the last few words with dread as I looked down at Liv. "Olivia, I need you to wake up!"

"Okay, the ambulance is already on its way. You said she's still warm?"

"Yes, I don't know when she took these. I walked in here to give her the phone and found her. Is there something I can do until they get here?"

"Are her lips or fingers blue?"

Grabbing her limp arm, I brought her hand closer before gently releasing it. "No. Come on, Liv!" Shaking her shoulders, I looked for some kind of reaction, but there was nothing. "I hear the sirens," I said to the dispatcher. "I'm going to open the door. Thank you."

As soon as he acknowledged my thanks, I ended the call and ran to the front door, threw it open, and waited for the EMTs to follow me back to Liv's bathroom. They asked countless questions about her health, her mental stability, and if she'd shown signs of being suicidal in the past as they loaded her onto the stretcher and took vitals. Once she was loaded into the back, I got in my SUV and pulled out my phone as I followed behind.

"Hello?"

"It's Brody."

"You worthless piece of shit," Mr. Reynolds growled. "Tell me where my—"

"She's loaded up in the back of an ambulance on her way to

Memorial because of you and your wife. Thought you'd like to know." Without waiting for him to respond, I ended the call and focused on getting to the hospital. There would be time to yell at them later.

I STOOD AND held back an eye roll when Olivia's parents walked into the waiting room almost two hours later. They lived fifteen minutes from the hospital, and they were both so dressed up, they looked like they were ready to go to a race.

"What have you done to her now?" Mr. Reynolds bellowed, and the other people in the large room looked between us.

My face heated, but not with embarrassment. Clenching my hands into fists, I refused to speak until they were standing in front of me, and when I did, I spoke so that only the two of them could hear me. "What have *I* done? That must be a joke considering Olivia is going to be put on a twenty-four-hour suicide watch once they're done because she overdosed on antidepressants that were prescribed to your wife!" I hissed.

Mrs. Reynolds scoffed and crossed her arms. "Now you're trying to lay blame on us?"

"What antidepressants?" Mr. Reynolds asked.

Grabbing the bottle from my pocket, I tossed it at his chest and said the information from memory. "Duloxetine, otherwise known as Celexa. Thirty pills prescribed to Cathy Reynolds, filled four days ago. All thirty were gone, and the bottle was next to Liv when I found her unconscious in the bathroom this morning." I turned and took two steps toward the chairs before turning back around to face them. Throwing my arms out, I leaned forward and whispered sardonically, "Which, by the way, is probably why she wasn't answering her phone."

Mrs. Reynolds took a step closer to me. "Those are in my name because she was too scared to get them herself. She was afraid of what you would do to her if you knew she needed them."

I laughed, but I didn't know if it was because Olivia's parents were so blind, or because I was just that much closer to breaking down after all this time. "Are you—are you fucking kidding me?" I said through gritted teeth. "I have *never* hurt Olivia. I told you she was suicidal, and you didn't listen. I have been trying to get her help! I have been *trying* to get her to realize on her own that she needs help. The other night she called me saying she needed to be with Tate, that she couldn't live without him anymore, and then she hung up on me. When I got home, she was talking to you on the house phone like nothing was wrong except for the fact that I scare her and shattered her phone. When she got off the phone with you, she told me she broke her cell herself because she wanted a new one. How do you not see that there's something wrong with her? How do you not see what she's doing? She's trying to turn you against me because she knows you'll give her what she wants. I'm the only one who's trying to fucking help her! And how do you repay me? You put in a formal complaint with my chief?"

"Excuse me, sir, I'm going to have to ask you to step outside if you want to continue this conversation."

I turned to look at the security guard standing there with one of the nurses, and my shoulders sagged. "It's fine. I said what I needed to say."

We sat on opposite sides of the waiting room for another two hours until the director of a psych ward in a hospital in Portland called me back. Stepping outside, I talked with him for well over an hour about Olivia, what had been happening since Tate passed, the escalation in the last few weeks, and what had happened that morning. He told me about how things were run on his ward and the benefits for Olivia of being treated there; once he got the report from Olivia's doctor, he told me, we could talk again about the possibility of her going to his Portland facility for care.

Once the call was over, I hovered over Kamryn's name for a few seconds before putting my phone in my pocket. I wanted to tell her what was happening, but I wanted to be able to hold her when I did. I was finally going to get Liv help, but I'd almost been too late. And my stomach dropped every time I remembered how last night and this morning I'd been wondering if all this had been a game to her.

Walking into the hospital, my steps quickened when I saw Liv's parents speaking to the doctor. He eyed me warily, and my forehead creased in confusion. We'd spoken twice that morning, and he hadn't been back out since the Reynoldses arrived. I didn't know why he'd be talking to them and looking at me like I had no place in being there.

"What's going on? How's she doing?"

Mr. Reynolds's back stiffened, and he turned to glare at me. "You disgusting piece of trash. What was this going to accomplish for you?"

"What?"

"You think throwing a childish fit and trying to make us believe you're the only one who wants to help her would make any of us believe that our daughter would have done something so tragic?"

I shook my head slowly as I tried to comprehend what he was saying, and why his wife looked like she was about to kill me. Looking past him, I asked the doctor, "What the hell happened?"

He glanced at Liv's parents, and her mom urged him to tell me. With a slow breath out, he squared his shoulders and looked at me. "Your wife's toxicity report came back. There was no trace of the antidepressants, or any narcotic for that matter, in her system. We're running tests to see why she fainted. There's always the possibility of a seizure, that kind of thing."

My jaw dropped and I shook my head once. "No . . . she was completely unresponsive. Her breathing was too shallow. I was with her for five minutes trying to wake her up, the EMTs couldn't wake her up. And if she didn't take the pills, then what did she do with them so that they were all gone and the bottle just happened to be there next to her?"

"Or what did *you* do with them," Mrs. Reynolds said under her breath, and my head jerked back. "She said she was afraid of what would happen if you knew she needed them. I find it disturbing that *we* get her help, and she winds up in the hospital just days later."

"This has got to be a joke," I said, breathing hard.

Kamryn

June 16, 2015

"I THINK IT needs to be Sunday every day of the week," Kinlee blurted out.

Laughing, I dipped my spoon back into the pint of ice cream

and ignored her laughing when I moaned through my next bite. "Shut up," I grumbled.

"Oh, whatever. It's cute!"

"Lee, it is *not* cute! You try moaning like this when you eat sweet stuff! Think about never being able to try something sweet when you're out. Never being able to try flavors at the frozen yogurt shop, just having to hope you'll like it. Think. About. It."

Kinlee's face morphed into a look of horror. "No fro-yo samples?!"

"Exactly." I pointed the spoon at her.

Jace was working, so we'd spent all day at her house in our pajamas, doing nothing but eating and watching movies. I felt so sick. So fat. So lazy. And so ridiculously happy.

Putting the half-eaten pint on the coffee table, I rubbed my eyes under my glasses and sat back into the cushions on the couch. "You're trying to kill me with sugar."

"You found me out," she said around one of my cookies. "Took you long enough. What's this?" she asked, nodding her head at the TV.

"How am I supposed to know? You have the remote."

"Well, I can't find it. What was coming on after *Harry Potter*?"

I rolled my head to the side and raised an eyebrow at her. "Really? You're really asking me this right now? There were two on in a row. How the hell am I supposed to know the answer to that?"

"Meh, whatever. It has Cameron Diaz. I like her." Kinlee shrugged and sat back. "I don't want to watch this," she whispered a few moments later.

"What? Why?" I looked at her, alarmed by the tone of her voice.

"I just don't. Can you help me look for the remote?"

I watched as she turned and shoved her hand in the side of the couch, and I glanced back at the inoffensive movie playing. "I don't—what's wrong with it?"

"I just don't want to watch it, all right?!"

Jumping back from her now-shrill voice, I sat there stunned for a few seconds before nodding my head furiously. "Yeah, okay. Let's find it."

I helped her look for the remote while sneaking glances back at the TV. "*What to Expect When You're Expecting,*" I said, reading the title out loud. Why would Kinlee be so against watching this?

Looking back at her, I watched her eyes flutter shut and a deep breath left her. Her shoulders hunched forward like she was curling in on herself, and my chest ached for my friend.

"Are—are you and Jace having a baby?" Wouldn't that be a happy thing?

She sighed sadly and opened her eyes, but didn't look at me. She just continued staring at the back of the couch. "No."

Glancing quickly at the movie still playing, I moved to sit on the floor next to her and grabbed her forearm. "Did you have a miscarriage, Lee?" She shook her head, and my confusion grew. "I—what happened? I don't know what's wrong."

For long minutes she just sat there staring until she finally cried out, "I swear to God, it's like it all comes at once. It can't just be the same amount all the time. I either don't see babies, don't see pregnant women, and don't see commercials about them . . . or I see them everywhere!" Fat tears fell down her cheeks, and my mouth hung open as I sat there helplessly. "In the last week I have seen dozens of commercials about babies, about pregnancy tests. There has been at least one pregnant woman or one woman with an infant who comes into the store every day, and did you notice the group of women at Starbucks on Thursday?" she asked, finally turning to look at me.

I shook my head as I thought back to Thursday.

"Pregnant!" she spit out. "All four of them were fucking pregnant, and two had toddlers." Hard sobs racked her small body, and she wiped at her eyes with the heels of her hands. "It's like it has to taunt me constantly for weeks until I finally break. It's like the universe realizes that I'm okay with my life, and happy with Jace, and wants to remind me of what I can't have and make me miserable all over again!"

"You—you can't have kids, Kinlee?" I asked softly.

"Do you—" She cut off, trying to suck in air. "Do you realize how *hard* it is knowing you *can't*? Knowing it's not even an *option*?" she cried. "Do you know how badly Jace wanted a family? That's all—" Her words stopped as the sobs took over her body, and she slumped into the couch.

Pulling her over to me, I wrapped my arms around her and let my hand run over her back as her body shook uncontrollably.

"That's all he wanted. That's all *I* wanted! And I can't give us that," she whimpered, her body sagging as the sobs calmed.

"Kinlee, I'm so sorry. I had no idea," I said as I continued to hold her. "I'm sorry."

We sat there on the floor, in front of her couch, for countless minutes as she cried and my heart broke for her. When her tears stopped and she sat back, I grabbed her hand and looked at her red-rimmed eyes.

"When did you find out?"

She sniffed and wiped at her face. "Right before we got married. We got in this huge fight because I was sure he wouldn't want to get married anymore. It was our first fight, and it was so dumb, but I'd been terrified and heartbroken when I'd found out."

"Have you ever thought about adoption?" I asked cautiously. I wasn't sure if this was a sore topic for her.

"I mean, yeah. But it's expensive, and people can go years waiting to adopt."

"Would Jace want to?"

Kinlee laughed and shook her head. "He's the one who's pushing adoption. I mean, we could, I know we could afford it. But"—she glanced at me—"what if we never get the opportunity, and I get my hopes up? I don't know if I can handle that," she whispered.

"Kinlee," I choked out.

"I just want to be a mom. That's all I've ever wanted."

My chin quivered as I watched more tears fill her eyes. "Then don't be afraid to try. You don't want to look back in twenty or thirty years and wonder what *would* have happened if you had just gone for it now. Right?"

Just like how I hadn't wanted to lose myself in a life I hated with Charles, so I'd run away. Just like how I had done something I never would have seen myself do so I could be with the man I needed in order to breathe. In both cases, I hadn't wanted to look back in twenty or thirty years and wonder what would have happened if I had done those things . . . I'd wanted to know what *did* happen.

12

Brody

June 17, 2015

"I JUST NEED to know if you think I should get an attorney, or what the best way to go about this would be."

Chief sat there with a dumbfounded expression on his face, and after a few seconds blinked his eyes quickly and shook his head. "Honestly, I'm lost, Saco," he said as he threw his hands up. "So, according to the reports, she didn't take the pills. Then she refused to go home with you when she was released from the hospital. And now already the next day is demanding to come back to *your* home *with* you?"

"Do you see why I'm so close to breaking? I almost took your advice yesterday morning, Chief. I was *this* close to saying screw the whole thing and stepping back from trying to get her help. Then I found her on the floor of her bathroom unconscious, and now all this is happening. She. Needs. Help. And all her parents are doing is enabling her crazy fits. I don't know if all three of them are in on this, or if I'm honestly just missing something."

"Play the voice mail again."

Leaning forward, I tapped my screen and hit the voice mail that Olivia's dad had left me two hours before. He'd called thirty minutes after Olivia's constant calling and sobbing voice mails had stopped to let me know that he was calling his attorney and they would be coming after me for spousal neglect because I couldn't afford to pay for the hospital while she was in it, couldn't afford her lifestyle, and refused to provide shelter seeing as I wouldn't let her back in the house.

I hadn't paid the ER fee at the hospital because Mr. Reynolds had told the administrator not to bother asking me for payment since I couldn't afford bread, much less a hospital visit; then he more or less threw his credit card at the woman. I couldn't afford Liv's lifestyle because she wanted to be like the fucking Cunninghams and thought $100 shoes were for homeless people. And it wasn't that I wasn't letting her back in the house. She still had her key, and I sure as shit hadn't changed the locks. I just hadn't *asked* her to come back, and Liv, being the girl she was, wanted me to beg her to come back. Seeing as how I couldn't stand the woman and was trying to get her help before I divorced her, I had no desire to beg her to come anywhere near me.

So if that was spousal neglect, then yeah, the attorney definitely had a reason to go after me. While I knew he didn't, I knew Liv and her family, and I wouldn't have put it past them to somehow find a way to have something on me.

"I can't do this anymore," I whispered as Mr. Reynolds's voice drifted to an end on my phone.

"I don't blame you, but you have to be strong. Don't let this break you, not after everything you've been through. Have you—" Chief cut off and eyed me for a moment. "I know you're not happy. Have you ever thought of leaving her?"

"That's what I meant just now. I've been wanting to for over a month now, but I wanted to get her help first. I can't, though. I can't help her if this is how they come back at me. You have no idea how responsible I feel for the woman Olivia has turned into, but I've been done with her for years. And now . . . well, now I'm done being responsible for her too. If they want to make it seem like *I* faked *her* suicide attempt, and then threaten me with their attorney because I'm not asking her to come back home the next day, then her parents can take care of her."

Saying the words out loud, even if just to my chief, made this crushing weight slowly begin to lift from my chest. And suddenly, I couldn't wait any longer. I'd dealt with her for far too long, I'd made Kamryn wait for this for too long, and now that I knew that Olivia was a lost cause, there was nothing else to wait for.

I stood up quickly, and Chief gave me an odd smile. It was happy, but still somehow pained. Like he knew this was something I'd agonized over, but needed nonetheless. "Well, I guess you'll probably be getting an attorney regardless, then. Just let me know if you need tonight off."

Shaking my head, I grabbed my phone and headed toward the door. "I'll be in. Thank you for listening."

As I drove to an attorney's office in town I called Kamryn, but she didn't answer. Knowing she was either near Kinlee or too busy at work, I didn't bother leaving a message and tossed my phone in a cup holder. I tried to calm my anxious shaking as I drove and focused on what was to come. I was finally going to do what I should have done long ago.

I walked in, told the receptionist what I needed, gave her my name, and took a seat in the lobby. Not three minutes later, a woman in a suit walked out.

"Mr. Saco?"

"Yes." Standing, I offered my hand, which she shook.

"I was told you were looking to file for divorce. Is that correct?"

My hands started shaking even harder, and my stomach tightened in anticipation. "That's correct."

With a smile, she nodded once and took a step back. "Okay, just making sure I knew what to be ready for. I'm finishing up something that needs to be sent over to a client. It will only take a few minutes, if you don't mind waiting."

"That's fine, I'll be here."

"All right then. Ten minutes tops!" she said with a smile and hurried back down the hallway.

Thirty minutes later, a man in a suit that had to cost more than I made in a month walked into the building.

"Brody Saco, what a pleasant surprise seeing you here."

I raised my eyebrow and straightened in the chair. "I'm sorry, do I know you?"

"Oh, well, not exactly. But you're about to if you decide to continue on with what you're about to do. I'm J. Shepherd, but I'm sure you would have figured that out sooner or later in this conversation."

I locked my jaw and my eyes narrowed as I recognized the

familiar name. Olivia and her parents threw it around enough, there was no way *not* to know it. He was her parents' attorney.

"You know what I just find absolutely hilarious?" he asked as he took the seat next to me. "Other than the fact that you really thought I didn't have enough pull in the surrounding cities to have them watching for you and to call me when you finally came in? And to file for divorce too. I had bet it would be for a defense attorney." He clucked his tongue. "Guess I lost out on that three hundred dollars."

"What do you want?" I said through gritted teeth.

"Right. So this is what I find funny. A man who was driving when an *accident* occurred, which resulted in killing his son, and the same man who tried to make his wife's fainting look like a suicide attempt . . . is now wanting to file for divorce. I'm seeing a pattern. If I'm not mistaken, Mr. Saco, you only married Olivia Reynolds because she was going to have your baby. Is that correct?"

I didn't say anything. I just sat there trying to control my breathing.

"I'll take your silence as a confirmation. So that means you never really wanted a life with her, and that includes a family. It is *quite* convenient that your son is out of the picture. And now, after waiting a long enough time that it wouldn't seem suspicious to most, you try to get your wife put in a psych ward before divorcing her. Now *that,* Mr. Saco, seems very suspicious, if you ask me. And since we *are* asking me . . . I'll just inform you now that if you continue with your filing, we *will* press charges for trying to make Olivia look suicidal so you could force her into a psych ward, which will only bring up the question of whether the car accident was actually an accident or not."

My breaths were coming fast, too fast. It felt like I was going to be sick. This couldn't be happening.

"We wouldn't want that to happen, now would we?"

"What game are you all playing at? No one in that family, including Olivia, can stand me. She's always making bullshit accusations about things I've done that have scared her. She's said I've hurt her. For Christ's sake, her parents put in a formal complaint to get me fired for it. They made this huge, dramatic scene at the hospital yesterday about not letting me near her because of what I had allegedly done. And now suddenly it's the opposite? They want to file something against me because I haven't called begging her to come home when she can willingly do it herself? They have you watching for me, and you're coming in here threatening me if I file for divorce? What is the point of all this back-and-forth bullshit?"

"Ooh." He held his hands up and winced. "*Threatening* is such a harsh word, Mr. Saco. As a lawyer, I'm not threatening; I'm simply strongly advising you against something you would regret immensely. Most people pay me five hundred an hour for this kind of advice. You're lucky I'm giving it to you for free."

I stood and started to leave, but stopped when he grabbed my wrist.

"Mr. Saco, I am *strongly* advising you that you go home and take care of your wife the way you're supposed to. You don't want the Reynoldses to have to call me again. We wouldn't want to see what would happen to your career, or your brother's, or heaven forbid your house, his house, or your parents' house if you decide to ignore my advice. I'll tell you once again, this is merely advice. You don't want to see what happens when I start threatening."

Slowly, I turned to look down at him and watched as his challenging eyes met mine.

"Now you have a nice day, Mr. Saco."

Kamryn

June 17, 2015

I HANDED OFF a tray of pastries to Grace to take up to the front and turned to begin filling and icing a few dozen cupcakes when the shop's phone rang. Looking around the counter until I spotted it, I grabbed it and put it between my shoulder and cheek.

"KC's Sweet Treats," I said by way of greeting.

"Hey."

I stopped reaching for the cupcakes as my body heated and tingled, my stomach simultaneously started churning, and I held my breath. One word. One simple word and I felt like I could easily faint from the effect his voice had on me—or get sick because of the stress I could tell he was trying so hard to hide.

"Brody, what happened?" I asked, my voice barely above a whisper.

"Nothing. I, uh, I'd just called you earlier and never heard back. I wanted to be able to get ahold of you before I went in to work."

"You called?" I patted my apron and pockets and sighed. "I don't have my phone on me. It's either in my purse or my car, I'm so sorry."

"Don't—Kamryn, don't ever say you're sorry."

My forehead bunched together in confusion and worry. "Brody, what's wrong?"

"Nothi—"

"Don't lie, what you just said is not something you would say in normal conversation. And besides that, you never call me before work, and I can hear it in your voice—something happened. So tell me."

He was silent for a few heavy moments, and in that time I felt the blood draining from my face.

"There are just times when I need to hear your voice. I need to be able to talk to you because I can't see you . . . and I just need you." He cursed away from the phone. "For so many reasons."

I worried my bottom lip as I waited for anything else he might have to say, but there was nothing. "You're scaring me," I admitted softly.

"I want to be able to give you everything, Kamryn . . . and it kills me that I'm in a situation where I can't. But you know what makes it that much harder? I feel like I don't know how to get out of the situation and get through all this bullshit without you right there. Right. Fucking. There. By my side. But because of the circumstances, I have to find a way."

"Brody . . ."

"And sometimes that just feels impossible."

My chest ached for him, and it felt like I was struggling to stay standing as I listened to him admit all this to me. "Tell me what happened," I pleaded.

"Nothing," he finally replied. "Nothing happened, sweetheart. I'm just trying to figure out a way for this all to go away for us, and some days it seems harder than others. I wanted to vent and hear your voice. That's all."

My lips tilted up slightly, but that sickening feeling like he wasn't telling me everything wasn't lessening.

Brody

June 17, 2015

STEPPING INTO THE kitchen late that night after work, I froze when I saw Olivia sitting at the table.

"Brody, I—" She cut off on a sob and dropped her head into her hands, her entire body shaking with the movements. "I'm so sorry."

I didn't make a move toward her, and I didn't say anything. It was all I could do to keep from clenching my jaw so hard that it felt like it was about to break. My hands curled into fists, and I crossed my arms over my chest to keep them close. I wouldn't touch her, but I didn't trust myself to not throw whatever was closest to me right now.

"They made me do it, you have to believe me. They made me say you planted it! I didn't want to, but you know how my parents are."

My eyebrows shot up at her desperate plea for me to believe her. Tears included, this was the sanest I'd seen Liv in years. "What are you saying, Olivia?"

"I didn't—couldn't do it anymore. I wanted to be with Tate," she sobbed and clutched at her chest. "I can't deal with this pain, Brody. It's killing me! So I-I-I just took them all."

Walking over to the kitchen table, I pulled out the chair closest to her and sat down. Leaning forward, I grabbed her arms as gently as possible, and pulled them back when she tried to cover her face again. "Olivia . . . what? No, the report came back. The doctor said you didn't have any of it in your system."

"They must have something on him, or paid him off . . . something! They told me they couldn't have this ruining their family name, so they needed to make it seem like a medical condition. But, Brody, I swear I didn't know they were going to try to throw the blame on you! I'm so sorry."

I shook my head back and forth and leaned back in the chair. "No. No way. Liv, you're just as manipulative as they are. The things you've been telling them—no. I'm not falling for this shit again," I said as I stood to leave.

"Brody, *please*!"

"How do you expect me to believe you after everything you've done since we got married, Olivia?!" I yelled, and she flinched back in her seat. "I've excused your behavior, I've looked the other way, and I've tried to get you help. But no matter what I do, you and your parents are right there trying to screw me over for it."

"I didn't want to admit I needed help! I didn't want to admit I was that *weak*!" she cried, her voice breaking on the last word. "I'm telling you, and I've told you—I can't do this. But my parents . . . they don't understand, and—and—what was I supposed to do, Brody? I couldn't tell them that I wanted to die! I couldn't tell them I didn't have the will to live anymore, so I just put it off on you. I'm sorry for that, but it just seemed easiest at the time."

"Seem—seemed *easiest*?!" Raking my hands roughly through my hair, I turned and took a few steps before turning back toward her. "Are you fucking kidding me? They tried to get me fired! They tried to get my peace officer license taken away, Liv!"

"They may have acted on things too harshly, but they were doing what they thought was best for their name, and for me. They're just trying to protect me!"

"I don't give a shit what they *thought* they were doing! The three of you—no! The four! You, your parents, and their attorney have been ruining my life. All of this has got to stop, do you hear me? You need to tell your parents what's happening with you. You need to tell them that you're suicidal, Liv. And you *need* to let me get you some help!"

She cried harder and shook her head back and forth. "I can't! It would be such an embarrassment to them!"

I flung my arms out to the side and my voice got even louder. "Tell me how it could be a fucking embarrassment for their daughter to get help? How could that be worse for them than her being dead, huh? They'll just have to get over it! Why are you acting like your parents are in the spotlight or something? They're just normal people. No one is going to know, or say anything, if you get help. And I swear to you, your parents will both be much happier to have their daughter alive and not sick any longer."

"You don't understand, Brody! You've never understood!"

"Stop with that bullshit! I *do* understand! No, I didn't grow up in some goddamn country club neighborhood. I didn't grow up being given everything I ever wanted. But I do understand what it's like to lose a fucking child. And I sure as hell know that I would rather Tate be in a hospital than in the ground. So I know your parents would feel the same."

Her shoulders shook, and her blond hair covered her face as she cried into her hands.

"Olivia. This is the last time I'm offering this. Let me get you some help, please."

No words came from her, but she nodded her head a few times.

A relieved sigh blew past my lips, and I walked back to sit in the chair next to her. "All right, then that's what I'll do." Lifting her head with my hand, I looked into her bloodshot eyes and made sure she understood every word. "You *need* to tell your parents what's going on. You *need* to tell them you've been lying to them about me. And you *need* to tell them to get their attorney off my back." My jaw shook as the words I wanted so badly to say to her sat on the tip of my tongue, but instead, I simply said, "I need to be able to live my life without him threatening me at every turn."

Olivia's blue eyes narrowed the smallest fraction, but I still saw it. She knew something was coming; she wasn't stupid. We'd grown too far apart for her not to know it was coming eventually. And with that statement, she had to know it would be coming soon.

"If you need my help in telling them, let me—"

"I don't," she choked out and shook her head. "We have races out of town this weekend. I'll tell them then."

"Okay." For the first time in days I had hope that my life with Kamryn would be starting soon.

13

Kamryn

June 22, 2015

"YOU SOUND HAPPY, baby girl."

I smiled and lowered myself onto the couch. "I am happy, Barb. Things are going really well with the shop, Kinlee is still as crazy as ever . . ." I drifted off and smiled at Barb's belly laugh, but the smile faded as the words I couldn't say played through my head. *Even though you warned me against it, I'm dating a married man.*

"Is she still trying to set you up with someone?"

Barb's psychic! "Eh. Sort of. She's backed off a lot, but that's just because she and Jace really want me to be with Aiden."

"From what you said, I don't see what was wrong with Aiden."

I chewed on my bottom lip and thought back to just last weekend at Kinlee's birthday party. Once Aiden and I were inside the house, he hadn't made any more comments hinting at an *us,* and I'd been thankful for that. Because, other than completely ignoring him, I wasn't sure what more I could do.

"Kam, honey?"

"Hmm?"

"That Aiden boy—is there something wrong with him? You stopped talking."

"Oh, no." I shook my head, even though Barb couldn't see me, and sank into the cushions until I was comfortable. "No, there's nothing wrong with him. He's gorgeous, has a very admirable job, he's polite . . . I'm sure you'd love him. He's just not it for me, you know? I went on that one date with him, but there was nothing more than a friend bond for me."

Barb stayed silent for a few moments, and just as I was about to ask if she was still there, she spoke softly. "I know you'll find a good man, Kamryn. You just have to. Your life is finally going how it always should have, and I just know there's a man lined up in there somewhere. But you're only twenty-three. You have plenty of time to find him."

I'd found him, there was no question about that. "Right."

"Okay, sweet one, I need to get up early to get your parents' Sunday brunch started, so I need to get me some sleep. You have a good rest of your weekend, all right?"

" 'Kay. Love you, Barb."

"I love you too."

I pressed END and let my phone fall to the cushion as I stood to find something in the kitchen. Just as I hit the end of the couch, my phone chimed. A chime I'd reserved specifically for Brody.

Racing back to the phone, I pulled open the text.

B:

I'm coming over

Olivia? No hotel?

The only response was the sound of my garage door opening. I quickly ran to the door leading to the garage and watched as Brody's black Expedition pulled in. The second he was in the clear I was shutting the garage door behind him. My body was humming as I watched him exit his SUV and walk over to me.

"Olivia?"

"She left with her parents for Washington and won't be home until Monday."

A smile crossed my lips at the thought of having him to myself for more than a day. "What about the hotel?"

He shook his head once, his dark gray eyes never leaving mine. "I didn't have the patience to wait any longer."

Before I could respond, his hands were grabbing around my waist, pulling me to his body, and his lips were pressed firmly against mine. A small giggle bubbled up my throat, and I wrapped my arms around his neck.

"I missed you," I said against his lips.

"God, I've missed you too." Pulling away from me, a sharp laugh left him when he saw me frown, and his fingers traced my bottom lip. "Don't pout. There's something I need to tell you, something I should have told you long before now."

My forehead scrunched in confusion, but I didn't say anything, just waited for him to continue.

"I love you, Kamryn."

Those four words washed over my body, and a shiver ran down

my spine. I'd known Brody loved me; it was unmistakable when we were together. What I hadn't known was that I'd been waiting to hear those words from this man my entire life. A smile broke across my face, and I threw my arms around his neck again as I crushed my mouth to his.

Pulling back just enough to speak, I looked up into his eyes and replied with every fiber of my being: "I'm so in love with you, Brody Saco."

My body tingled with the truth and rightness of those words, and I wanted to say them over and over again, but Brody's mouth silenced anything else, and soon he was walking us back toward my bedroom.

"WHAT IS IT?" I asked Brody late the next afternoon after we'd finally left my room to eat something.

Brody turned and looked at me confused, his eyebrows pinching together as he set his mug down. "What is what?"

I took a few calming breaths and forced my hands apart when I started nervously playing with them. "About Olivia? What is it about her that's kept you together all these years?" Brody's confused expression turned pained, and I hurried to continue. "I know this will sound horrible coming from me, but I've always thought divorce was bad . . . but that's only because the people around me who I saw getting divorced were doing it because they grew tired of who they were with." *Or the men wanted someone younger and the women wanted someone with more money. That's just how it was in the racing world.* "From what everyone has said, that's not what's going on between you and Olivia."

Brody stayed silent, his body still as stone as he stared down at the granite countertop on the kitchen island.

"I know *why* you married her, and it's honorable, Brody, but if you're so miserable—and if she's as evil as everyone says she is—why would you stay with her all these years?"

He didn't answer for a long time, and he never moved. When he did finally speak, his eyes wouldn't meet mine, and his body seemed to somehow tighten even more. "Because I ruined her," he said on a breath, the words haunting, matching the torture in his eyes.

When he didn't say anything else and minutes ticked by, I asked softly, "Ruined her how?" He didn't respond, but I watched as the torture in his eyes washed over the rest of his features. "Does this have to do with you needing to make sure she'll be okay?"

Another five minutes passed, and all Brody had done was nod. Knowing he wasn't comfortable with this conversation, and knowing I wouldn't get my questions answered, I slid off the stool and walked around the island toward him. Wrapping my arms loosely around his rigid frame, I placed a kiss on his chest and took a step away from him. My chest ached when he didn't look away from the spot on the island he'd been staring at. Turning, I walked quickly from the kitchen and into the bathroom to clean up.

My movements were slow as I moved to the bedroom to put on some clothes, and while I was hurting for whatever pain Brody was in, I was terrified that I'd just pushed him away somehow. It had felt like he was a thousand miles away in the kitchen, and I couldn't help but worry that feeling wouldn't go away. I'd strained to hear the door closing, or the garage opening as he left, but there had been nothing. No sound, no indication that he'd even moved from his spot against the counter.

"I haven't been in love with Olivia for a long time."

I jumped at the sound of Brody's voice and instinctively covered myself with the shirt in my hands as I turned to face him. "I know." Sliding my arms into the sleeves, I pulled the shirt over my head and went to sit on the end of my bed. Brody wasn't looking at me again, but if he was going to talk, I wasn't going to rush him.

"But before meeting you, Kamryn, leaving her seemed like the cowardly thing to do. She's not a good person. She's always been manipulative, vindictive, and a person who will do anything to make sure she gets her way. And there's still that side of her . . . but I—I absolutely destroyed her. And to destroy her that way, and then leave her?" He raked a hand through his hair and kept it there. "I just couldn't do it. Since meeting you, whenever I see the scheming side of her, I don't know why I bother trying anymore . . . until I see the broken side again, and I know that I still owe it to her to get her help. Because everything that happened to her was my fault." Looking at me sadly, Brody shrugged helplessly. "She's this fucked-up shell of the woman that she'd been before, and it's all my fault," he whispered.

I watched as his body settled back against the wall, like he couldn't handle standing on his own for another second. I wanted to go to him, to comfort him . . . but I couldn't force myself to move.

"When Liv gave birth to our son, I guess it went bad. There was a lot of bleeding, she had to go into surgery, and afterwards she was told that she'd never be able to have another baby. That alone was hard for her to deal with, and then . . ." He cut off, and a single tear ran down his cheek.

"Brody?" My voice was barely above a whisper, but I couldn't manage anything more. I was terrified of what came after the "and then." Brody had told me they didn't have children . . . and with how this story started, and how tortured his face was, I knew it didn't end well.

"My son was only six months old . . . I had to go to the store for Olivia, and she wanted time alone, so I took Tate with me. It was really icy that morning, and we were stopped at a red light. The guy who came in behind us couldn't stop, and when he hit us my car slid into the intersection."

Tears slid down my own face at the pure anguish in Brody's voice. I'd never heard the kind of torment that I was hearing from him now, and my heart broke for him as I tried to prepare myself for what would come next.

"A car had been flying through and clipped the back of us, and I couldn't stop the car from spinning no matter how hard I tried. And God, I tried so damn hard," he cried. "We hit a median, but another car that had been trying to avoid us ended up swerving into us instead. I don't remember anything after that until I woke up in an ambulance. I freaked and tried to get out, to get to Tate, but they kept me on the stretcher and shut the doors. They didn't tell me until after I woke up again in the hospital that he was gone," he choked out, and more tears fell down his face as he slid down the wall. "The car that had hit us up against the median rolled my car over it, and more cars coming up to the intersection slammed into us. He was dead before another driver could come and try to check on us."

Moving from the bed, I went to where he was sitting on the floor and kneeled between his legs. Grabbing the hand that wasn't in his hair in mine, I placed my other hand on his cheek and attempted to brush away the wetness there. His body was trembling, and the guilt that crossed his face had a sob tearing from my own chest as my heart seemed to break even more for him.

"Liv was never the same after that," he said and finally opened his eyes to look at me. "I can't say if she's depressed or bipolar, because the way she acts is so unlike anything I've looked up. But she's not well, and that's my fault. And Tate . . . I killed him after only having him for a few months."

"Brody, no. It's not—you can't put this on yourself. It was an accident, and what happened when she gave birth was something no one could have stopped from happening."

"I did this to them, Kamryn! I did this to *her*," he yelled as he let his head fall back to the wall. "I've taken everything from her."

"No! None of this is your fault." Cupping his face, I waited until he looked at me again. "You can't do this . . . you can't blame yourself for any of this. What happened—I can't imagine how difficult it was to go through that, Brody, and I'm so sorry you've had to. But it's *not* your fault. You have to see that," I cried when I saw the look in his eyes. He didn't believe me—the guilt that poured off him said it all. He'd been carrying around the knowledge for years that he'd ruined his wife and ended his son's life. But he was so wrong—how could he not see that?

"That," he began, "is why I need to make sure she'll be okay. She's not well, and I need to get her help . . . I owe her that much after all I've done."

I shook my head for long moments, trying to figure out the right words. Kinlee and Jace had said it was like everything that made Brody *Brody* had been gone for years. I didn't see that side of Brody, because I didn't know what he was like before everything happened. But he was never going to heal from this if he kept blaming himself. "And what about you, Brody? You've lost just as much as she has. Who's supposed to help you?"

"Do you not see that that's what you've been doing?" he asked. "I've never felt as alive as I do when I'm with you. And even when I'm not, I feel like I finally have something to live for again. I was just going through life, going through the motions, just to get through the days. Nothing mattered, and all I ever felt was pain. You've changed that. You *are* helping me."

MY EYES HADN'T left the clock since Brody had fallen asleep two hours earlier. With each minute that passed, my body grew more and more tense, as it did every night he fell asleep with his arms around me. It hadn't mattered last night or tonight that I'd known Olivia wasn't coming home until Monday. She always found some way to interrupt us when she wasn't supposed to be home. I had no doubt she'd do it again this weekend.

Some part of me thought Olivia had to know what we were doing, because there was no other explanation. Brody said she only called if he wasn't home, but then there would be days at a time when she was gone and he wouldn't see or hear from her. It never failed, though, every night we were together—whether it was at the hotel or one of the nights we risked staying in my condo—she called.

I knew I had no right—since technically, Brody wasn't mine—and I knew it only made it harder for both of us, but that didn't stop me from begging him to stay. My pleas never made a difference, because we both knew he had to leave. But it was in those moments, as I begged Brody not to go back to his wife, that I felt exactly like what I was. A mistress. A home-wrecker. The other woman. And every time he left another part of me died. I would get physically sick from the guilt of our secret, but my love for Brody would have us in the same heartbreaking situation the very next time we got the chance to be together.

I couldn't stay away from him, and I couldn't say no to him no matter how much I hated this.

How many movies, stories, and songs had been written about people like us? And how many times had I wondered why the girl in my situation couldn't see that the man would never leave his wife? That my character was just a plaything and, in the end, would be left alone and shattered? Every time the girl would be so sure that he would choose her in the end, and it never happened. Still, no matter how many red flags there were in our situation, I knew Brody and I were different.

My body flinched as another minute went by on the clock, and I prayed for sleep to find me. Another minute gone, and I began counting Brody's deep, rhythmic breaths to soothe my tightly strung nerves. Another minute . . . when it happened, I squeezed my eyes tightly.

"Please, no," I whispered just as Brody jerked awake and searched wildly for his phone.

"Liv?"

I crawled off the bed and began searching for my clothes, not wanting to hear her cries for him to come home.

"I had too much to drink at Jace's, I crashed on the couch."

My stomach rolled at how easily our lies had started coming. He'd been with me since last night, but the sure tone of his voice would've had me believing that was exactly what had happened.

"You told me you weren't coming home until tomorrow night. I didn't know it would matter to you if I went to hang out with my own brother, Liv." His eyes searched my face and a deep sorrow filled them. "All right, you're right. I'll be home in a bit." Brody ended the call and tossed his phone on the bed. "Babe, please don't cry."

I hadn't realized I was until he said that. "Don't go, Brody, *please* don't go."

"Kamryn—"

"What do I have to do to keep you here with me? Name it and I'll do it—just don't leave," I begged with a sob and curled into his arms when he pulled me back onto the bed.

"I have to, you know I have to. Just like you know I don't want to. I'd do anything to stay here with you forever."

Normally, this was where I would have stopped, but the words were out before I could stop them. "But you aren't doing anything to change this, and you won't! We wouldn't have to keep doing this, Brody, if you would just tell her."

Cupping my cheeks in his large hands, he held my head back and stared at me in shock. "God, I hope you don't really think that. I *am* trying. I told you earlier, I need to get her help first."

A sob burst from my chest, and I let my forehead fall to his chest as I shook my head back and forth. Brody held me until I was able to compose myself again, the entire time telling me how sorry he was and pressing soft kisses to the top of my head.

With a hard kiss to my lips, Brody got out of bed and collected his clothes. My body and heart felt numb as I watched him prepare to leave me again. Once his clothes were on, he looked at me with the most devastating expression and leaned in to kiss me one last time.

"One day, Kamryn, I swear to you. All of this will be behind us, and it will just be you and me." With that, he turned to leave and I continued to stare at the empty space he'd just been occupying.

Tears slipped down my cheeks again as I realized I no longer believed his words.

A knock sounded on my door not even ten minutes after Brody left, and I cautiously left my bed and walked to the front door. It was late, I didn't know anyone other than Brody who would show up at this hour . . . but he used the garage. And seeing as how he'd just left, I doubted it was him.

Making my steps as quiet as possible on the hardwood floor, I held my breath and looked through the peephole.

"Lee?" I gasped and hurried to unlock the door. "What are you doing here? It's late. Are you okay?" I grabbed her in a hug when I saw her pale white face.

"Jace and I were on the phone when the sirens sounded for a fire. It's all over the news, it's a huge fire at an apartment complex. They're calling trucks from other cities to come help, and knowing that he's there is freaking me out."

"He'll be okay. Come on, let's go hang out in the kitchen. Do you want ice cream?"

She nodded, but looked at the living room. "I want to keep watching the news, but I can't watch alone."

" 'Kay. Go get comfortable, I'll bring you something."

Part of me was relieved Brody had left, the other part was screaming at me to tell Kinlee about our relationship. She could have gone to anyone on a night like tonight, and she'd come to me. She'd helped me more than she'd ever know when I moved here, and I cherished our friendship . . . but I had to be the worst friend ever since I couldn't seem to do anything but keep my real life from her.

I walked back into the living room to see Kinlee's face whiter than when I'd opened the door. Turning to look at the TV, I almost dropped the bowls of ice cream when I saw it.

Oh, Christ.

Kinlee hadn't been lying. This wasn't your average call for the fire department, nor was it one of the more intense structure fires I'd ever seen on the news. But this fire was out of control. The news reporter let out a yelp and ran toward the camera when the noise behind her startled her, and her soft words echoed my thoughts. Part of the first building had collapsed on itself, and as the reporter tried to straighten herself out she said the words no one wanted to hear.

"We won't know for some time if anyone was still in the building . . ."

Kinlee and I watched the news in horror for the next three hours as firefighters worked relentlessly on the nine buildings in total that ended up catching fire. The entire time I kept her hand clasped in mine and wondered if Brody knew what was happening. Did his time in the Army, and now as a police officer, have him always prepared for situations like this? Situations where the lives of his brother and friends were at stake and the outcome unknown.

Once the fires were put out, we both held our breath as we listened for the reporters to say anything about the lives of the firemen and residents. Just before the reporters came back on the air, Kinlee's phone went off and she grabbed it. A relieved cry left us both when we read the words.

Hubby:
Love you, baby. See you in the morning.

14

Kamryn

July 4, 2015

"Is there anything else you need help preparing or setting up?" I looked around Kinlee's kitchen and living room covered in food, red, white, and blue, and prayed to God that was it. I didn't know if the house could hold much more.

"No, I think that's everything. Thanks for bringing the cupcakes and puffs."

I glanced at her and laughed. "You say that like I wouldn't normally."

"True. Hey, Aiden!"

"Hi, Kinlee. Need help with anything?" I stiffened when I felt his arm go around my waist. "Hey, Kace, you look beautiful," he mumbled into my ear.

"Thanks." Guilt ate at me, but what else could I tell him? He knew how I felt—he knew my heart belonged to someone else. I felt horrible, and I hated that I couldn't give Aiden what he wanted. But Brody had my entire soul.

"How've you been?"

"Pretty good. I heard about your rescue of that little girl. That's amazing, Aiden, you saved her."

Aiden's cheeks went red, and he looked down at the floor as he shook his head faintly. "Any one of the other guys would've done the same thing."

I doubted that, but that was typical Aiden—he didn't want to be seen as a hero. The night of the fire, when Kinlee had come over, they'd all been told they couldn't go back in the first apartment building because the fire had already done too much structural damage, but Aiden pushed his chief away and ran inside and up the stairs. He'd saved a four-year-old girl's life seconds before that building had collapsed. And he'd gotten written up, but that part didn't matter to him.

"But they didn't."

He was still shaking his head and looking completely embarrassed. "I was just doing my job."

"Well, I'm proud of you, and I'm glad you're safe."

His brown eyes searched my face and he smiled sadly. "I'm here, Kace. Whenever you're ready."

"I'm sorry," I whispered.

Instead of pulling away, he just looked down until his eyes were holding mine. "Don't be sorry—then it makes me think I'll never get my chance. I have to stay positive."

"Aiden—"

"Don't, KC, you told me how you feel. Doesn't change the way I do."

I sighed and stepped away from his nearness. Not knowing how to respond to that, I just smiled softly, touched his arm, and turned to go talk to Kinlee and her mom and mother-in-law. I'd barely gotten over there when there was a commotion and Mrs. Saco went running toward the door.

Turning in that direction, my breath caught in my throat and it felt like I was that much closer to feeling whole again. Just seeing him made the empty feeling subside a bit, but I knew until I could be with him again, I wouldn't be complete. Brody hugged his mom and his eyes bounced around the living room until they hit me and his face softened.

We said the polite hellos, both of us knowing this night was going to be torture, but worth every second of it. For the entire evening it seemed like someone in his family was constantly questioning Brody, and the majority of our glances happened across the room from each other. Our words were almost all through texts, and I had to make sure Kinlee didn't notice that I couldn't keep my eyes off him.

I was putting more food out on the table when he came up behind me and grabbed my hip. I immediately set down the food and reached back to touch him, a sigh leaving my chest when I did.

"How did you get off work?" I asked quietly.

"Practically begged for the night off. I knew you would be here, and any opportunity like this to see you, I'll take." He was silent for a minute as he pretended to look at the food. "This is killing me, Kamryn."

I kept my gaze on everyone else as I whispered back to him, "I know."

One of Jace and Aiden's friends started walking by us and toward the kitchen, so I dropped Brody's hand and he grabbed at some food. "Everyone's going to know about us tonight if I see Aiden Donnelly touch you again," he growled under his breath and let his hand run over the curve of my back, past my butt, and down my thigh. "This is mine."

"He knows there's someone else, Brody. He's just hoping to one day get his chance."

"Brody, honey, come here, there's someone I want you to see." We both looked up to see his mom, and I pushed around a few trays. "Do you remember Savannah from high school? She's here and she's single, Brody."

I tensed and noticed Brody do the same. "I'm married, Mom."

Until that moment, I'd never seen Mrs. Saco look at anyone like she wanted to smash their face into a gravel driveway and dig in with her stiletto heels for good measure. And I'm guessing that look wasn't directed at her son, but had to do with the woman she refused to call her daughter-in-law. "*Again*, Brody, it's to that bitch of a woman who doesn't deserve you and is manipulating you into staying with her. You don't owe her anything except a stack of papers to sign to get out of your damn marriage. Why don't you just come talk to Savannah? Maybe you'll realize what you're missing out on, honey."

"I'm not interested," he growled, and then groaned, "Fuck."

I looked up at him seconds before I heard her.

"Ohmigod, Brody! I haven't seen you since high school, you look amazing!" A tall woman with dark hair and dark eyes threw herself at Brody and clung to him for far too long. Even when he stopped hugging her, she kept her arms around his neck.

"Savannah. You haven't changed."

"Your mom was telling me all about you. Army and then the police department? Wow, you've been busy since graduation."

He pulled her arms from around his neck, and shit you not she put them around his waist. Brody sighed but didn't attempt to remove her again. "Savannah, I'm married to Olivia."

She shrugged. "Details."

My eyes about bugged out of my head until I realized that I was no better than her. But I wasn't so careless about it. Even with his horrible wife, what we were doing killed me a little more every day. I didn't want to be the other woman; I didn't want to be the reason a marriage ended. But I needed Brody to breathe. This girl didn't care about any of that other than hooking up with him. Surely Mrs. Saco couldn't want this more than Olivia. I looked over and realized that Mrs. Saco was gone and I'd just been standing there staring at Savannah and Brody.

"Olivia used to tell us all how wild you were. I can't wait for you to show me just how wild you can be."

I was going to throw up. I finally figured out how to get my feet to move and bolted away from them. Was this what it felt like for Brody when he saw Aiden touch me? Like he was going to die? But I always pulled away from Aiden. Always. Even when Brody wasn't around. I had just been standing right freakin' there! I slapped my hand over my mouth when a pained cry burst from my chest and tried not to think about what Brody was letting her do. Or what she was suggesting to him. She was probably telling him how they'd make freaking gorgeous Italian babies and how she would bake him manicotti instead of cupcakes.

"Oh, Kace! There you are, I've been look—whoa. You look pissed. Are you okay?"

"I'm fine. What's up?"

Kinlee tilted her head to the side as she studied me. "Uh, the fireworks from the park are going to start in about half an hour. We always light a few of ours before, and then a bunch after. Want to help me get everyone outside?"

"Yep!"

"KC"—she grabbed my arm and stopped me when I turned—"are you sure you're all right?"

"I'm fine. I'll help you get everyone out there." As soon as I was away from her someone grabbed my arm and pulled me down the nearest hall. I didn't need to see him to know who it was. The way my heart raced and goose bumps covered my body told me all I needed to know. "Can I help you?"

"You had to have seen how uncomfortable I was," he whispered in my ear, and I hated that my knees went weak. I wasn't done being upset.

"No, what I saw was that you didn't even try to get away from her."

"Kamryn—"

"I always step away from Aiden, even when you aren't around. And I was close enough that your arm brushed mine when you went to hug her. I was standing *right* there. Do you know what it was like having to watch that? Do you know what it was like listening to your mom trying to set you up with someone else *again* and having Savannah assume you were going to hook up with her?"

"I can't stand that girl, never been able to. And you know I don't want anyone if it's not you."

"I can't do this right now, Brody. Your family is here." I took a step away, but he pulled me close, his lips brushing my ear.

"Don't do this. I never get you, Kamryn. Tonight is already hard enough staying away from you. Don't pull away from me too."

Tears pricked my eyes, and I blinked them back before turning my head to look up at him. "You're right. We don't get to be with each other a lot, and it is hard staying away from you. But we have to, and why is that? Oh, that's right, because you're still fucking married." I jerked my arm from his hand and stormed off down the hall and right into Aiden. *Seriously?* I immediately took two steps away from him.

"Kace, are you crying?"

"No, no, I'm fine," I said a little too brightly judging by the way Aiden's eyebrows shot up. "Just got something in my eye and it's killing me. Hey, we need to get everyone outside for the fireworks, can you help me?"

"Uh yeah, sure." His eyes darted behind me, and I turned to see Brody watching us. "Hey, Brody, everyone's headed outside for the show."

His face remained impassive as he nodded once, but the pain in his eyes cut straight through me. If Aiden hadn't been standing there, I would have thrown myself into Brody's arms and apologized for everything I'd said.

The guys didn't move, just stood there staring at each other, so I lowered my head and walked past Brody toward the front door. Everyone was setting up chairs and unfolding blankets as they got ready to watch our fireworks and the park's, and I quickly made my way toward Kinlee and Jace. I sat on their blanket next to Kinlee and somehow I made it through the next fifteen minutes of our starter fireworks without looking back at where I knew Brody was sitting. Even when I felt my phone vibrate, I never checked it.

Savannah and two other girls around her age sat down next to us when the park's show started, and I froze when she told them about how she was taking Brody back to her place that night.

"Isn't he, like, married?" one girl asked, and I'm pretty sure I heard Savannah snort.

"And? It's fucking Olivia. She's a train wreck these days, and everyone knows their marriage is over. Besides, Brody and I have always had a connection—this was bound to happen."

"What if he never leaves her?"

Savannah straightened and flipped her long black hair over her shoulder. "He will, I'll make sure of it. I'll trap him the same way that bitch did."

The other two girls looked at each other and let out soft, but harsh, laughs. "Oh, my God, you're going to get pregnant?"

Savannah turned and blinked her eyes rapidly. "I swear I'm on the pill, Brody."

I turned to see Kinlee's reaction to all this, but she was practically lying on Jace, watching the show, and they were whispering to each other. I wanted to scream at Savannah that he was mine, but honestly, what could I say? Our relationship was a secret. And though Brody's family hated Olivia, I couldn't do that to him. Until he left her, I couldn't be seen as what I was. Oh, God, I was a home-wrecker. I curled an arm around my stomach and stopped breathing when Savannah spoke again.

"I just blew him in the bathroom before we came out here. That man is *hung*."

"Oh, my God!" The other two laughed and pushed at her. "You are so bad! His family is here."

"Who cares? They want him to be with me."

I knew she was lying, but I couldn't continue to sit there and listen to her talk about him like that. He was *my* Brody. I wanted to rip her freaking extensions out. Standing quickly, I bolted for the house and didn't stop until I hit the bathroom. Gripping the countertop, I attempted to take deep breaths in and out and forced my tears back through the sobs that tore through me.

The door flew open, and before a scream could build up in my chest, Brody was pulling me into his arms and locking the door behind him. "Babe, what's wrong?"

I gripped him as hard as I could and buried my face in his chest. "She said you're going home with her and she's going to trap you into marrying her the same way Olivia did. She said she was just blowing you in the bathroom."

He pushed me back to look directly into my eyes. "Kamryn, you know that's not true."

"I know! You're *mine,* but no one else knows that, Brody. I couldn't say anything, I just had to sit there and listen to it."

"I know that I'm yours. As long as I know that, I'll never be anyone else's. And Kamryn, I'm gonna be yours forever. You understand?"

I nodded, and he slammed his mouth down onto mine. He pulled me closer, and I clutched his shirt in my hands while throwing everything I had into that kiss.

"I love you, Kamryn," he promised against my mouth, and I tugged against his bottom lip, earning a low growl that made my knees go weak.

He backed me up to the sink, lifted me, and sat me down on the counter. I smiled against his kisses and whispered my love back to him. He pushed my skirt up my thighs, and my hands quickly released their death grip on his shirt and fell to the button on his jeans. I'd just hit the zipper when his fingers slid inside my lacey underwear and trailed over me.

"Oh, Brody," I moaned and his forehead hit the base of my neck.

"Jesus, you're so wet."

I finished with his jeans and roughly pulled them, along with his boxer-briefs, down low enough so I could take him in my hands.

"I'm sorry, Kamryn, I'll buy you a new pair." Before I could question his apology, he ripped my underwear and put his arms under my legs, pulling me closer to him and the edge of the counter.

We both groaned and stilled when he pushed his length into me. "Please don't stop."

I felt him grin against my neck before biting softly there. "I just like hearing you say 'please.'" He pulled out and pushed in twice before pausing again and I was on the verge of screaming at him.

"Brody, *please.*"

Pulling out almost completely, he slammed back in and crushed his mouth to mine when my scream filled the bathroom. Thank God for the fireworks outside, or I'm positive someone would have come running in there. The burning tension I'd been craving started building, and I leaned back, knowing Brody would keep me in his arms, and I whimpered at the feel of the changed position. The knot low in my stomach tightened as he continued to fill me over and over again, and I begged him not to stop as I went crashing over the edge and my body shattered around his. Brody pulled me back up and kissed me roughly to quiet my moans, and his fingers tightened almost painfully when he found his release inside me.

I don't know if it was the boom of the fireworks outside, the fact that someone could have caught us, or not having been with him in over a week, but bathroom sex was now my new favorite.

Brody laughed out loud, and I whimpered when his body left mine. "Guess we'll have to do it more often."

My eyebrows pulled together before it hit me. "I said that out loud, didn't I?"

"Yeah, babe. You did." He kissed my lips softly and pulled me off the counter before putting himself back in his pants and bending down to pick up my torn underwear.

I watched as he shoved it into his jeans pocket and smiled to myself knowing they'd be there the rest of the night.

Tilting my head back so he could look into my eyes, he whispered softly, "Don't ever doubt my love for you. Don't ever doubt our relationship. We're going to get through this, and when we do, everyone will know that we're together. No more hiding, no more Aidens or Savannahs. Just us. Got it?"

"Yeah." I didn't say anything else. I just pressed a kiss to his chest and let him hold me a little longer before pulling back and making sure I was okay to go back outside.

"Go out first. That way, if anyone is waiting, I'll handle it. If I don't get another chance to tell you tonight, you look so beautiful. And I love you."

"I love you too, Brody." *I hate this. I hate this so much it physically hurts.*

Forcing myself not to say anything else, I made my way out of the bathroom and back outside to watch the rest of the fireworks. Brody and I didn't get a chance to talk for the rest of the night, and I wondered as I drove home how much more of this I could take.

My phone had died at Kinlee's house, and I was racing to get home so I could call Brody, knowing I probably wouldn't be able to talk to him for another few days. But as I turned onto my street I saw Aiden's truck parked outside my condo and Aiden sitting on the steps leading up to the porch. I didn't pull into the garage before turning off my car and getting out. I figured it'd be awkward to have to come back around to him, and if I went through the house, I'd have to invite him in.

What is he doing here?

He stood as I made my way toward him, and I instantly knew this wasn't a visit where he hoped for a relationship to start. Aiden looked hurt, confused, and beyond pissed.

"Brody?"

Oh, God. I froze a dozen feet away from him. "W-what?"

"That's who it is, right? The other guy. The guy you aren't seeing but you *belong* to." He laughed harshly and ran a hand over his buzzed hair. "Because, you know, you can't really say you're in a relationship with a married guy."

"Aiden," I whispered, silently begging for him to understand.

"I was inside grabbing a drink when you came running in crying. I started to go to you when he raced in after you. At first, I thought he'd said something to upset you, so I waited . . . kinda hard to mistake the sounds you started making, Kace."

"Please, just—"

He threw an arm out to the side. "He's fucking married!"

"I know that, Aiden! I know! Do you think I enjoy this? That I like being the other woman? It *kills* me, Aiden. God you have no idea how much this kills me every damn day. I wanted to stay away from him, and I tried to start a relationship with you. But after meeting Brody, it was over for me. There is no one in the world who will ever be able to make me feel what he does just by saying my name. Not a day goes by that I don't hate myself for what we're doing. Not a day goes by that I don't hate myself for breaking up someone's marriage even though everyone already knows it was over. And yet, at the same time, not a day goes by that I don't wonder why, if he is so miserable with his marriage, won't he leave his wife for me." Tears were streaming down my face and a loud sob burst from my chest. "Judge me all you want, but you have no fucking idea how insane this is making me and how much this is killing me. I would never want to be a part of this, but he is married to someone else and I can't breathe without him, Aiden."

"Shit, Kace, don't cry." He took a few steps toward me, and even when I held up my hand to stop him, he pulled me into his chest. "I'm sorry, I shouldn't have attacked you like that. I told myself I was going to be calm—I just, I don't know. When you told me there was someone else, I had no clue it was Brody. Why didn't you just tell me?"

I pushed out of his arms and wiped at my cheeks. "And what was I supposed to tell you? That I was sleeping with a married man? I know what this makes me, but I couldn't stand anyone else knowing that. I couldn't have Brody's family seeing me that way. I'm not normally this person."

Aiden ran his hands over his hair and down his face as he shook his head. "Couldn't you have at least waited until he divorced her? KC, it's not a secret that Brody and Olivia are done, but this just looks so bad."

"There's no way for me to explain it so you'll understand. You can't understand without being one of us, but there was no waiting for us. It just wasn't possible. And he swore he was going to file for divorce, he swore to me," I cried and covered my face. "But it's been almost two months, and he hasn't even told her he's leaving her. The longer this goes on, the more I start to doubt if he will, and I just—I don't understand. He loves me and he can't stand being in that marriage, so why am I not enough for him?" I was rambling about things that no one else should have known. But I couldn't stop. Once my fears had been given a voice, they all wanted out.

"Fuck. I'm sorry. Come on, let's go inside and we can talk about this more."

I didn't want to talk to Aiden, but at the same time I did. Keeping this from Barb and Kinlee had been making everything that much harder to deal with—and deep down I knew I'd been craving to have someone know the truth so I would have someone to talk to. Despite how unconventional it was, it seemed like Aiden was going to be that person.

Brody

July 4, 2015

I SENT THE text to Kamryn, wishing I'd said something when we'd been together earlier. I was telling Olivia we were over tomorrow. I was done waiting for Liv to be ready to get help. I could only drop so many hints and could only deal with so many nights of her breaking down and then screaming at me before I had to just step back. And I couldn't keep hiding my relationship with Kamryn when she was the best thing that had ever happened to me. I couldn't keep doing this to her, and I couldn't keep living day to day without her by my side.

But all of that would change after tomorrow. My life with Kamryn was about to start.

I checked my phone to see if she'd responded before walking into the house and had to bite back a groan when I shut the door. A barely dressed Olivia was standing there with a look I knew too well.

"Where've you been?"

"Jace's. Where I said I'd be when you told me you were going to the club with your parents."

She pouted and sauntered up to me, letting her hand trail over my chest. I could've just gotten it all over with at that moment, but she reeked of wine and I knew it would be pointless. I'd just have to tell her all over again tomorrow anyway.

"But it's so late. I've been waiting for you."

"Good night, Liv."

"Brody," she whined and dug her fingers into my chest and arm as she pulled herself closer. She pressed her lace-covered breasts against me and breathed in my ear. "I'm so horny, Brody. I want you." The hand on my chest dropped to my pants, and I gripped her thin wrist in my hand.

"I said, good night. You've taken care of yourself for years, tonight doesn't need to be any different." As gently as I could, I pushed her back and turned to walk toward my room.

"Why don't you love me anymore?" I could already hear the tears starting and was determined to keep moving until she spoke again. "Is it because of Tate? Or is it because I can't have kids—you think I'm worthless now, don't you?"

Or maybe I'm not going to wait until tomorrow. I stopped walking when she mentioned Tate and had to grit my teeth to keep myself from lashing out at her for bringing him into this *again.*

"You would still love me if I could have more children, Brody, I know it."

My head slowly shook back and forth as I turned to look at her. There was already makeup streaking down her cheeks with her tears as she hunched in on herself. "You and I both know that's not it," I said. "We've drifted too far apart, and it started long before Tate."

"But—but it didn't!"

Holding back a sigh, I put an arm around Olivia's waist and led her to one of the large couches and sat down next to her. "We both know you only stayed with me to piss your parents off. Just like we know that we would have never stayed together or gotten married if you hadn't gotten pregnant."

"No, I don't know that!" she cried and wiped miserably at her face.

"Liv, you refused to see me. You wouldn't let me see our son. You didn't want to live with me . . . you and I hadn't loved each other for a long time before we got married. It had nothing to do with Tate or you not being able to have more kids."

"That's not true! I love you! I do."

"You don't. Olivia, I want a divorce." A loud sob left her, and her face hit her hands. "We're both miserable," I continued. "We can't keep doing this to each other. Let's just end this on good terms and go our separate ways."

"You can't just stop loving me all of a sudden!"

"Olivia, this isn't sudden. How haven't you noticed that we

haven't even been going through the motions of being married? Do you even see that I've been sleepwalking through the last five years of my life?"

"I don't care—"

"And that's just it," I said, interrupting her. "You don't care. You don't care about me, you don't care about my life, you don't care about what I want. I want to be able to live my life, Olivia, and you and I both know you're happier without me too, so this is the obvious thing for us to do."

"I've lost everything! I lost Tate, I lost the ability to have more children . . . I can't lose you."

I ground my jaw at the umpteenth reminder of Tate that night and shut my eyes.

"Our baby is *gone,* Brody. You've already taken everything. Don't take *you* from me too. Don't tell me I lost you with Tate."

Goddamn it; stop bringing up what I did! "Olivia—"

"Please, Brody. After everything you've done, you owe it to me to stay with me."

Pinching the bridge of my nose, I tried to hold back the tears that had begun forming. "I can't, I—"

"I'll die without you, Brody! Do you hear me? I. Will. Die. Do you want my death on your hands too?"

"Olivia, stop!"

"You promised you'd help me! You promised you were on my side. No one else knows what it's like to go through this, no one else knows that I can't deal with this pain. And you swore you were going to get me help. And now you're just going to leave me?" she shouted. "How could you do this to me? After everything else you've done, Brody?!"

"I have tried, Olivia," I said, exhaustion coating my voice. "I have tried so many times to get you help. You say you want it, but I know you don't."

"It's because of this! It's because I know once you put me in that fucking mental institution you're going to leave me there forever. You'll never come back for me. You'll never check on me. You won't love me anymore; you're going to leave me. I know it! You're just trying to throw me in there so you don't have to deal with me anymore."

"No, what I'm trying to do is make sure that you get the help you need so that when I leave you, you won't kill yourself, Olivia!" I shouted before I could stop myself.

Olivia's eyes and mouth went wide, and her tears fell impossibly harder. "I knew it! You're going to leave me as soon as I'm in there! I won't go. I won't fucking go! And if you leave me, I swear to God I won't be alive the next day! Do you hear me?"

My shoulders sagged in defeat and my breath came out in a hard rush. "Liv—"

"How do you think Daddy's attorney would like that?" she asked, her lip curling in disgust.

My eyes narrowed on her for a long moment before I shook my head and stood. With a hard swallow, I turned and walked toward the hallway. "Go to bed, Olivia. You're drunk."

"No! You're going to leave—"

"I'm not leaving you. You're fucking sick. I'm gonna get you help. Just like I said I would."

15

Kamryn

July 5, 2015

THE BELL CHIMED, and I made my way to the front of the bakery. After Aiden had gone home last night, I'd barely been able to force myself through a shower before falling asleep. Yesterday had been draining in so many ways, and for the first time since I'd opened the bakery I didn't want to be at work.

We should have put up the MONDAYS SUCK board this morning.

A beautiful woman not much older than me was talking on her phone when I walked out, and she did a double-take when she saw me, her eyebrows drawing together as she studied me. I pulled off my glasses and realized I probably looked weird to her with flour on my face and glasses. I looked around for a napkin so I could clean them off.

While I was cleaning my glasses, she stopped her phone conversation abruptly and pointed at me. "Do I know you?"

"Uh, no? I don't believe so."

"Huh." She gasped and snapped a couple times. "Are you a member at the Stockton Country Club?"

"No." *Lord no, no more country clubs for me.*

"What's your name?"

"KC."

Her eyes widened with recognition, and her glossed lips formed a perfect O. "Oh, this is *your* bakery?"

"Yes, ma'am. Do you know what you were wanting?"

Her head was still tilted to the side as she looked at me. "I'll just take two. Anything chocolate." She rummaged around in her massive Coach purse as she hissed into her phone, "No, I swear I know this girl. Anyway, so like I was telling you. He may have been planning on leaving before, but he's definitely not now. Not after last night." She handed me her card, and all the blood left my face.

Olivia Saco. Olivia . . . oh, my God! My boyfriend's wife is in my bakery, and she recognizes me! How does she know who I am? Has someone seen Brody and me together? Did she know Brody was having an affair? As the room swirled around me, I was positive this was what Barbara was going through when she had hot flashes. Somehow I managed to stop staring at the credit card, and my eyes shifted to watch Olivia's back as she stood next to the window whispering on her phone.

I suddenly hated that my shop had amazing acoustics.

". . . with him lately. He's different. But I played the whole guilt-trip thing . . . Of course, he bought it, he said he wasn't leaving me, didn't he? God, it really is pathetic how easy he is to sway, though . . . Oh, I know, right? How he hasn't realized by now that I can cry at the drop of a hat is beyond me. I never wanted the damn kid anyway. Shit, I'm probably going to hell for saying that, aren't I? . . . Ha! Love you too, bitch. Be there in thirty . . . I know, I know, I'm getting you a cupcake too."

My throat burned and my hands shook as I grabbed a little plastic container and put two cupcakes in it. It took everything in me not to scream at her and break down in the middle of my store for Brody's sake as I realized the amount of guilt and manipulation he'd lived with for years. I'd heard enough stories from Brody's family and Kinlee, but my God I'd had no idea. Three minutes in her presence and I wanted to get Brody as far away from her as possible. And what did she mean he said he wasn't leaving her? My gut churned as I replayed Olivia's words: *"I never wanted the damn kid anyway." I have to tell Brody. I have—*

"That's not your natural hair color."

I jumped at the sound of her voice so close to me and looked up at her. "Excuse me?"

"Your roots are starting to come in. You're not naturally a brunette, are you?"

Thank God for my appointment tomorrow, I didn't realize anyone could see the blond. I couldn't even see it. "Um, no. I'm not." I swiped her card and handed it back to her. When she didn't take it, I looked up.

"I swear I know you, but I would remember that accent of yours."

I really hope you don't. I put the credit card on top of the cupcake box and slid it toward her. "I must just have one of those faces,

I guess. Thank you so much for coming in, please stop by again soon." *Don't. Don't. I never want to see you again.*

"Oh. My. God! K-C, like initials, you're—are you—oh, my God, you're Kamryn fucking Cunningham!" she screeched, then did a high-pitched, girly squeal.

"Oh, shit," I breathed and took a step back.

"I have to call my mom, she's going to flip! Everyone thought you'd been kidnapped! Why are you here? Did you just, like, move here? Your parents and Chad—oh, my God, Chad. You left him! Why would you just leave him?"

"Please don't! Don't call your mom, don't tell anyone. Shit. This is not happening, how do you know who I am?"

Olivia leaned across the counter, a massive smile on her face. "Wow, you just look so different. You really shouldn't wear glasses, they don't look good with your face." She grabbed for a chunk of bangs and I took a step away from her hand. "All your blond hair is gone. I loved your hair, I've always grown my hair out to look like yours. See?" She turned to the side to show me her long blond hair before facing me again and screeching, "I can't believe Kamryn Cunningham is *here* in Jeston, Oregon!"

"Olivia, please don't tell—"

She reared back. "How do you know my name?"

Oh, shit. "Your credit card."

"Oh, right." She waved it off and slapped a hand on the counter. "We have to go out for drinks at the club. I can't believe you didn't become a member of one when you moved here."

"Look, please, I don't want anyone to know I'm here. Just, please . . . tell me how you know who I am."

"Everyone knows who you are in the racing world. It was a huge deal when you disappeared. They thought you were kidnapped."

"So your family has horses?"

She nodded and flipped her hair back. "We keep them at a place a few hours north. Oh, you've probably heard of us! The Reynoldses."

I hadn't, but I just smiled and pulled my shirt away from my body a few times. This day couldn't get any worse.

"I have to run or I'm going to be late, but oh, my God, I can't believe you're here! Here's my number. Call me anytime and we'll get drinks!" She grabbed the pen and wrote it on the back of the receipt before doing another squeal-screech and grabbing her cupcakes and card.

"Olivia, please don't tell anyone," I begged when she hit the door.

She winked and pushed the door open with a hip. "Your secret's safe with me."

What the hell just happened?

Brody

July 5, 2015

I FELT LIKE I was losing my mind. After telling Liv I wouldn't leave her last night, and not hearing from Kamryn after texting her that I was telling Olivia I wanted a divorce, my mind was going in a thousand different directions. I didn't know how to explain to Kamryn about what had happened last night without her thinking I still wasn't trying to end things with Olivia. It felt like someone was sticking thousands of knives in my body just thinking about not being with Kamryn. But she had to understand. She had to understand how Liv and her parents were. And even though I'd done everything I could to keep what had been happening away from Kamryn, I knew it was time to tell her about their lawyer, what he'd been threatening, what Liv and her parents had been doing to me, and Liv's alleged suicide attempt.

She will understand, I told myself again.

"Bro." Jace kicked at my foot, and I glanced up at him. "What's up with you today?"

"Nothing."

"Not nothing. I haven't seen you look like this in months. What's going on? Is it something with Olivia?" A pained laugh left me, and Jace actually muted the TV. "I thought things with her were getting better, you've been happy lately. Not that I *want* things with her to get better, don't get me wrong. But hell, you've been around, and if you're happy, that's all we really want."

I shook my head and rubbed my hands over my face. "Things aren't better with Liv," I groaned. "Jace, I . . ." *What? I'm having an affair?* Jace and Kinlee would never look at Kam the same way again. I couldn't do that to her.

"What? Dude, I'm your brother. You can tell me anything."

"I told Liv I want a divorce last night."

His eyebrows shot up, and though I knew he was trying to hold it together, a smile was tugging at his lips. "Are you for real? Brody, I know that must have been hard for you, but I'm proud of you."

I grimaced and had to swallow an imaginary lump in my throat. "We're not getting a divorce."

"What? And why the fuck not?!"

"She kept bringing up Tate. Saying I took everything from her and I couldn't take our marriage too. I don't know, Jace. I just . . .

fuck! She was saying she would kill herself if I left her. What the hell was I supposed to do?"

"Are you shitting me? She's such a bitch! You can't let her keep doing this to you, Brody! She's manipulating you!"

"I—no. I don't know. I need to get her help, I know that. But it's just been so fucking difficult trying to get her help with her family and her dad's damn attorney trying to get me at every damn turn."

Jace eyed me. "What are they doing?"

I waved him off. "It's nothing."

"Brody. Tell me. It can't be *nothing* if you're staying with her! Do you need an attorney? Do you need us to help you pay for one?"

"Jace, what? No . . . no, I don't." An attorney couldn't help me. Not when J. Shepherd had them all watching for my name. "I can handle it, I just . . . it doesn't even matter. I don't know why I'm telling you any of this anyway. I'm not leaving Olivia. I need to get her help. I owe her at least that much."

"You don't need to do shit. None of it was your fault; it was an accident. And she's fine! Olivia is fine, Brody. I know you only see her during her crazy rants at home, but you haven't seen her in public. That girl hasn't changed a bit, and she is still living it up off her parents' money."

"I do see her in public, Jace. She's normal Liv in public, I know that."

"But you don't see her when she's not with you," Jace said, looking at me like I was missing something important.

"And how would you know what she's like in public?"

Jace held my stare before admitting, "We've seen her out a few times. Followed her for a while after Tate died."

"What the hell, Jace? Why would you follow her?"

"Because you can't keep living like this! She was lying to you and ruining your life, and we wanted to prove it! The crazy shit you tell us about at home, there's none of that when she's with her parents or friends out in public. I've tried talking to you about this, but shit, other than the past two months, we were only seeing you maybe twice a year. And whenever we tried bringing up what she was doing to you, you just kept pushing away what we were saying because you thought we were making shit up so you would leave her. But she hasn't changed. She's not suffering—far fucking from it. She's just normal bitchy Olivia," Jace grunted. After a few silent minutes, he stood up. "Let me grab us some beers. I'll tell you everything we've seen, and we'll talk this out."

My phone vibrated, and I slid it out of my pocket.

K:
I need to see you. Now.

Work?

K:
I closed up early. 732

I have work tonight, but I'm on my way

I stood up just as the front door opened and Aiden Donnelly walked in. His eyes narrowed into slits when he saw me, and Jace called out his greeting from the kitchen.

"Hey, man! How'd it go at KC's last night?"

The words were out before I could stop them. "You went to her place last night?"

My thoughts flew. She'd never texted me back last night after the party. I didn't hear from her until two minutes ago, and Aiden went to her fucking house last night?

"You mean she didn't tell you?" Aiden sneered low enough so Jace wouldn't hear, but I didn't ask what he meant by that. I was too pissed to even think about his question.

Kamryn was already waiting for me at our hotel, I was three seconds from punching Aiden in the face, and instead of leaving Olivia I'd done the exact opposite. "Jace, I gotta go."

"Brody, c'mon. Don't leave like this again."

"It's important, I have to." Forcing myself not to look at Aiden, I turned and ran out to my SUV.

I didn't even care this time if Olivia called me screaming because I wasn't home tonight, and I didn't care that my sergeant was pissed because I'd just called in claiming to be sick. Kamryn was my world, and I wasn't about to lose her to Aiden or Olivia. I'd figure out a way to still get Liv the help she needed, but I'd do anything to keep Kamryn. Fucking anything.

I sped the entire way there, and after thirty minutes sighed in relief when I pulled into the parking lot. The workers standing behind the main counter shot me a look when I ran through the lobby to the elevators, but I barely spared them a glance as I pushed the buttons furiously. When I reached the seventh floor, and after going the wrong way, I sprinted down the hall until I found the right room and Kamryn opened the door almost as soon as I knocked.

"I saw Olivia," she blurted at the same time I asked, "Did you sleep with Aiden?"

"What?!"

"Wait, you saw Liv? When?"

Kamryn's mouth was open, and she shook her head fiercely. "Why on earth would you think I slept with Aiden?"

For the first time since Kamryn and I had decided we were going to do this, we weren't pulling each other closer as soon as we were alone. She had one arm out as if to keep me away and kept taking small steps back. I would have given anything to start the last minute over.

"He stopped by when I was at Jace's today, and he said he went to your place last night. Why was he there, and why didn't you tell me? You never responded to me last night, and I hadn't heard from you since the party. That's not like you. So did you sleep with him?"

She looked like I'd slapped her. "How dare you," she whispered. "How dare you accuse me of *anything* when you have yet to leave your wife after you promised—you *promised*, Brody—that you would. It's been months, and you obviously have no plans to divorce her since you told her you're not leaving her!"

When had Olivia and Kamryn talked? How did they even know each other? "How did you know about that?"

"Oh, my God, she wasn't lying."

"I can explain, Kam—"

Kamryn stumbled back, and the tears that had been filling her eyes finally spilled over. "You can explain? You can explain to me how for the last two months you've been lying to me and making empty promises of a future together? What was last night, Brody? One last round of pity sex?"

"Of course, it wasn't! Tell me how you know Olivia and what else she told you." Kamryn grabbed her purse off one of the large chairs and started walking toward the door. Before she could reach it, I grabbed her arm to stop her. "Kamryn—"

"What does it matter, Brody?!" she cried and pulled against my hold. "I'm just the stupid mistress who believed all your bullshit and thought you really loved me. I'm done, Brody, I'm so done. I can't do this anymore—what we've been doing has been killing me, but I would've stayed with you because I love you and I trusted you! I trusted that you were filing for divorce, that you were telling Olivia that you were leaving her, that you were planning our future together. But you never had any plans to leave her, did you? I was never anything to you but a convenient fuck."

She yanked her arm free and grabbed the handle of the door. Her assumptions about our relationship, combined with thoughts of her and Aiden together, had my anger winning out, and before I could stop myself I was lashing out at her. "You wanna talk about accusations and trust?! How are you going to talk to me about trust and tell me what our relationship did and didn't mean to me when you were screwing my brother's friend last night? Yeah, Kamryn, let's talk about convenient fucks. Starting with Aiden and me. Is it just us or is it any guy who happens to be around?"

As soon as the words were out, and before her palm could connect with my face, I felt like the worst kind of asshole. I couldn't believe those words had just left me. I couldn't believe I'd just purposefully hurt her that way.

"Go to hell, Brody," she seethed and took a step into the hall.

My hand reached out in search of hers. "Kam, I'm sor—"

"Aiden found out about us! He came over to confront me about it, and we talked about my relationship with you. I begged him not to tell anyone else—that was all. I've never even kissed him, you asshole."

I gripped the door frame when the door slammed shut behind her and let my forehead fall hard against it. How had I screwed this up so much? It felt like my life was slipping through my fingers and I was rapidly grasping at anything to keep me there. If I lost Kamryn, I lost everything.

I flung the door open and took off down the hall, but she was already stepping onto the elevator so I turned and sprinted toward the stairs and rushed down the flights. Bursting out the side exit door near the stairwell, I searched for Kamryn's car as I made my way toward the front of the parking lot and looked for her.

When I saw her racing into the lot, I took off after her, calling out her name. She didn't stop, but I caught her just as she got to the driver's side door of her car. Pulling her into my arms, I dropped my forehead to hers and held her there.

"I'm sorry. I'm an asshole, I know. I didn't mean what I said to you about Aiden. God I'm so sorry. Please don't leave, we need to talk about this."

"I can't, Brody, I can't keep doing this with you. You don't even trust me. You thought I would be with Aiden? I know I'm in a relationship with a married man, but regardless how society views our relationship, I'm not a whore! And you—you didn't even deny that you told Olivia you were staying with her."

"I can explain that, Kamryn, but we need to talk about it. We need to figure something out. You need to know what happened when I went home last night. And Aiden—I'm sorry. When I found out he was there, I just flipped. You're mine, and the thought of anyone touching what is mine drives me insane."

"I *am* yours, Brody," she whispered and tried to step back from me. "But you're not mine. You never were. I can't keep being the mistress in a relationship that I give my everything to, when you're only giving a fraction of yourself."

"You're not a mistress, you're my world." I pulled her close and rested my forehead against hers again. "I can't lose you. I'm so sorry. I love you, Liv."

An agonized cry left her before she could cover her mouth with her hand, and I thought I would die right in that moment.

"Good-bye, Brody."

"Pl—" My breaths were coming too fast and strong. "Please! Kamryn! I didn't mean—"

"It's over. Go back to your wife and stay there. I'm done sharing you with her."

She turned, and my arms fell away from her. I couldn't reach for her again even if I tried. I stumbled back until I hit the car next to hers and slid down to the ground as I watched her get in her car and drive away. My end couldn't come soon enough. In less than twenty minutes, I'd insulted and lost the girl who meant everything to me, and I'd called her by another woman's name. This had to be the worst nightmare I'd ever experienced. I needed to wake up and have it be yesterday morning all over again.

16

Brody

July 15, 2015

"Olivia, can you come here for a minute?"

"Kinda busy, Bro. We can talk tomorrow. I need to get to my parents' so we can get to the club on time."

I blew out a deep breath and tried to remain calm. "This will only take a few minutes, and you've been blowing me off for the last couple days."

She tsked, and I knew she was rolling her eyes. "Poor Brody wants attention," she mocked. "Go get it from your friends."

"Olivia, sit in the fucking chair for a minute!"

"Oh, so you have a temper now too? Do you want me to tell

Daddy about this?" She sat roughly in the chair and immediately began drumming her fingernails on the table. "Well, what did you want? I need to go!"

I huffed a laugh and couldn't help but smile. *Jesus, why did it take me this long to do this?* "You're making this a lot easier than I—"

"What?" she snapped.

"I filed for divorce three days ago, Liv."

"You what?!"

"And I should've done it years ago."

She stood quickly and began pacing. "You can't divorce me! My dad will ruin you. I will take everything you have, Brody!"

"The house is in my name only, and you keep draining our accounts, so I have no money. You've already completely ruined my life, what more could you do?"

"You're about to find out."

"Save your threats, Liv. I'm done with all of this."

Tears poured down her face, and her shoulders hunched. "You can't do this to me! You killed our son."

"Stop using that against me! Goddamn it, Olivia! I will have to live with that for the rest of my life, but I won't fucking live another five years of you constantly reminding me of what happened to Tate. If you had an ounce of respect for his memory or me, you wouldn't keep doing this. And don't try the suicide thing with me again. I see your bullshit—fuck, Olivia, I see it now, and I hate myself for not seeing it a long time ago. You love yourself and your life way too much to ever jeopardize it. And another thing—since this is *my* house, I put it on the market this morning. I don't want anything that reminds me of my years with you, and I want you out of here by the weekend."

"You bastard! Where am I supposed to go?"

"Your parents have a mansion, and you spend the majority of your time there already. Shouldn't be hard to take the rest of your stuff there."

Her tears had stopped just as fast as they'd started, and I wondered why it had taken me so long to notice that everyone was right. She was an amazing actress. Liv deserved a fucking Oscar. "How can you be so heartless?"

I laughed and stood up from the table. "How can *you*? And don't bother trying to drain our accounts again, Liv. I had all the money moved and those accounts closed."

"You can't do any of this!" she screeched and threw her keys across the kitchen. "There has to be a law! That's my money, this is my damn house!"

"That's the beautiful thing about being the only name and signature on the house and all our accounts, Liv. None of it is yours. You haven't worked a day in your life, all you've done is blow my money on useless shit like a Lexus to match your Mercedes, couches when we already had new ones, and a tanning bed . . . to name a few."

If it hadn't been for the fact that I hadn't heard back from Kamryn for a week and a half and I felt like she'd taken my soul with her, this would have been one of the best moments in almost five years. It felt like a huge weight had been lifted off me. Even as Olivia sat there threatening to sue me and make my life miserable, I was so damn happy I'd finally done it.

"Olivia"—I spoke over her and waited for her to stop talking—

"you know this is what you want too. It's not a secret that this is what we want, or what we should have done long ago. So stop acting like this is a shock and pretending you're brokenhearted over this."

"I am!"

I pulled up one of dozens of pictures I'd been sent of her on my phone and turned it toward her. "I had a long talk with my brother the other day. Just a thought, Liv: when you're married and have boyfriends, it's best not to be seen in public with them. But at least for you, your parents seem really happy with you and the guy in this picture."

Her eyes narrowed as she marched past me to grab the keys she'd launched. "You'll be hearing from Daddy's attorney."

Considering I'd spent a week searching for an attorney who would actually help me instead of calling J. Shepherd, I'd been waiting for the moment when I heard from him again. "Looking forward to it," I mumbled when the front door slammed shut.

I tapped the screen on my phone to pull up Kamryn's number and immediately called her. Like it had done the other hundred times I'd called her since that afternoon in the hotel parking lot, it went straight to voice mail.

"Kamryn." I sighed and dropped back into the chair at the kitchen table. "Please call me. I'm sorry for everything I said to you. You have every right to hate me, but I can't live without you. I will spend every day of the rest of my life making it up to you. Call me. I'll always love you."

And there went my momentary good feeling. Divorcing Olivia was a must, but until Kamryn was back in my life, nothing would be okay again.

Kamryn

July 15, 2015

"You're going to stay for dinner, right?"

"I'm not sure, Lee. It was a long day. I kinda just want to go home."

I knew she was studying me, so I continued to stare at the road. It'd been ten days since I'd left Brody in the hotel parking lot. He'd left at least a dozen messages, and more texts, every day, but I just deleted them all when I turned my phone on for a few minutes late at night to see if there was anything from Barb. Ten days, and it felt like ten years. I felt hollow without him, but I couldn't go on like that anymore. Especially after everything I'd found out and how he'd reacted at the hotel. I had been stupid enough to think he would leave Olivia, and even more so for thinking he actually loved me. But I had spent more than six years with a guy who treated me like a possession and like I was beneath him. I wasn't about to spend any more time with a man who didn't treat me like I was his everything.

A small part of me whispered that Brody did treat me that way when we were together, but I pushed it aside. It had been a lie. Some sick joke he'd played on me, and a betrayal of his wife that I'd taken part in.

"Kace, Kace!"

"What?"

Kinlee looked worried as she touched my arm. "I've been sitting here talking to you, and it's like you didn't hear me at all, and why are you crying?"

"I'm not," I choked out and blinked rapidly to keep more

tears back. "It's just allergies or something and my eyes keep watering."

"That's such bullshit and you know it. What is going on with you these last couple weeks?" When I didn't respond, she began angrily tapping on her phone. "I'm going to make sure Jace doesn't let you leave our house. You're staying with us tonight, and you're going to talk to us. KC, you're scaring me."

I rolled my eyes and tried to laugh, but it sounded wrong. "I'm fine." Reaching over to the stereo, I turned the volume up and tried to get lost in the Pandora country radio.

Two songs later, a song by Sugarland I'd never heard came on. When a line in the first verse about praying *she* won't call poured through my speakers, my eyes widened and flashed over to look at the title. "Stay."

Kinlee started talking again, and I shushed her as I hung on to every haunted word of a song about being the other woman in a relationship and wanting the man you love to stay with you.

With tears streaming down my face, I pulled over into a parking lot. All I could do was listen to every word like she was singing about my life with Brody. Kinlee squeezed my hand, and I looked at her through blurry eyes as the chorus filled the car again.

I couldn't hold back the sobs that burst from my chest, and I fell forward until my forehead hit the steering wheel. Kinlee kept brushing my hair away from my face as she mumbled words I couldn't hear. All I could focus on were the words of that song, ten days prior with Brody, and how my world felt like it was crashing down around me. At some point her phone rang, and when she ended the call, she made me look at her.

"KC, *please* tell me what's going on. You're scaring me. The way you've been acting lately, and then whatever just happened with that song . . . what is it?"

I shook my head and cleared my throat. "You're going to think I'm horrible, Kinlee."

"Why?" she whispered and gripped my hand. "Kace, I'm here for you, just tell me."

Another loud sob filled the inside of my car, and my body began shaking so hard that Kinlee's eyes went wide. "I'm hav—I was . . . Brody and I—"

"Did you say Brody?" she asked when I couldn't continue.

I just nodded and buried my face in my hands as my body was overcome with all the pain I'd been feeling the last week and a half and the realization that we were over.

"Jace just—you and Brody wha—oh, holy shit! KC, you're *with* Brody? Brody . . . like my brother-in-law?"

"N-no . . . not anymore. He wasn't—he lied to me. He wasn't going to leave Olivia."

"What the hell? When did all this happen, and how did I not know about this? I'm your best friend! How did you not tell me?"

"I couldn't!" I cried out and pointed toward the screen where just minutes ago the name of the song had been sitting. "I didn't want you to think of me like that! That isn't who I am. I'm not that person. I don't ruin marriages, but I love Brody—" I cut off quickly and sucked in air at saying those words again. "He called me 'Liv,' Kinlee."

"He what?!"

"He was trying to get me to stay. I was breaking up with him last week, and he said, 'I love you, Liv,' and I—I just couldn't. That was it for me, I can't be with him when he's in love with someone else."

Kinlee sat back against her seat and just stared blankly ahead. "Oh, my God, how did I not know? How long has this been going on?"

"Almost two months," I whispered and wiped furiously at my face.

After a long silence, she finally shook her head and huffed a sad laugh. "I can't believe you didn't tell me."

"Kinlee, I had an affair with a married man—"

"I don't care."

"How could you not?"

Her eyes searched around, like the answer was somewhere between us. "You said two months, so this started right after you first met Brody at my house?" I nodded, and she did the same as she continued: "I haven't seen Brody this happy since his son, Tate, was alive. You don't know what it was like watching him emotionally die a little more every time we saw him—*when* we saw him. We've seen him more in the last two months than we have in the five years since Tate died. You gave all of us our Brody back. How could I even begin to care that you had a relationship with him?"

"Because it's wrong!"

"It is, but Brody is a different case. He should have left Olivia long ago, and he definitely should have left her when you guys got together . . . but you've seen his mom, she's always trying to set him up. No one views Brody's marriage as a marriage. They view it as a death sentence for him. And I know you, KC. You're not a home-wrecker at heart. I doubt going through this was easy for you . . . and the only thing I'm upset about is the fact that you felt like you couldn't tell me." She held a hand up when I opened my mouth. "I understand, but it still hurts."

"I'm sorry," I whispered. "I'm sorry for so much, Kinlee. For lying about Brody, for not telling you about my past . . . all of it. Other than Barb, you're the only friend I've ever had, and I feel like I don't deserve your friendship with the way I've kept everything from you."

She looked at me with confusion. "Barb isn't your aunt, is she?" she asked so softly I almost didn't hear her.

Shaking my head, I blew out a deep breath, and then told her everything as I drove us back to her house. I told her about Kentucky and the horse-racing world. About my family's status in that world, and what people expected from a family like mine. I told her about my parents. How detached they were, how they expected perfection, and how they viewed me as property instead of as a daughter. I told her about Charles, how ridiculous he was, and how hard it had been to go through years of pretending to even like him. But mostly I told her about Barb. How she'd been my maid, how she'd raised me and been the only person on my side growing up, and how she'd been the one who helped me get away.

"Holy shit," Kinlee breathed when I was done. "No wonder you never told anyone. You're finally getting to be who you want to be. And for the record, I think I like KC a lot more than I would like the princess of the Kentucky Derby."

I laughed sadly and turned onto her street. "I like KC a lot more too."

"You're really from Kentucky?"

"Yeah."

"Damn it." She hiccupped and sucked in a couple breaths before wiping at her tear-streaked face. "Don't tell Jace. I bet him two hundred dollars you were from Alabama." A startled laugh bubbled up in her throat as she wiped at more tears.

"How can you be so calm about all this? I just told you I was having an affair with your brother-in-law. I just told you that I'm really someone else. And you're joking about it?"

She looked at me sadly and shrugged. "I love you. I'm not going to judge you for wanting to run away from a shitty life. And though I wish you'd told me, I'm not going to judge you for falling in love with Brody and acting on it."

"Kinlee, what we did was—"

"It was wrong. Yeah, sure, I get that. But you're wrong about all this too, you know."

My head whipped to the side as I put the car in park. "Wait, what?"

"Brody. I don't know what happened between you two last week. But he doesn't love that woman. And what happened between the two of you, well, it's never been an option for him before. Which means you have to be special to him. So maybe he made a mistake, and maybe he's still in love with you. Don't shut him out. Because if you've been shutting me out, then I know you're doing it to him too."

I rubbed at my aching chest. "It . . . it doesn't matter anymore. He chose her, Lee. So whether I'm wrong or not, it's over."

Brody

July 15, 2015

"EVERYTHING OKAY WITH Kinlee?" I asked when Jace hung up and tossed his phone back on the table.

"Yeah, I couldn't really understand what she was saying other than something was wrong with one of her friends and she was on her way home. She was just blowing up my phone with texts I didn't understand, but there was loud music playing in the car. So, I don't know, I guess we'll find out when she gets here."

"Do you need me to go?"

"What? No, she'll be happy you're here. She misses you just as much as I do. Anyway, sorry about that. So what happened with Olivia after that?"

I ran my hand through my hair and settled back into the couch. "Well, the tears stopped, and she turned into an ice queen in less than a second. And there was no argument or denying the picture I showed her. She just up and left, saying I'd hear from her dad's attorney."

"Bitch," Jace huffed and drained his beer. "I'm proud of you, Bro. I know that must've been difficult."

"A week and a half ago, I would have thought it would be too," I said. "But as soon as it was out today I felt lighter than I have in years. I just don't know why it took me so long to see that this was all bullshit. I mean, even at the end there were times when I knew she was lying but she'd do something to make me actually believe she was suicidal and needed help. I just don't get why I couldn't have realized long ago all of this was typical of her games."

Jace stayed silent for long minutes as he rolled the empty bottle back and forth between his fingers. "I hate to say this, but it's because of Tate. Because of your view on what happened that day, you weren't able to see what she was doing to you. You just knew that your world had shattered and figured hers had done the same, so you weren't seeing her clearly."

"You're probably right," I said. *And because of that, because I*

wanted to help a woman who needed anything but that, I've ruined ev-
erything with Kamryn.

"Did you at least get some of Olivia's psychotic episodes recorded?"

"What?" I snorted. "No."

"What about her dad's attorney? You can take that shit to
court and use it against them for this."

I frowned and sank even deeper into the couch. "My attorney
already mentioned that. With Olivia, half the time I wasn't even
expecting to see her, she'd just be home all of a sudden, or she'd
rant at me over the phone. Now that it's over, it's easy to think
I could have pulled out my phone and recorded it, but I know
that's bullshit. I was always so blown away with whatever was
happening, and trying to keep my shit together, that it was taking
all my focus. And besides, do you really think she wouldn't have
noticed if I started recording her? She would have stopped whatever she was saying immediately."

"Yeah, I guess you're right." Jace sighed and stared straight
ahead—seeing nothing for a few minutes before he stood up.
"Do you want another?" He held up the bottle, and I shook my
head.

Two days after Kamryn had left me in the hotel parking lot,
I'd gone to see Jace and demanded to know everything he'd seen
from the times he'd followed Olivia. Not only did he have stories of the handful of times he or my parents had followed her,
but he had pictures. Olivia shopping with friends, on dates with
other guys, out at brunch or dinner with her parents and one
of the guys. One of the best pictures was the one of a guy who
just happened to be Liv's doctor when she'd "overdosed" on the
antidepressants. And not once did she look like the emotion-

ally unstable woman I'd grown to know over the last four and a half years since Tate died. Jace had been right—she looked like normal Liv.

"You know," he said, "it's a good thing you have those pictures, though."

My forehead creased and I took another sip of my beer. "And why is that?"

"That way, if she tries to come after you in court, you can say she was unfaithful. We have more than enough pictures of her in . . . *interesting* positions with other men. You throw that into it, the judge isn't going to rule in her favor, no matter who her 'daddy' is."

I started choking on my beer and had to force it down my throat before I spit it out everywhere.

"You good?"

I held up a hand and took two deep breaths after it was all down. "I, um, I can't use that against Liv."

"Of course, you can! You know she's going to come after you with whatever she can get her hands on just to be a bitch. You need to have something against her, and now you do."

"Yeah, but it goes both ways," I whispered and stared at the carpeted floor.

"What does?" When I didn't answer, he prompted me. "Brody. What does?"

"I'm—I *was*—having an affair," I admitted softly, and heard Jace exhale.

"What. The. Hell. With who?!"

I shook my head and finally met his bemused stare. "It doesn't matter."

"The hell it doesn't! We've been trying to get you away from

Satan in female form and this entire time you've been with some-one else?"

"Not entire. The last two months."

"What—I don't—how the fuck didn't we kno— Oh, wait, ac-tually, yeah, that makes sense now. You've been different over the last couple months. You and I just talked about that a couple weeks ago."

"Yeah." My chest felt like it was being ripped apart thinking about that day. I would give anything to do that all over again.

"Well, Brody, if *we* didn't know, then chances are Olivia didn't know."

"I wouldn't be so sure about that. The day Ka—uh, the day she broke up with me, she'd seen Olivia that morning, and they'd talked. I don't know what about, I never asked Liv. But the girl knew about how I'd told Olivia I wasn't going to leave her, so I'm guessing Olivia knows about her."

"Wait, whoa . . . back the fuck up. When did all this go down?"

"Ten days ago." Ten of the longest fucking days of my life. I looked back up at Jace and explained, "That's why I left so sud-denly a week and a half ago."

"Damn, Brody. And you didn't tell me? So who is she? You said she knows Olivia?"

"No, I honestly don't think she'd ever met Liv until last week." Jace motioned for me to continue, and I shook my head. "It doesn't matter who she is."

"Yes, it does! Do I know her? Did we go to school with her?"

I blew out a hard breath through my nose and met his stare. "It's because you know her that I won't tell you her name. I can't do that to her."

"Come on—" He cut off when the front door opened, and

his brow scrunched together. "What the hell happened to you two?!"

I turned around and was off the couch as soon as I saw the beautifully broken girl Kinlee had secured to her side. "Kamryn." I automatically took a step closer to her.

Jace had been walking toward them and stopped when he heard me. "Who?"

"What did you just call her?" Kinlee's tear-streaked face was full of surprise as she looked from me to Kamryn, and Kamryn tried to break away from Kinlee's side as new tears quickly fell down her cheeks. "No, no. You're not leaving."

"You knew he was here and you didn't tell me?" Kamryn cried and avoided looking at me as she continued trying to get free.

"Don't go," I pleaded, and Jace inhaled sharply next to me.

"Oh, shit, no way! KC's the girl?"

Kinlee gasped. "You knew about it and you didn't tell me?"

"I just found out! How long have you known, and why didn't you tell me?"

"Because I've only known for, like, ten minutes!"

Kamryn wrenched her arm from Kinlee's grasp and took off for the door, with me right behind her. I caught her and slammed her body to mine before she could reach the door and held her as her body started giving way to sobs.

"Kamryn, I'm so sorry," I spoke into her ear as I continued to pull her back closer to my chest. "I'll never be able to explain how sorry I am for what I said to you and for letting you walk away from me."

"I can't do this with you," she sobbed. "Please just let me go. You have to let me go, Brody."

Knowing I was the reason for her tears was gutting me, and each word was like a new knife in my chest.

"I can't let you go. I'll do everything in my power to keep you with me for the rest of my life. So letting you go isn't an option. I love you. I've loved you since you ran into me in this entryway. And I will love you until I die."

"Olivia—"

"No Olivia. Just you and me. I told you, Kamryn, I'm gonna be yours forever. I know I fucked up, but I will do whatever it takes for you to be mine again."

Her cries filled the entryway, and her hands went to grip where mine were holding her tightly. "But you lied." Her voice broke, taking my heart with it.

"I never lied to you. I don't know what Olivia told you that morning, but I'll tell you everything that happened and why I told her what I did. But I didn't lie. And you were never a mistress. I had every intention of leaving her to spend the rest of my life with you. She made things complicated, and it was just going to take longer than I'd originally planned."

"I can't do this." She huffed and pushed against my hands.

Keeping her wrists locked in one hand, I turned her body and pushed her back until she hit the door. "Kamryn." Pressing her joined hands to her chest, I stepped close enough so our noses were touching and waited until she looked me in the eye. "I'm meant to be with you. If I thought for a second that you actually wanted me to let you go, then I would. But I've wasted enough time living without you as it is, I'm not going to waste any more."

"And what makes you so sure I don't want you to let me go?"

I smiled at her defiance and brought my other hand up to

wipe tears from her cheek before cupping it. Her eyes shut and a heavy breath left her at my touch. *That's why I'm sure.* "Because right now you're guarding yourself so I can't hurt you again. And I don't blame you for it. I know I don't deserve you after everything I've put you through. But no one will ever love you as fiercely as I do. If you believe anything, Kamryn, please believe that."

Her head shook back and forth. "I don't . . . I can't. I can't do this with you. Brody, I love you, but . . . I just can't." Forcefully removing my hands from her face, she moved for the door again. I trapped her against the wall.

"Please just hear me out." If she was going to leave now, she needed to know everything. "I filed for divorce three days ago. I told Liv this morning and said she needed to be out of the house by this weekend. I was wrong to do what I've done with you." A harsh breath left her, and I spoke quickly. "I will never regret being with you, but I hate that I made you wait for me. You didn't deserve that, you deserved all of me from the beginning, and for *that* I'm sorry. And God, baby, you will never know how sorry I am for what happened last week. I don't love her, I haven't for a *long* time. I'm not going to try to make an excuse for why I said her name, because there is none. It just came out."

"You thought I'd cheated on you," she said through her tears.

"No. No, I was being selfish, and jealous, and let my thoughts get away from me before asking you. But, Kamryn, I knew deep down that you wouldn't cheat on me. I was just already stressing about telling you what happened with Liv the night before. I was afraid of losing you, and when I heard he'd been at your place . . . I snapped."

Her eyes had hardened when she looked up at me. "And what exactly happened with you and Olivia that night?"

Letting my hand trail back up to her face, I rubbed my thumb back and forth over her cheek and looked directly into her blue eyes. "I texted you on my way home. I had decided I couldn't wait anymore and I was going to tell her the next day. But she ended up being home, and was drunk, and when I turned her down—"

"Turned her down?"

I just raised an eyebrow at her and traced the line of her jaw when she clenched it shut. "I've been turning her down for years, it was nothing new. But when I turned her down, she started yelling at me. Saying I didn't want her because she couldn't have kids, and kept bringing Tate into it. She said I would still love her if that hadn't happened. I told her that she knew we hadn't loved each other before Tate ever came into the picture, and that I wanted a divorce. She flipped. Said I'd already taken everything from her, I couldn't leave her too. She said she would kill herself if I left her, and then I'd have her death on my hands too."

"What the fuck?" Kamryn whispered. Her expression had turned to one of complete shock.

"That's just how she is. I kept telling her I'd tried getting her help, and I would still get her help if she would let me, but she just kept saying I would leave her so she was refusing to get help. And if I left her, she would be dead the next day. So I told her I wasn't leaving her, because at that point I felt like I didn't have a choice. The next day it was killing me that I didn't know how I could leave her and I'd just told you I *would,* and then when I found out about Aiden . . . I just basically said, 'Screw it.' I knew

I would do anything not to lose you, I didn't even care if Olivia found out about us. But something happened on the drive over there, and I ended up getting more pissed off about the Aiden thing. Like I said, I let my mind get ahead of me . . . and then I fucked up everything."

"Brody, I just don't think I can keep doing this. You keep promising me our forever. But hasn't enough happened that you're starting to second-guess this 'forever' too? Too much happened with Olivia, and I can only imagine it's about to get worse with you filing for divorce. Brody, what if all this is a sign? What if—what if we're not supposed to be together?" she asked, her voice breaking. "So you filed for divorce. That means we should just go on with our relationship now? Brody, you promised me for *months* that you would divorce her, and you only did it after I left you."

"No, no. Don't start thinking about it like that. There's so much that happened that you don't know about. So much with Liv, her parents, and her father's lawyer that I kept from you so you wouldn't have the added stress. What we were already going through was stressful enough. I saw what it was doing to you—what it was doing to us. But if I had told you what was happening, Kamryn, you would have left me just so I wouldn't have had to go through what I was going through with them. I know it. I wasn't *not* leaving Olivia because I didn't want to. Trust me, Kamryn, there was nothing I wanted more than to leave her and start my future with you."

Her eyes had widened with dread. "What was happening?"

Shaking my head, I cupped her cheeks and leaned close. "I'll tell you everything, just not right now. Right now I need you to know that I love you, and I need to know that I haven't lost you."

Kamryn's jaw quivered, and she looked down to where our chests were pressed together.

Putting my fingers under her jaw, I lifted her face until I could look in her blue eyes and I whispered, "Please. You . . . *you* I can't lose."

A sob broke free from her chest, and she shook her head back and forth. "Brody, I love you. But if we do this, then I want all of you."

"Done," I vowed and pressed my lips to hers, only moving back far enough so I could speak. "Done, Kamryn. Completely, one hundred percent yours. No more calls in the middle of the night," I swore against her lips. "No more leaving. No more hiding. I'm yours."

"I'm done sharing you."

I brushed a thumb against her trembling lips and looked back into her eyes. "I hate that you felt like you were. If only you knew that it's always been only you. I was never hers; she's never had a part of me. But God, Kamryn, I'm so damn sorry for making you wait so long."

"Can we please have our forever?" she begged, her voice so soft and broken, I wanted to die for ever making her go through this pain and doubt in our relationship.

"Yeah, babe. We can have our forever."

17

Kamryn

July 18, 2015

A PAIR OF arms slid around my waist, and I smiled when Brody's lips pressed firmly against my neck.

"What are you making?"

"Breakfast."

"Really now?" he asked as he grabbed a sausage patty from the plate and took a bite. "Is breakfast for dinner a normal occurrence for you?"

I took the rest of the sausage from his fingers and spoke around it. "No, but you made me miss it the last few mornings, and I'm a breakfast-food person."

"Are you really mad at me for making you miss breakfast?" he asked softly. The combination of his soft lips and rough stubble against my neck caused my stomach to feel like it was melting.

"Hmm?"

He laughed huskily, and I leaned against the rumbling in his chest. "I'll take that as a no. Can I help?"

"You touching me and kissing me like that is the exact opposite of helping."

Running his hands over my stomach, he played with the top of my pajama shorts and hipbones before bringing his hands back up to pass over the swell of my breasts. "Touching you how?"

"Uh." I licked my lips and tried to control my breathing. "T-touching me like that."

"So you want me to stop?"

"Hmm?" I didn't even know where we were anymore. All I could focus on were his hands moving slowly back down my stomach and his lips on the dip between my neck and shoulder.

Suddenly his body was gone from mine, and I stumbled back a step before he caught me.

"What the hell?"

He laughed loudly and leaned around my body to kiss me chastely. "I'll finish the sausage," he said as he moved in front of me to check the cooking sausage.

"But—you—what—not fair!"

"Sausage, sweetheart. Breakfast for dinner. You have a ton of fruit and a waffle iron out. Any of this ringing a bell?"

I just stood there staring at him like he'd stolen an ice cream cone from a child. "That was so hateful!"

Brody barked out a laugh and wrapped an arm around my waist to pull me in for another kiss. "God, I love that accent of yours."

"I don't have one," I grumbled and moved away from his hold to begin cutting up fruit.

It had been three days since we talked out everything in the entryway of Kinlee and Jace's house, and in that time . . . there had been nothing but us. No Olivia, no Reynoldses, no J. Shepherd . . . just us. It had been beyond amazing and felt like a dream that I wasn't ready to wake up from. While we'd spent most of the time in the bedroom, we had done a lot of talking. He'd told me everything that was happening with Olivia's psychotic family that he'd kept hidden from me. He told me about J. Shepherd's threats, and his worries about what they might come back with now that he had filed for divorce, even though he had a lot of evidence on Olivia. But mostly he told me about everything he wanted to do now that we were about to start our forever. Including being reintroduced to his parents as his girlfriend. I'm not going to lie—that one was scaring me.

Jace and Kinlee had taken the news well—too well—but that was because they hated Olivia and wanted Brody back. Well, and probably because they both knew me and liked me. But while I'd met Brody and Jace's parents, I don't think they'd ever given me a second thought. So even though I knew they would be happy Brody had left Olivia, I had no idea how they would react to me. My bet was that it wouldn't be good. In my mind I was still a home-wrecker. I was still "the other woman." And I still didn't understand how anyone could see me as anything *but* those things.

"What are you thinking so hard about?"

My body tightened as Brody's voice broke through my inner freak-out, and I focused on loosening it as I continued cutting fruit. "Your parents. I'm still scared about that conversation . . .

about how it's going to go, and how it might be for a long time after that."

Brody was about to pour batter on the waffle maker, but stopped and frowned at me. "It's going to be okay, Kamryn."

"Just because Kinlee and Jace were okay with it doesn't mean your parents will be."

"I'm not expecting them to be okay with it. I was never expecting anyone to be okay with it. Hell, my two closest friends more or less said they were glad I was happy but didn't approve of what I was doing."

My eyebrows rose, and my eyelids blinked slowly. "Um . . . who?"

"When Hudson and Steele came down for Tate's—"

"Oh, my God, they know?!" I didn't even know these men, and they'd known that Brody and I had been having an affair? My cheeks heated in embarrassment. Whenever Brody mentioned them, he always told me they were guys he wanted me to meet someday . . . but I doubted, because of what they knew about me, that this meeting would ever happen.

"They're not really the kind of guys I can keep things from. Steele figured it out on his own, Kam." He stepped closer to me and cupped my cheeks in his large hands. "Don't be embarrassed. They don't think any less of you, and they weren't judging you, I swear. They were mad at me for making you wait for me to leave Olivia."

I breathed out heavily and dropped my head. "This is a disaster. Your best friends and family are always going to think of me as the woman you had an affair with," I grumbled. "Even if you think they won't judge me," I said before he could say anything.

"I'm sorry, Kamryn," he said simply. "I'm just sorry."

Looking up into his gray eyes, I placed my hands over his and sighed. "We went in this thing together. Please stop saying you're sorry." Leaning up to kiss him softly, I smiled against his lips and said, "We just have a few more things to get through, including telling your family, and then one day this will all just be a memory."

"You know what I'm scared about?" he asked seriously, and my eyebrows bunched together. "When you tell Barb. From what you've said, I'm afraid she'll come after me with a wooden spoon or something."

I laughed, and he kissed me hard before releasing me.

"We'll get through it, Kamryn. But until I go to work tomorrow, let's just keep pretending like we have nothing to deal with and nothing waiting for us out there. All right?"

I studied his worried eyes and nodded. "All right, Brody."

After our breakfast-for-dinner, we cleaned up the kitchen, but that took a little longer than expected when flirtatious touches and quick kisses started lingering and growing hotter. Soon the dishes and leftover food were forgotten as we got lost in each other on the cool hardwood of the kitchen. Once everything was finally cleaned and put away, we moved into the living room, turned on the TV, and lay down on the couch together as the shows played in the background. Sometimes we talked, sometimes we kissed, but we were always holding on to each other like we couldn't get close enough—and I loved every second.

It was all so stress-free, so normal, and so perfect.

Later, my eyelids cracked open when Brody removed my glasses and put them on my nightstand. Running my hand over the fabric, I realized we were on my—*our*—bed, and I watched groggily as Brody removed his shirt and crawled onto the bed.

"I fell asleep?" I guessed.

"Little bit," he said, his voice warm and rough with exhaustion. "Snoring and drooling all over the place."

"Shut up." I pushed at his bare chest, and he caught my hand in his, his laugh filling the otherwise quiet room.

"No, you looked adorable." He kissed me gently and pulled my body closer to his. "Go back to sleep, Kamryn."

And I did, so easily, just as I had done the last three nights. There was no fear that he would leave. There was no watching the clock. There was no Olivia. Again, it was just us. It was perfect.

Brody

July 21, 2015

"I DON'T KNOW if I can do this!" Kamryn hissed and dropped her phone into one of the cup holders in my SUV.

I sent her a reassuring smile and picked up her phone, searching for Barb's number.

Kamryn refused to go out in public with me until my family knew about us, and I wasn't about to keep hiding us. So we were having brunch at Kinlee and Jace's with my parents, and I was making her call her aunt Barb on the way so we could get it all done at once.

"I'm going to be right here with you. None of them will be easy to tell, but it needs to be done. And the sooner we do it the sooner we can start our forever. Then it will be done, babe. We won't have to hide, we won't have to worry about them finding out . . . it'll all be over."

She nodded her head a few times and roughly swallowed as she looked out the window.

Pressing Barb's number, I let the call go through my car and watched as Kamryn jumped at the first ring. For a few seconds, I didn't think Barb was going to answer as the phone continued to ring. Just as I was about to end the call, I heard an accent that put Kamryn's to shame come through the phone.

"Baby girl, are you all right? You never call me!"

My brow furrowed, and Kamryn started biting on one of her fingernails—something I knew she didn't do.

"I'm fine," she said shakily.

"What's going on, I'm getting your—"

"Barb, I'm not alone."

There was silence for a few seconds, and I wanted to ask why Barb said Kamryn never called her, and why the start of the call was already weird as shit.

"Is Kinlee with you?"

"No. I, uh, we're on our way to Kinlee's house, though," Kamryn responded and glanced at me.

"Well, all right then. Who is 'we'?"

Kamryn started breathing roughly, her chest moving up and down rapidly.

Squeezing her hand, I waited for her to look at me. "Kam," I prompted her when she didn't.

Her head whipped to the left, her eyes were wide and worried as she tried to control her breathing.

"Kamryn, honey?" Barb asked.

"You don't have to do this," I whispered. "I'm sorry."

Kamryn bit down on her bottom lip and squeezed my hand back. "Barb, do you remember when I told you that Kinlee kept trying to set me up with that guy Aiden?" she began, her blue eyes locked on mine. "And I was trying to explain to you why I didn't want to be with him?"

"Yes," Barb said cautiously.

"Do you also remember me telling you about Kinlee's brother-in-law?"

"Kamryn, no." Barb gasped and whispered something I couldn't make out. "Baby girl, tell me you didn't do anything with that married man."

"Barb, you have to understand, I love him—"

"Kam, young lady, do you realize what you have done?"

Kamryn covered her mouth as a sob worked its way out of her chest, and though Barb couldn't see her, she nodded her head.

"He is married. He made a vow before God, and you helped him destroy that vow! You think he will leave his wife for you? And even if he does, how do you know that he won't go and do the same thing to you?"

Kamryn cried harder, and I grabbed the phone from the cup holder, took the call off speaker, and spoke to Barb through the phone.

"Ma'am, this is Brody Saco, and I know I'm probably the last person you want to hear from or speak to, but right now Kamryn's too upset to respond to you, and I need you to understand something."

"You should have never approached that young girl, do you hear me?"

"I know you can only think the worst of me right now," I said calmly. "But you have to know I'm in love with Kamryn. I married the woman I did because she got pregnant, and before you ask, I do not have a child with her—he died almost five years ago. But she and I stopped loving each other long before we got married, and for the last five years she's been manipulating me into thinking she was suicidal and bipolar so I would stay with her. Her parents' attorney has been threatening me into staying with her, and recently I've come to find out that there's absolutely nothing wrong with her and she's been cheating on me with numerous men . . . including men her family used to try to get me fired." I paused, waiting to see if Barb would yell at me some more, but when she said nothing, I continued. "I have been trapped in a marriage. I have felt like I was drowning for almost five years now, and it wasn't until I met Kamryn that I finally knew what it felt like to be alive again."

Kamryn reached over to grab my arm, and I looked back over at her.

"It's my fault Kamryn had to keep our relationship from you, and for that I'm sorry. I know you can't think highly of me because of the little you knew about me before. But please, don't be upset with her about this. Kamryn saved me. And despite how we may come across to people because of how we began our relationship, I will cherish her and love her until the day I die."

"While that was a well-thought-out speech, sir, you will have to understand why I don't trust you," she said after a few beats of silence. "Please put Kamryn on the phone."

It felt like a weight settled in my stomach as I handed the phone over to Kamryn.

"Barb? . . . I—yes, ma'am." Kamryn blew out a deep breath as she ended the call and put her phone in her purse.

"What'd she say?"

"That she hoped I knew what I'd gotten myself into, and that she needed time to think about it," she responded, her voice completely monotone.

"Fuck," I whispered. "I'm sorry. We can go back to the condo—we don't have to tell my parents right now." I leaned forward to put the SUV into gear, and Kamryn sat up as she cleared her throat.

"No. You were right. I want to get all of this over with at once. And your family is already expecting to see you. I know your mom is going to be so upset if you don't show up. So let's do this."

Cupping her cheek with my right hand, I leaned forward and kissed her forehead gently. "I love you."

"I love you too. Come on," she said and sat back. "I'm ready. Let's do it."

Putting the car in drive, I drove down the last couple streets to Jace's house and breathed out heavily when I got out of the car. I wasn't worried. Whatever they said wouldn't affect me. I'd gone years with them hating whom I was with. I was just terrified of what their response would do to Kamryn.

Walking up to the door, I grabbed her hand, hoping to reassure her, but her body continued to tremble the closer we got. "Breathe, Kam. We'll get through it togeth—"

The door was flung open, revealing my mom and dad, and Jace with an apologetic expression. My mom glanced down at our joined hands, looked up at me, then over to Kamryn, and screamed excitedly as she threw her hands up and rushed us.

I WATCHED AS my mom grabbed Kamryn's shoulders hours later and spoke softly to her before kissing her cheek and walking out the front door with my dad. For a few seconds Kamryn stood there looking stunned—like she had all morning—before shutting the door behind them and turning to walk into the living room.

"You okay?" I asked against her forehead before placing a kiss there and wrapping my arms around her.

"Yeah, just . . . so weird."

"Not what you were expecting?"

She was silent for a few seconds before breathing out. "No."

"Me neither," I replied honestly.

I hadn't known what to expect. Even with my mom pushing girls I'd grown up with on me whenever she saw me, I still hadn't known how she'd react to Kamryn. I didn't know if she'd look at her the same way I knew Kamryn's aunt Barb was judging me. I didn't know if she'd let this change the way she'd come to know Kamryn. And I didn't know if Mom would accept her the way she'd accepted Kinlee. But I definitely hadn't been expecting my mom to *thank* Kamryn.

It hadn't been hard to guess that my parents would be happy with the news that I was divorcing Olivia. My dad—who had always been a man of few words—simply smiled and nodded his approval. And my mom began crying before turning to Kamryn and thanking her. She hadn't wanted to know the details, she was just happy that Kamryn had come into my life and given me the motivation to get myself out of my life with Olivia.

"Kace—um, Kamryn . . . sorry, that's still hard to get used to," Jace began, and I moved so I could pull Kamryn's back into my chest. "You have to understand something. It's not that any of us *wanted* Brody to have an affair, and it's not that any of us are really happy that this is how the two of you started. But Kinlee and I already love you, and honestly, knowing you and knowing

Brody, I can't think of any two people more perfect for each other. And I know all you've ever heard was that we hated Olivia, but it was so much more than that. We all saw what she was doing to him, and we all watched what looked like Brody slowly dying because of her. He never saw us because of what was going on with them, and it was like we were waiting for the day when we lost him too," he choked out. I looked down and noticed the tears falling down Kinlee's cheeks.

I hated that I'd put my family through this. I hated that by trying to do the right thing, I'd hurt so many people other than myself.

"So to have someone come into Brody's life and change him so drastically and bring him back to us . . ." Jace trailed off as he searched for the words to say. "How are any of us supposed to be upset about that?" Kinlee nodded, and Jace continued: "It's like Mom said: she didn't want to know the details, because she doesn't want to think of you that way. And I know Kinlee and I don't think of you that way. You saved my brother, you saved their son, and that's the only way any of us want to see it. We love you, Kamryn, end of story."

Kamryn grabbed and squeezed my hands, where they were resting on her stomach, and nodded a few times. " 'Kay," she managed to choke out.

Jace looked up at the ceiling and blinked back the wetness in his eyes before looking back at us and letting out a loud breath. "Gah. Can we stop with the mushy now? I'm going to spontaneously grow a vagina and have to stay for the girls' nights with you two if we keep this up."

Kamryn laughed and wiped at her face, and Kinlee elbowed Jace.

"Can we go back to celebrating the fact that Olivia is gone? Jesus Christ, I've been waiting for this moment since Brody went into the Army eight years ago!"

I rolled my eyes, but smirked when Jace winked at me. Kissing Kamryn's neck, I whispered in her ear, "I'll get you something to drink," before releasing her and following Jace into the kitchen.

"I *am* happy for you, Bro, I hope you know that," Jace said quietly once we were grabbing beers out of the fridge.

"I know you are. I am too."

Straightening, he shut the fridge and took a step in the direction of the living room before looking back at me, his face reflecting the sincerity of his next words. "But I wasn't lying when I said Kinlee and I love that girl in there. You hurt her again, I won't think twice about beating the shit out of you, big brother."

Laughing, I nodded and bumped his shoulder as I passed him. "Noted. But you won't have to carry out that threat."

"I better not have to."

Looking at Kamryn talking to my sister-in-law, a calm I hadn't felt in years settled over me, and I knew I would go through hell and back to make sure I gave that girl the forever I'd promised—the one we both deserved.

18

Kamryn

July 26, 2015

I RELAXED DEEPER into Brody's side and smiled as we walked through the marketplace downtown almost a week later. Brody had been trying to make up for the time we'd lost in the beginning, so while I'd been working during the weekdays, he'd randomly show up at the shop just to say hi, bring me coffee, or steal a cupcake and a kiss before running errands as he tried to sell his house and everything in it. At night we'd done everything from grocery shopping to going out for coffee to going for a run together, and tonight we were on our first *real* date.

After a long dinner followed by a movie, we were walking

through downtown Jeston looking at the shops and just enjoying being out together. We'd done everything so backward from the very beginning. These dates should have been done then, but they hadn't been. And somehow, after all we'd been through, it made them that much more special.

Knowing we didn't have to hide made an indescribable feeling swell inside me. Like I was happier than I'd ever been. Like I was on some high you couldn't even get from drugs. Like I could do absolutely anything in the world . . . and like, if I stopped touching Brody, all of it would come crashing down around me in a second. This feeling made me want to scream in excitement—and then cry because all the hiding and stress was finally behind us.

"You want to do anything, or do you want to go home?"

I smiled up at Brody and tried to not roll my eyes. "I love being able to be in public with you just as much as you love it," I said, "but I kind of just want to go back home." I kissed him quickly and skipped a step ahead of him so I could turn to face him. "I was thinking we could curl up on the couch and watch another movie, or maybe you could feed me something sweet . . ." I trailed off, and his eyebrows rose. "Maybe a shower together . . ."

He grabbed at my waist and pulled me back into his arms, his lips falling lightly onto mine. "All of the above," he said against my mouth. "Come on, let's go."

Brody turned us around to walk in the opposite direction, picking up the pace as we made our way back to his SUV. The entire time we walked he whispered into my ear what he wanted to do when we got home, and by the time we got to the car I was practically running to get inside—and was almost positive we would be skipping the movie and couch time.

"Eager?" he asked, and I winked as I laughed, but the laugh

stopped short when I noticed Brody's expression fall.

"What?" When he didn't respond, I rounded the front of his Expedition. "Brody, what is it?"

He swallowed hard and looked around us as he tore off the note that had been taped to the driver's side window.

"What is this?"

"Get in the car, Kamryn."

"But what—"

"Get in the car first, then we'll talk about it."

His tone left no room for discussion, but even still, he put his arm around my shoulders and walked me to the passenger door to let me in before going back to his side and getting in.

"What—" I cut off quickly when he handed me the paper, and I hurried to put my seat belt on when he started up the car and tore out of the parking spot and onto the street. "Jesus, Brody."

"You know what Olivia looks like, right?"

"Uh, yeah . . ." I said uncertainly, drawing out the word like it was a question. I knew exactly what she looked like, but I didn't understand. Flipping over the paper, my mouth fell open and I felt dizzy when I read the words.

"Have you seen her at all in the last week when we've been out?" Brody asked when we stopped at a light. "Kam, baby, have you?" He turned my head so I was facing him, and then pointed down at the letter. "Don't worry about the lawyer and court bullshit. I'm not. It's just, until I saw that, I forgot she'd been to your bakery, and I don't trust her not to pull some stupid shit with you."

"I haven't seen her," I said breathlessly.

I wasn't worried about the words on the paper either. After telling Brody to show up on Tuesday for a meeting with their lawyers so they could settle things or she'd take him to court, she ended the letter with:

By the way, cute girlfriend you have there.

xo Liv (your wife)

And like Brody, when I read those words, I remembered that I'd already met Olivia. But my first thought hadn't been fear that she might try to make my life hell by showing up at my bakery. My first thought was that she knew who I was.

"Brody," I began, taking deep breaths as I prepared myself to tell him about my past—about Kamryn Cunningham.

"Yeah? Shit, hold on." He grabbed for his ringing cell phone, and I snapped my mouth shut, taking that as a sign that now wasn't the time to tell him.

I RAN TO the door of my bakery on Tuesday morning, thankful that today wasn't one of the days Kinlee and I drove together. But I didn't know how long this would continue, or if it was even something I should tell her.

We should totally go for drinks . . . you can bring my worthless, cheating husband!

Every day since Saturday morning there had been a note on the front of my bakery from Olivia—Monday there had been two since we were closed on Sundays. Brody knew about them, and every day I'd tried to tell him about my life in Kentucky before I'd moved here. But it never failed that something happened when I started to tell him, and then, when we were talking later, I wouldn't have the nerve to bring it up. I wanted to keep living as though that time in my life had never existed.

But the more Olivia left me notes, the more I worried she would mention something to Brody.

As of right now, he only knew about Barb, who he still thought was my aunt. Barb had called once since we told her about our relationship, and while it was better between her and me, it wasn't how it had been. She'd even asked to talk to Brody, and apparently she'd been nice to him. But even Barb thought it was better if everyone in Jeston thought of her as my aunt. She didn't want me to have to think of my old life any more than I wanted to.

I left it for a reason. It's not like I'm hiding a criminal history. I just don't want to be Kamryn Cunningham anymore! And I couldn't believe I was actually standing outside my bakery with my head to the glass door, trying to justify not telling Brody.

"Uh, KC?"

I rolled my head to the side, still letting it stay on the glass as I turned to look at Grace.

"You going to go in or stay out here?"

"Did you forget your keys?" Andy yelled as he walked across the parking lot.

I held up my keys without responding and looked back at Grace. "It feels like a Monday, and Mondays suck."

"Oh, my God, is it a 'Mondays suck' day?" Andy asked excitedly as he finished running up to us. "Let's do this!"

I smiled at my employees and unlocked the door to the bakery to let us in.

Sometimes you just need to throw some cake.

Brody

July 30, 2015

"KAM?" I CALLED out over the loud music as I stepped into the bakery. I looked at the large chalkboard with the bright words MONDAYS SUCK . . . SO THROW A CUPCAKE! on it, and shook my head. "Babe!"

Kamryn bounced out of the back room with a large smile on her face, and I couldn't help but laugh. She didn't have just flour and icing on her, she had pieces of cake plastered to her arms and glasses, and she couldn't have looked more adorable if she'd tried.

"Is this helping?" I asked, nodding at the chalkboard.

She sighed happily and leaned up on her toes to kiss me. "Like you wouldn't believe. Do you want to throw one before you go into the meeting?"

"No, but I'll probably come back after and throw some."

"Okay, good, I want to know what happens anyway. So I'll make sure to save you a few . . . or a dozen."

I smiled and looked at her meaningfully. "Do you have anything for me today?"

Her happy expression fell, and she jammed her hand into her apron before pulling out a piece of paper covered in red velvet cake. I raised an eyebrow, and she shrugged. "I threw it with a cupcake."

"God, I love you." Opening up the letter, I bit back a growl and folded it up before putting it in my pocket. "This is getting ridiculous."

"There's something . . ." Kamryn began at the same time I said, "Okay, I need to get going, I'm already running late."

". . . I wanted to tell you about Olivia," she mumbled and looked down at the floor, defeated.

Cupping her cheeks in my hands, I waited until she looked up at me again. "Did she do something to you? Because now is definitely the time to tell me since I'm going into this meeting."

"No, she didn't."

"Okay." I kissed her hard before releasing her face. "Then tell me when I come back, all right?" Kamryn nodded slowly, and I smirked at her, hoping to see her face light up again. "Throw a cupcake for me. I'll be back soon. I love you, Kamryn."

Her lips slowly tilted up until she was smiling wide. "I love you too, Brody Saco."

"THIS WAS RIDICULOUS," I whispered. "What was the point of this meeting, Liv, if you were just going to have your lawyer go around in circles about things you both know you have no case on, and then take me to court anyway?"

"I'm sorry," she choked out, holding a hand up toward me before covering her mouth with it. "I can't talk to you, it's just too hard seeing you."

"Save your tears for the judge. Maybe you will have screwed him too and you'll have his sympathy."

Olivia's eyes darted left and right for a second before shrugging. "No, I don't think any of the guys were judges."

"God, this is—do you hear this?" I asked J. Shepherd, who was standing on the other side of the room with my lawyer. "She's admitting to sleeping with other guys in front of all of us, and you're still going to play it so she was the victim and I was the cruel husband. Got it. Makes sense to me."

Olivia slapped her hand on the table. "You're really going to try to put words in my mouth even now when we're all in the same room, Brody? My God. Acting like I told you my parents paid off the doctor was one thing, but this is taking it to a whole new level."

"You fucking said—"

"Don't go making more accusations when you have no proof of any of these so-called conversations with my client, Mr. Saco. As for just now? I'm afraid I didn't hear anything," J. Shepherd said with a shrug and smug grin, and my lawyer just sent me an apologetic look and put his hands up in a gesture showing he hadn't heard a thing either.

"This is bullshit. I'm leaving." I stood to go and had just made it around to the other side of the table when Olivia spoke again . . . and stopped me in my tracks.

"Don't you think the judge will be interested in your little cup-cake girlfriend? Poor Olivia, kicked out of her home . . . her pos-sessions taken from her so her husband could buy his girlfriend a bakery."

"You have got to be fucking kidding me." Bending down, I rested my hands on the table near her. "You don't go near her," I growled low enough that my voice wouldn't carry. "You hear me?" When Olivia only responded with a slow malicious smile, my hands curled into fists. "Don't forget I still have all the evi-dence of you and your boyfriends from when we were still to-gether, and now, thanks to you, I have the notes you've been leaving us. What do you have? Kamryn and me out on dates after you and I were already separated? Yeah . . . good luck with that one, Liv."

"Bro—"

"Do not contact me or Kamryn again. I only want to see or

hear from you when we're in front of a judge. Any more notes or evidence that you were near her bakery or our place, and I will get a restraining order against you faster than you can fuck your way into trying to get me fired again. You ruined the last six years of my life, Olivia, I'll be damned if I let you touch my life with Kamryn. Stay. The hell. Away."

Her smirk fell, and she looked to the side. "He's threatening me!" *Oh, Jesus Christ.*

Both lawyers looked at us, but before either could say anything, I straightened up and walked toward them. "Threatening? Hardly. I was simply strongly advising. Isn't that right, J.?"

J. Shepherd's face fell before he could compose it, and he looked past me at Olivia. "Olivia," he said in warning.

I tried to control my shaking as I left the room. I wasn't worried about them actually finding out and having proof that I'd been having an affair with Kamryn before I filed for divorce. I had enough on Olivia, in addition to the threats her attorney had made on me if I *did* file, that they wouldn't be able to get much off the fact that I'd been having an affair too. But I knew Olivia, and I knew how vindictive she was to people she saw as a threat. Even though Olivia didn't want me just as much as I didn't want her, Olivia had lost her control over me because of Kamryn— and she knew it. To her, that was exactly what Kamryn was—a threat. And I wasn't about to let Liv come near Kamryn.

"Mr. Saco," my attorney called after me. "I know the things you've told me, but I strongly suggest you don't speak with Mrs. Saco unless Mr. Shepherd and I are moderating or we're in front of the judge. There's too much she can make up, and we won't have anyone who can verify either way."

"I understand." I nodded in the direction of the room. "All I told her was that I would get a restraining order put on her if she came near my girlfriend or me again. She's been leaving notes on our cars and on my girlfriend's place of business. I've kept them all, and I'll scan them and send them to you in the morning. You can let J. know that, by the way."

My attorney raised one eyebrow, and a small grin crossed his face as he nodded and began backing up toward the room. "Perfect, send me everything. I'll talk to you in the morning, Mr. Saco."

Taking off my tie and rolling up my shirtsleeves, I walked quickly to my car. I was done with Olivia. I was done with her family. I was done with their entitled view of themselves because of their money, and the way they could sway people and look down on others because of it. I was just done. I only wanted to get back to Kamryn, throw a fucking cupcake, and go home with her tonight and try to forget all about Olivia until I had to see her in court.

19

Kamryn

August 1, 2015

PRESSING MY LIPS to Brody's cheek two days later, I laughed softly against his skin when he reached for my waist and kissed him again before moving away from his searching fingers.

"Mmm, nu-uh. Come back," he mumbled into the pillow.

"I have to go to the shop. I'll see you later."

He propped himself up on one elbow, and I had to force myself to stay away from him. *I wake up, and I look like I got in a fight with a Weedwacker. Brody wakes up and looks like he's ready for a photo shoot. Asshole.*

"Do you want me to come help you?"

I laughed and pulled on my Converses. "You mean, do I want you to come and eat everything I make?"

"Basically, yeah."

"If you want, you can. But I need to leave right now, so you'd have to bring your own car."

As Brody crawled out of the bed, I stopped tying my shoe-laces. My body warmed, and I might have started chewing on the inside of my cheek, but I couldn't be sure of anything anymore, other than the sight of him naked and what I wanted to do to him.

"Are you sure you don't want to be a little late and help me get ready?" he said softly into my ear, his gravelly voice making my already unsteady breathing even more ragged.

"You don't play fair," I whimpered when he made a trail down my neck.

"Never claimed to. And I want you in the shower . . . now, Kamryn."

Just as I started to say, "Okay," my phone started ringing and I jerked back. "Shit! Kinlee! I'm supposed to pick up Kinlee today." Brody grumbled his dislike, and I laughed as I grabbed his head and brought it down to kiss him soundly. "I'll see you when you get to the shop."

"Drive safe, see you soon," he said as he walked into the bath-room.

Grabbing my phone, I saw the missed call from a number I didn't know and decided I'd wait to see if the caller left a voice mail before calling back. Shoving my cell in my back pocket, I finished tying my shoes and grabbed my purse as I ran to the garage.

After picking up Kinlee and getting us to the shops, I rushed around to make sure my employees had gotten everything ready up front before going to the back.

"I'm so sorry, Grace! I forgot I was picking up Kinlee, and then Brody was trying to make me later than I already was, and . . . well, obviously, I'm super late."

Grace laughed and waved me off before going back to icing more cupcakes. "You're the boss, I'm pretty sure you're allowed to be late."

I frowned and tied on my apron. "You know I want to be here, I don't like being late . . . especially when y'all are here and having to do everything." Looking around, I walked back out to the front before glancing at Grace. "Where's Andy?"

"Restroom," she said just as Andy came up behind me.

"Right here, gorgeous!"

He blew me an air kiss, and I sent him one back before grabbing my ingredients and some bowls. The chimes sounded, and Andy turned right back around from where he'd been about to do dishes and walked toward the swinging doors. "I'll get this one. I know how you are if you don't start your morning off with baking." He winked and breezed through the doors.

I'd barely gotten started when he walked back into the kitchen, a confused look pinching his face.

"Uh, I think that one's for you, KC."

I smiled at him, and my stomach started warming. "Brody?" I asked as I walked past him.

"Not exactly."

I stopped so suddenly midway through the swinging doors that Andy ran into me from behind. "Can I help you?" I asked the reporter and two men with her. One was holding a camera.

"Are you the owner? Are you KC?"

Glancing at the camera, and then back to Andy and Grace, who was now directly behind him, I slowly nodded my head. "I am. Again, can I help you?"

Her perfectly painted face lit up and she walked toward the counter with a hand outstretched. "Meg Schwartz with KXJN News, what a pleasure to meet you."

I stepped forward to shake her hand, but kept my eyes on the cameraman and the second man who had just retreated from my shop, his phone going to his ear. "Pleasure. I'm sorry, but may I ask what y'all are doing here? I'm not comfortable having cameras in my shop."

She winked at me and stepped back. "I'm sure you're not."

Uh, what?

"We were wondering if we could do a piece on you and your journey to opening up this beautiful bakery?"

"No, I'm sorry. I'd really prefer if you didn't. Sorry you came all the way down here, you should have just called." I knew I was coming across as rude, but I wanted to avoid anything that put me in the news in any way. Someone would see me and recognize me just as Olivia had. I couldn't chance that. "But, please, pick something out to eat. On me." I walked over to the case and waited for them to decide on something.

"You're very sweet, but we couldn't possibly."

My eyes were back on the cameraman. The camera was pointed directly at me, and I was straining to see if there was any sign that it was recording.

"Okay, then, I'm sorry, but I need to ask you to leave," I said as I stepped back to the swinging doors. Why the hell is he following my every move with that thing? Suddenly, he shifted the camera down, and I released a heavy breath as they backed up to the door.

"We'll see you soon, Miss Cunningham."

I just nodded and smiled, no longer watching them. The second man who had left on his phone was standing directly in front of my shop, staring at me, his phone still pressed to his ear. "Back, back, get back in the kitchen." I pushed Grace and Andy back before closing the swinging doors and setting the latch so they couldn't open.

"What's going on?" Grace asked, and I shakily turned to face them. "Why wouldn't you want to do a story? It would give the shop so much more business. More than just people in Jeston probably."

Exactly. I couldn't have that. "Maybe, but I don't, uh . . ." I trailed off when I finally realized it. *Miss Cunningham. The reporter called me Miss Cunningham! Oh, God, this isn't happening. No, no, she must have found out my name another way, she can't know who I am! "I'm sure you're not."* I gasped and started rambling to cover the look of horror that was probably crossing my face. "I don't like cameras very much, or news stations. They tend to clip and rearrange your words to make you look worse, and I'm just not a fan. Okay? Okay. What was I doing? I need to bake."

Andy grabbed my hand, and he and Grace were now wearing matching concerned looks on their faces. "Sweetie, you look like you're about to pass out. What is wrong? Why did you lock the doors?"

"No, I'm fine. Nothing is wrong. I just—just locked the doors in case they came back in. But that was stupid." Forcing myself to unlock the swinging doors, I stood there facing them with my head down. I wanted to go home. Needed to. The camera had made me nervous, but I shouldn't have been this freaked out about it. I had a bad feeling, and Andy was right . . . my legs and arms felt like Jell-O.

"KC?" they both asked right when the chimes sounded again.

I jumped away from the doors and pointed at them. "Andy, please help them. If it's the people who were just in here, ask them to leave and then lock the front door."

He brushed his hand against my shoulder as he passed, and while the doors were still swinging shut, I heard his voice. "Holy shit."

Oh, Jesus.

"Uh . . . Kace?"

On shaky legs, I walked to the doors and pushed them open, afraid of what I might find and somehow already knowing. Once I was through the doors, I heard dozens of the all-too-familiar clicks and saw bright lights flashing. I heard too many people talking and knew that it was over. They knew I was here, and I had no doubt that Olivia was somehow behind their knowing.

"Oh. My. God. Kamryn, what have you done?"

My head snapped up, my eyes widening when I heard my mom's voice. I found her immediately. She looked disgusted for all of three seconds before she pulled it together and started dramatically crying.

"My baby! We've finally found you!"

I couldn't move, I couldn't speak. The cameras were still flashing, the same reporter who had been in the shop a few minutes before and another one were speaking toward their cameramen, and there, next to my mom, were my dad and Charles.

"Hey, move. Everyone move. News crews, get out of here.

What the hell? I said get out!" Brody's voice rose above every-thing else, and in that moment I wanted to die. "Jeston PD! I said get out! If you want me to call backup, I will!"

A few of the people, along with one news crew, quickly left. Brody made his way to me behind the counter.

"I said get the fuck out!" He held his badge out to them and pulled me close to his side, moving so his back was facing the cameras. "Baby, are you okay? What's going on?"

"Get your goddamn hands off my fiancée!"

My eyes shut, and a harsh breath left me. Brody stilled, and the hand around my waist tightened as he turned to look behind him. "You need to leave too . . . wait, do I know you?"

"I'm sure you've heard of me, and I'm not going anywhere without her," Charles said with a confidence you only learned when you'd grown up the way we had. "Kamryn, come here, babe. Get away from him."

"Kam," Brody said softly, "who the hell are these people, and why did he just call you his fiancée?"

"Who are you, and why are you touching our daughter?" Mom asked, her voice holding the same disgust her face had shown earlier.

"Shit," I mumbled and looked up at Brody's wide eyes.

"Kamryn?"

I shook my head and choked out, "I'm so sorry." Moving to the side, I faced my parents and forced myself to keep my head high.

"God, Kamryn, what have you done with yourself? You look awful!" Mom chastised as she moved closer to me. "All your beautiful hair is gone! Why would you do this? Is this the man who stole you?"

I hadn't planned on responding, but when she brought Brody into it, I couldn't keep quiet. "He's my boyfriend, and he didn't steal me. I left! And honestly, I don't care if you don't like the way I look. I hated the way you made me look. I'm happy like this."

"Kamryn, what is your last name?"

I turned to look at Brody when his horrified question filled the space between us.

Charles laughed condescendingly. "How wonderful. You have a boyfriend who doesn't know you're engaged, doesn't know who your parents are, and doesn't even know your last name. Cunningham—her name is Kamryn Cunningham."

Brody mouthed my name, and his face fell as recognition and horror filled his eyes. "This has to be a joke." His words were barely audible.

"Brody, I'm so sorry. I should have told—"

"Do *not* apologize to him." I flinched and looked at my dad. "If you owe anyone an apology, it is us. We thought you were dead, we thought you'd been kidnapped. Do you know what your mother and I, or what your fiancé, have been through over the last year?"

"I am not engaged to Charles! And I know you didn't care! You used my leaving to get more publicity, so don't act like you're so happy to see me now."

Charles stepped closer to the counter, his eyes on Brody. "You should leave. This is a discussion she should only be having with her family."

"Don't. Talk. To him," I seethed as I looked at Charles. My stomach rolled at having him this close again.

Brody pushed past me, and I turned to grab his arm.

"No, don't, please don't go!"

His nostrils flared as he looked down at me. "Olivia . . . she worshiped you, she never stopped talking about you as we grew up. I can't believe I didn't realize before. She freaked when you disappeared. You're—you're just like her."

"Brody! I'm noth—"

"She wanted to *be* you! I've dealt with the way her family is for *years,* and I finally get away from that . . . only to find out that my girlfriend and her family are the people who Olivia's strived so hard to be like?" A sneering laugh left him. "Fuck this. I can't go through this again."

"Can't go through what? Brody, don't do this!"

"This!" He flung his arm out to my parents and Charles. "Having my girl's family look down on me because I didn't grow up in country clubs, having her dad constantly remind me that I don't make enough to keep her happy." He took a few steps away from me before turning and pointing at himself. "I told you everything, I never kept anything about myself from you. I knew you wanted to forget where you were from, so I never pushed it. And now I find out that you're not only engaged but you're the— what the fuck did Liv call you? The *princess* of the racing world? Tell me, do you view me the same way Liv did? Someone to keep around because you knew your family wouldn't approve? Someone beneath you who you could try to control?"

I was sobbing so hard that I couldn't say anything. Shaking my head back and forth, I took a step forward as I reached for him. But he stepped back and rushed away from the counter to leave the shop. I'd started to follow him when my eyes fell on Kinlee standing there at the entrance of the store with a pained look on her face as she watched Brody leave.

Turning, I found Grace and Andy standing there staring at me in shock. "I'm so sorry. If y'all want to go home, I understand."

Grace looked at Andy, and Andy gave my mom a disgusted once-over. "I think I'm going to go make some cupcakes. It feels like a Monday, and don't Mondays just suck?" he asked and turned to shoot me a smile and wink.

"I think I'll help you." Grace turned to follow him, and in that moment I wanted to hug them both.

To find out you've been working for a complete stranger and then show your support the way they just had—that was something I'd never had in Kentucky. And I loved them even more for it.

"Where are you staying? We'll go and pack you up."

"What?" I asked my mom.

"We're taking you home. Where are you staying?"

"No." I shook my head, and the ache in my chest over having Brody leave turned into anger. "I left for a reason, I hated that life . . . hated everything about it. All the two of you wanted was a perfect daughter. You were the most detached parents a girl could have!" Looking at my dad, I raised my hand toward him. "And you? I *heard* you the day I left. You were talking to Charles and his dad about me marrying him so we could merge our stables? I only stayed with him as long as I did because y'all didn't give me a choice! I never would have married him— having him this close to me now is making me sick. The only reason I stayed in that house as long as I did was because of Barbara. She was more of a parent than either of you, and she was always there for me. If it weren't for her, I wouldn't have lasted in that fucking prison of a house!" I screeched, and my chest rose and fell roughly.

"How dare you—" my mom began, but Dad cut her off.

"Young lady, you have forgotten your place in this family."

"I haven't. I know exactly where I would be if I were still in your family. But I'm not. This"—I motioned toward my bakery—"is my life now. That man who just left, those two in the back, and this girl are my family now," I said, gesturing toward Kinlee.

Wiping the wetness from my cheeks, I glanced at Charles, who was studying me silently, then over to Kinlee, who still looked upset, but proud.

Looking back at my parents, I cleared my throat and squared my shoulders. "Now I need to ask you to leave. I'm sorry I left the way I did, but I didn't have any other option. I don't want anything to do with y'all, or racing. I just want to continue my life here."

"Kamryn—"

"Leave. Or I will call the police and have them remove you." Walking around the counter, I went to stand at the door and held it open. "Don't come back, and don't contact me."

"Charlotte," my dad said by way of an order.

Mom immediately began walking toward the open door, and at the last second turned to face me, her palm connecting with my cheek before I realized it was coming. I turned my head back to look at her, my eyes wide and mouth open. But I couldn't say anything else; I was too shocked by the force of her hand.

"You're an ungrateful little brat. When your world comes crashing down around you, don't come running home to us. You've made your decision, and as far as I'm concerned"—she raised her chin in an attempt to look down on me—"my daughter died a year ago. You have no place in our family anymore. Do you hear me?"

"Charlotte, we're leaving."

With one last look, my mom turned to leave, her eyes glimmering with unshed tears. Dad was right behind her, but didn't look at me as he walked out the door.

Charles walked up, his eyes glossing over Kinlee before coming back to rest on me. "Can she give us a minute?"

Kinlee grabbed my hand, and I huffed a short laugh. "*She* is here for me, and I don't want to talk to you. Please. Leave."

His lips pulled up in a small smirk, and one hand came to the back of my neck as he leaned forward to place a kiss on my forehead. I tried leaning back, but his hand held me in place. With the door still open, I could hear the clicks of cameras, and one of the news reporters talking—and I had no doubt Charles was doing this for them.

Moving his lips to the ear farthest from Kinlee, he whispered, "Do you have any idea how much you've embarrassed not only your parents but me as well? I won't be as harsh as your parents, Kamryn. You have a day to change your mind. And if you know what's good for you, you will," he said, his tone conveying his warning.

Releasing me so quick that I stumbled back a step from the force of trying to get away from him, he turned and walked away. Slamming the door shut behind him, I locked the deadbolt and turned to throw my arms around Kinlee.

"How the hell did they find you?"

"Olivia," I cried. "It has to be her. She's the only one who knew besides you."

"That stupid fuc—"

A hard sob was wrenched from my chest, and Kinlee tightened her grip on me. "Brody . . ."

"It's okay," she crooned softly.

"What do I do, Lee?"

"I thought you'd told him. Why didn't you?"

Pulling back, I wiped away new tears and shook my head. "I didn't want anyone to know, I wanted to forget about them. I told you that night because I hated that I'd been lying to you and keeping things from you. With Brody, he never asked other than the first or second time we saw each other. It was easy to forget about them."

"Did you think he would judge you differently? I just don't understand why you thought you had to hide this from him."

I shrugged helplessly as I thought about it. "I don't know. In a way, I guess I'm afraid everyone will judge me differently. I've always been treated a certain way because of who I am— well, *was*. I didn't want that. I wanted normal; I wanted a new start. And as you can see"—I gestured toward the crews still outside—"this happens as the result of someone figuring out who I am."

"Anyone can see you're not like them—well . . ."

"Kinlee, he looked like I'd crushed him."

"He'll understand, he's just upset right now. Go get him, Kam."

My eyes drifted to the back of my store, and she waved me away.

"I'll tell them, and they'll understand too. Just go get my brother-in-law back. You brought him back to us, I can't have him leaving us again now."

"I'll call you to let you know."

Unlocking the door, I ran past the news crews and hopped into my car, praying like hell that I would find him. I drove quickly through the streets on the way back to my condo. The entire time my body stayed tense as I worried about Brody's reaction and thought about the different possible outcomes of what had just happened. I called his cell a second time, but like the first time, it went straight to voice mail. Tears filled my eyes, but I refused to believe that Brody and I couldn't work through this too . . . after everything we'd already been through . . . there was no way this would be the thing to break us.

After looking at my condo, Jace and Kinlee's, and his parents' house, and not finding him, I finally drove back to my bakery, exhausted and defeated.

Grace and Andy didn't ask if I'd found him. I think they knew based simply on the fact that I was already back and probably looked like hell. After asking me to stop trying to hide my accent and whether I preferred Kamryn or KC, they handed me a few cupcakes, turned the music up loud, and pointed me toward our "Mondays suck" wall to let out my anger before we went back to baking like it was a normal day.

Every time the door chimed I ran out, hoping it would be Brody. And every few minutes I called his phone, hoping it would finally be turned on again. Every time my hope was crushed I felt like I was that much closer to losing him.

I gasped and almost dropped the cream puffs I was holding when the chime went off again. Putting the tray on a counter, I burst through the swinging doors, only to have anger quickly flood my veins.

"Leave. Now!"

Charles smirked and took long steps to the counter. "I decided a day was too much time for you to think and get more of your insane ideas in your head."

"Do you not understand? I want you to leave. I don't want to see you again. How is that so hard to get?"

His smirk was turning into more of a sneer. "Oh, no, doll. I got it. What you're not understanding is that you're making the wrong decision, and I'm trying to make all of this go away for you right now. Your parents and mine will forgive you, I'll forgive you, and we'll all move on the way we were supposed to. You leaving messed up more than you could imagine."

"Like the fact that you couldn't merge the stables? I don't care about the stables, Charles! I've never cared! I don't want to be seen as property to be sold off to a family. This is what I care about," I said as I waved my arms at my bakery. "Falling in love with someone who wants to be with *me*. Just. Me. That's what I want."

"You think I didn't love you, Kamryn? You think I don't *still* love you? You think your disappearance didn't kill me?"

"No! I don't! I think you've always seen me as an opportunity—"

"Bullshit!" he yelled, slamming his fist down on the counter. "If this is what you want, Kamryn, I'll give you it. I'll build you a goddamn bakery. You want your hair to stay this way? When you're my wife, your mom won't be able to say shit. Do what you want, I don't care. Just let me take you back to Lexington. You and I both know I will be able to take care of you better than anyone. Your parents' status, babe . . . we'll top that. We'll fucking rule the racing world," he whispered, his eyes brightening. "You and me."

"Oh, my God! Do you not see? That's all you want! You want me to help you 'rule.' I told you, you see me as an opportunity."

"Right now I see you as a spoiled girl who pulled some ridiculous stunt because she wanted attention. Now I'm giving you the attention you wanted, baby, and you're done playing this game." Grabbing a box out of his pocket, he opened it and put it on the counter. "I've held on to this for far too long, Kamryn. You will put that ring on. You will be leaving this shop with me tonight. And we will be going back to Kentucky together."

I glanced at the diamond that had to have cost as much as my bakery, and swallowed back bile as I looked up at Charles and saw the man walking into the bakery from over his shoulder.

"We're going to finally get married, I'll give you another bakery in Kentucky, and then we're merging the stables."

"Brody," I whispered as my eyes filled with tears.

Charles turned and hissed a curse. "Oh, Christ. Do you mind?"

Brody didn't move, and he didn't respond for a long moment as tears steadily fell down my cheeks. His eyes just stayed glued on the box sitting on the counter, with the ring fully displayed.

"I said . . ." Charles began when Brody's deep voice whispered, "You are engaged."

I shook my head, even though he wasn't looking at me as his mocking tone pierced my chest.

"We've gone through all this . . . all this shit, and I almost lost you because I was married. And you've been engaged the entire goddamn time?!" He looked up at me, and his face was twisted in anger, but his eyes couldn't hide the deep ache he was trying so hard to mask.

"So now your boyfriend's married?" Charles asked. "This just keeps getting better."

"I'm not," I choked out, ignoring Charles. "I left before he ever asked, I swear to you, Brody."

He laughed hard once and threw an arm out between Charles

and me. "How am I supposed to believe you? I knew you wanted to forget where you were from, but I thought—God, I don't even know what I thought anymore. But I knew you would tell me when the time was right. I just had no fucking clue that you were Kamryn fucking Cunningham. That you were some privileged girl who wanted to see what normal people lived like. That you were this *princess*"—he sneered the word—"who I'd grown up constantly hearing about from Liv. Her parents' goal in life was to *be* your family. Olivia's dream was to be *you*! They are the way they are because of your family, Kamryn, don't you get that? My wife was a nightmare because of you!"

A sob tore from my chest, and I had to grab the counter so I wouldn't fall to the floor. The entire time my head was shaking back and forth. His words were killing me. I was nothing like Olivia, and I'd had no part in making her the way she was. Part of me knew Brody was just hurt, but it didn't change the way each word he said felt like another punch to the chest.

"I was never enough for Olivia. I was never enough for her parents. But it didn't matter, because I didn't love her." His anger quickly faded, and grief replaced his hardened features. "I can't go from one Olivia to the next, Kamryn. I can't handle not being enough for you. When you realize you're done playing this game and you're done with me and want to go back to your old life, I won't be able to handle that."

"I won't!" I cried out. "I won't! I know you're hurt, and you have every right to be. I should have told you from the beginning, I know that. But I'm nothing like her, and you know it. This"—I gestured to my bakery—"us, our condo . . . all of it *is* me. I left because I was suffocating with those people, Brody!"

Brody shook his head and laughed sadly. "I can't give you anything like he can." He gestured to Charles. "That ring? *That* is who you are, and I can't give that to you."

"At least he understands," Charles mumbled.

"I don't. Want. The fucking. Ring!" I screamed. Grabbing the box, I snapped it closed and threw it at Charles's chest. "I don't need some massive diamond. Give me a band and I'll be happy. Jesus Christ, Brody, just give me your last name and I'll be happy," I cried. "I don't need or want any of what Charles or my parents have to offer."

"Yeah, you might say that until you realize everything I *can't* give you." Brody turned toward the door, and my body locked up in panic.

I couldn't let him leave. I couldn't lose him.

"I only stayed as long as I did because I was saving money so I could leave. I only stayed with Charles as long as I did because my parents didn't give me a choice. But the minute I heard him talking with my dad about asking me to marry him that night, I left. I was gone within the hour. And it was the best moment of my life!"

"This is ridiculous. Kamryn, let's go," Charles said with a sigh, and the highest, most unattractive screech left me.

"Leave! I swear to God if you aren't gone in the next minute I will call the cops!"

Brody kept pacing near the door, his hands running over his face and through his hair. I took slow steps around the counter as I continued talking to him, my voice rising as hard sobs threatened to choke me.

"I'm sorry you associate my name with your ex-wife and her family, and yes, my parents are probably just as bad as Olivia's, if not worse. But I am nothing like them. I hated everything about my life. It was all mapped out and scripted for me, I didn't have a say in any of it. It was a prison."

Brody scoffed.

"Don't do that!" I exclaimed. "Don't act like I'm some spoiled brat who had everything, and still it wasn't enough. I never wanted any of it." Charles grabbed my wrist when I went past him, and I shoved at him. "Get off me and leave!"

Brody turned, his eyes narrowed on Charles. With quick steps, he was in front of Charles and me and pulling him away by the front of his shirt. "She told you to get out. I suggest you do it before I arrest you or get myself arrested for showing you exactly what I fucking think about you."

"Don't touch me. Kamryn, you have until tomorrow to change your mind!" Charles yelled as Brody shoved him out the door and locked it behind him.

"You have to understand, Brody, and I know you do," I continued when he didn't turn to look back at me. "I was miserable with them, and all my daydreams consisted of getting away from that life and those people. Think about it. Think about how miserable you were with Olivia, how miserable her family is. Being married to her was your own form of a prison sentence!" Brody's body tensed, and I prayed I was getting through to him. "Right? You felt trapped. You felt like you couldn't breathe. But you didn't have a choice for a long time. Well, *I* didn't have a choice either!"

He finally turned to look at me, and the smallest spark of hope began to form in my chest at the look in his eyes.

"I couldn't just change my life. I couldn't just decide I wanted something different for myself. I had to *run*. I had to *hide*. That was the only way. And I can honestly tell you that I have never been happier than I am now, in this life, in that small condo,

with my perfectly imperfect clothes and hair, and with you."
I chanced taking a couple steps toward him, but stopped halfway. "We didn't have choices back then, but we've changed that.
We've changed our lives so we could finally be happy. This isn't
a game for me, Brody, this is my life. You are my life. You may
not be enough for my parents, but I don't care because I'm not
enough for them either. You're more than enough for me, and
that's all that matters."

Brody stood there, still as a statue, staring at me. His face was
blank, but his gray eyes were dark with emotion. I just didn't
know *what* emotion it was.

"I should have told you, and I'm so sorry. But I am *not* my
name. I'm the girl you fell in love with. Brody, please, I'll tell you
whatever you want to know, but don't throw us away. Not now.
After everything we've been through to get here, I can't lose—"

My words were cut off when Brody suddenly closed the distance between us and pulled my body to his, his mouth falling
onto mine roughly. A noise that sounded like a cry broke past
my lips when the kiss ended, and I dropped my head to Brody's
chest, his arms tightening around me as he pressed his mouth to
the top of my head.

"Please don't leave again," I choked out. "I'm so sorry!"

"Shh, it's okay."

I sobbed into his chest and gripped Brody's back. Like if I held
on to him tight enough, he wouldn't leave me. My tears continued to fall harder, and my shoulders hunched in against the sobs
that were being wrenched from my body.

"I'm not going anywhere, baby. It's okay," he whispered and
moved back to the counter so he could sit me on top of it.

I heard a choking sound behind me and turned to see both Andy and Grace standing there holding hands and crying. I smiled, and a relieved breath burst from my chest. "Uh, I think we can close early. I'll see y'all tomorrow."

" 'Kay," Andy sniffed, and Grace just nodded her head. When they turned to go into the kitchen, I looked up into Brody's eyes and sagged into his chest.

When I'd moved here, I knew I'd never been happier. Brody, Kinlee, and Jace made my life complete. But lying to them and keeping the earlier part of my life hidden had taken its toll on me. The stress of worrying that someone would recognize me— that my family would find me—was now behind me. It had happened, and for a while my world had felt like it would crash down around me, but now that it was over . . . now that everything was out there . . . it felt like a huge weight had been lifted from my shoulders. The relief was amazing, but at the same time I felt worn out now that months of hiding had finally come to an end. The exhaustion from the stress felt like it would consume me.

"I'm sorry," I said again.

His hand paused a few seconds from where it'd been moving gently up and down my back, before starting up again. "I know you are. I'm sorry for not giving you the chance to tell me, and for what I said. I—God, I'm sorry . . . I don't think you're like her, Kamryn. I know you. I just . . . when it finally all clicked who you are, I freaked. I was afraid it would be a repeat of her, I was mad that you'd kept that from me, and I was scared about what would happen now that they'd come for you. I've always been terrified of losing you, and then I almost took myself away from you . . . *again*."

"Please don't apologize," I whispered and looked up into his glassy eyes. "Not for this. You have every right to be mad, and I knew even when you said it that you didn't believe what you were saying to me. I knew it was out of anger. It hurt . . . but I knew. But don't apologize. This is my fault. None of this would have happened if I'd just told you."

He looked at me for a few seconds before asking, "Why didn't you?"

I shrugged as I tried to figure out the words to say. "A lot of reasons. Where I'm from, everyone knew me by name and the way I looked. So I changed those things, but I still was terrified that if anyone knew my real name, they would know who I used to be and somehow my parents would find out. I couldn't risk it; I'd worked too hard to disappear from them. But then Olivia recognized me that morning she came to my shop, and I have no doubt she's the one who told my parents. I told Kinlee about my past the night you and I made up at their house, and I was going to tell you that last day in the hotel room, but obviously, I never got the chance to because we were fighting about other things. When the letters from Olivia started, I tried to tell you then . . . and every time I tried something would happen. Your phone would ring, you would have to leave, Kinlee would show up . . . and I kept taking it as a sign that I shouldn't say anything. Then you came back from the meeting with the lawyers and said you didn't want to talk about her again. I don't know, I just kept making up excuses, but I know I should have just told you."

He brushed back my bangs and nodded slowly. "I understand. I wish you would have, but with everything that's happened . . . I get it, Kamryn. *Please,* though, if there is anything else, just tell me now."

I thought hard, trying to think if there was anything about me that Brody didn't know. I shook my head for a few seconds before blurting, "Oh! Barb isn't my aunt. She's my parents' maid, but she raised me. She helped me with everything so I could escape from there."

Brody's lips tilted up in a lopsided smile, before dropping. "Wait, why didn't she tell you they were coming? Is she still that mad about us?"

"No, no, there's no way she wouldn't have warned me about that. My parents knew how close I was with her. My mom had to threaten to fire Barb in order to make me stay with Charles. But once they found out that I hadn't actually been kidnapped or whatever, I doubt they even told her they were going out of town because I'm sure they figured she would warn me. They probably just left, and it's not an uncommon thing for them to do. Barb packs for my mom if they're going on vacation, but they'll leave to check out horses on a moment's notice and be gone for days, and they won't tell Barb they're leaving."

"Okay," he whispered and searched my eyes. "Anything else?"

"I love you . . . and I'm sorry. I can't say that enough."

Brody leaned in to kiss me softly, and I melted into his arms. "We've both said 'sorry' a lot," he said, "and there have been a lot of hard times we've had to get through to be together. I haven't regretted a single one of them, and there's not one of them I wouldn't go through again in a second. But I'm ready to start making good memories with you, Kamryn Cunningham. What do you say we get through this divorce, and then how about we focus on that forever?" he asked against my lips.

A short, relieved cry burst from my chest, and I nodded, my nose brushing against his. "Sounds perfect."

20

Kamryn

August 4, 2015

"So, no more notes, no more nothing?"

I shook my head and shrugged at Kinlee. "There hasn't been anything since the morning he went into the meeting with them. And Brody made up something about being able to arrest Charles for coming back to my bakery on Friday, and Charles bought it and told him that Olivia's dad was the one who called my parents. But that had been before the meeting on Tuesday, so . . . oh, well. Now we're just waiting to see when the court date will be, and then we'll deal with that mess."

"And then we'll all be done with Olivia Reynolds for—hopefully—ever."

I grinned and relaxed into the cushions of my couch. "Yes, ma'am!"

"I like that you aren't hiding your accent anymore," Kinlee said with the worst drawl I've ever heard.

"I don't have an accent," I grumbled.

"Whatever, Miss Kentucky!"

I rolled my eyes and kicked at her leg.

"Has Brody mentioned getting married or anything?"

My eyes went wide, and I sat up quickly. "Kinlee! No!" I shouted and laughed.

"What? Why is that such a definite no?"

"Really? Think about it. It has technically only been three months."

Kinlee's face fell, and her eyes looked up and to the side as she thought about that. "For reals?"

"Yeah. Just three months. It may have felt like it took years to get here, but . . . not so much." I sat back against the cushions and watched as she thought some more, knowing she was nowhere near done with this conversation yet.

"But you're different. From listening to you both tell the story, you met and the world stopped turning, and no one else mattered except for the two of you because you were made for each other!"

I glared at her.

"Whatever, you know what I mean," she said with a laugh. "But you had that instant connection. And it wasn't something you read about in fairy tales. Where they meet, fall in love, and live happily ever after. You met, you knew you couldn't be together, and still you knew you couldn't live without each other. Now you've both been to hell and back in the last three months, and you can finally live your happily ever after. Why would you wait?" She looked at me expectantly for a few seconds before sitting up and scooting closer to me. "It has been three months. When you put it that way, I totally get it. Any other couple and I would think it would be insane. But then again, any other couple and I would probably hate the fact that they were together. I would think you stole him from his wife and he was an asshole. With you? I couldn't be happier that the two of you are together, and I want this for you."

"Kinlee," I said softly when her eyes filled with tears.

"I didn't even know about the bad shit when it was happening. But knowing the story, knowing both of you, I just—I just want you both to be happy. You deserve this."

Leaning forward, I pulled her close and hugged her hard. "Thank you, Lee. Thank you for understanding us. And we will," I continued when we both sat back. "We will get married someday. But I think once the divorce is final, we both just want to be together for a while." I shrugged and smirked. "Or who knows, we might get married the day after it's finalized if she drags it out long enough."

Kinlee laughed and rolled her eyes. We both knew that was a possibility.

"Brody and I are both just happy that we can be together finally. So for now, this is enough."

"Okay." She nodded and looked away thoughtfully. "That makes sense. But promise me you'll try to have babies someday!"

I laughed and covered my face. "Kinlee, oh, my God! What? Yeah, someday. Like, way far away someday."

"As long as there's a someday, I can live with that! Because I want to be Aunt Kinlee, and I really want us to be moms together."

My head snapped up, and my eyes widened at her. "What?" I asked breathily.

"Jace and I have been talking ever since that Sunday at my house, and, uh . . . well, on Friday we started the really ridiculously stupid-long process of adoption."

"Really, Lee?"

She nodded and tried to bite back a smile, but soon it was covering most of her face. "I don't want to get my hopes up, but I'm just really freaking excited that we finally started it!"

"I'm so happy for y'all! It will happen, I know it will. And you'll be the best parents!"

"You think so?" she asked, her expression hopeful.

"I know so. Come on!" I jumped up, pulling her with me. "We need to go out and celebrate."

Brody

August 4, 2015

SHUTTING THE GARAGE, I closed the door and locked it behind me and made my way through the condo, turning off lights as I went. The house was unusually quiet, so instead of calling out for Kamryn, I walked silently toward the bedroom and smiled when I found her.

Leaning up against the doorjamb, I studied her for a few seconds before pushing off and walking the few steps to where she lay asleep, her Kindle on the bed beside her, her glasses still on. Taking the frames gently in my fingers, I slid the glasses off her face and placed them—along with the Kindle—on the night-stand before brushing her bangs back and kissing her forehead.

"Night, sweetheart," I whispered and stood to walk into the closet.

After ridding myself of my boots, radios, duty belt, uniform, and vest, I stripped out of my undershirt and boxer-briefs and went to take a quick shower. When I came back out with a towel around my waist, Kamryn was sitting up on her knees at the end of the bed with a soft smile on her face.

I smiled back at her curiously and opened my mouth to apologize for waking her, but she placed an index finger over her pouted lips, her blue eyes conveying her want. My body instantly warmed more than it had in the shower, and my need for her coursed through my body.

Kamryn sat up higher on her knees and, with the hand that had been pressed against her lips, reached out toward me. I took the last few steps between us, and a short, hard breath blew past my lips when her fingers pressed low on my bare stomach. The muscles there contracted involuntarily, and she bit back a smile as she shamelessly let her eyes move over every part of my body.

When I brought my hands up to her shoulders, her blue eyes flashed up to meet mine for a brief moment before she slowly reached out for the towel resting on my hips. A needy groan sounded deep in my chest when the towel dropped to the floor, she moved her hands up my length, and I bent forward to alternate placing openmouthed kisses and gentle bites up the side of her neck. Her head rolled to the side to give me more access, and I let my hands slowly fall down her waist until I hit the bottom of her shirt and pulled it off her body.

Wrapping her hands around the back of my neck, she leaned

back onto the bed so her bottom rested on her feet, taking me with her. I ran my hands slowly up her legs, starting at her bent knees and moving to her thighs, and pressed my mouth firmly to hers as her fingers dug into my back, trying to fuse our bodies together.

Moving my lips down her body, I gripped her underwear in my hands and hoped she didn't like this pair as I quickly tore them, then pulled the scraps off her and threw them to the floor. Her breathing hitched when I blew cool air on her wet lips seconds before I sucked her clit into my mouth. I smiled against her when I heard her hands hit the bed and a breathy exhale fill the room, then gave one slow lick before climbing back up her and kissing her before she could make any form of protest.

Placing one hand behind her back, I pulled her with me as I lay back on the bed so she was now lying on my chest, and I growled when she lifted up on her knees enough to bring herself back down on top of me. She whimpered as I slowly filled her, and once she was fully seated on me, I grabbed her hips and pressed her down even more. Kamryn exhaled hard against my chest as she rocked against me, and with a lingering kiss, she sat up as she continued to move on top of me.

Keeping one hand firmly on her hip, I brought my other to her clit and rolled my fingers around the sensitive bud I'd only teased earlier. Kamryn arched her back, and I felt her tightening around me as her movements got quicker and her breaths came harder. Her body trembled above me, and she tightened against me for long moments as I continued her through her orgasm, before she leaned forward to curl her body on top of mine.

Gently rolling us over, I cupped one of her cheeks in my hand, and pressed my other hand against the bed as I moved inside her.

Her eyelids were heavy, but her blue eyes were locked with mine as I told her a hundred things:

That I loved her, and would love her even after I died.

That there was no one else like her.

That I would do anything for her.

That I wanted to make her my wife.

That I wanted to spend the rest of our lives making up for the years we'd lost.

But through this, the only sound in the room was our ragged breaths as our bodies moved against each other.

I quickened my pace before stilling above her, and I realized that somehow, with no words, Kamryn and I had said more in that time than ever before. There had been trust, passion, love, and promises. And as I lowered my body and rolled us to our sides, we continued to not say anything as we stared at each other. There was no need. That soft smile that crossed her face just before her eyes closed and she fell asleep said it all.

I love you too, Kamryn.

Epilogue

Two years later . . .

Brody

KAMRYN LAUGHED LIGHTLY and ran her hands through my hair. Apparently I wasn't the only one who loved that sound. A little hand jabbed against mine, and I looked up at her with a smile crossing my face.

"Laugh again," I prompted her.

"I can't just laugh again, it wouldn't be genuine. She'll know."

I smiled again and pressed my lips to her large stomach. "Oh, will she?"

"She will . . . she has laugh-dar or something."

"Now your mom's just being ridiculous," I whispered against Kamryn's belly. Running my fingers gently across her stomach, I let my lips leave a trail as I continued speaking. "But you'll keep moving for Daddy, won't you, baby girl?" Letting my voice drop lower, I spoke softly. "Tatum, baby, move for Daddy," I crooned and was instantly rewarded with a few kicks.

"Show-off," Kamryn scoffed, but she smiled widely down at me.

"Nah, she's just a daddy's girl."

"Ugh, gag me," Kinlee said as she walked into the kitchen. "Can the two of you be any cuter? I'm waiting for you to get out of the honeymoon phase so I can watch the lovely drama unfold of you hating each other."

I stood and rolled my eyes before kissing Kamryn quickly.

"If I'm not mistaken," Kamryn began, "you and Jace have been married for five years, and y'all are *still* in the honeymoon phase."

Kinlee flipped her hair back and sighed dramatically. "Well, that's just because we keep it exciting in the bedroom."

I laughed and Kamryn started gagging. "Gross, Lee."

"Kinlee told me she's always telling you to join us, Kam! Even pregnant, I'll let you join," Jace said as he walked into the kitchen.

Straightening up, I glared at my younger brother.

"Oh, come on, Brody. You know I'm joking. It's just what Lee says when she's drunk."

My glare didn't waver, and his smile faltered as he moved to stand next to his wife.

"Still grossed out, losing appetite!" Kamryn gagged again. "Seems to be a recurring theme when it comes to y'all."

"Pfft, whatever." Kinlee bounced a few times on her toes and looked up at Jace with bright eyes. "Now?" she whispered.

Kamryn and I exchanged confused glances as she moved to

rest against my chest. My hands automatically moved to caress her swollen stomach, and I smiled when I felt Tatum moving.

Jace nodded twice and bent down to kiss Kinlee's forehead. When he was standing upright, I saw a look I'd never seen on my brother before, but just seeing the way his eyes and smile lit up had me anxious to know what was happening.

"Okay, so, we're going to be telling everyone at dinner tonight, but we wanted you two to come a little early so we could tell just the two of you first, since you're not only our family but our best friends," Kinlee choked out as a few tears slipped down her cheeks, and for whatever reason, Kamryn was already crying too.

Pregnant women. So confusing.

"Well," Kinlee said, drawing the word out and glancing up at Jace one more time, "we got the call yesterday, and we're going to be adopting a baby boy in three months!" she cried out and began jumping up and down.

"Oh my God! Are you serious?" Kamryn grabbed at one of my hands, and the other went to her chest as she watched her best friend. And when Kinlee nodded, she moved to pull her into a hug. "Oh my God! I don't know what else to say except, oh my God!"

Kinlee choked out a laugh. "I know! And you know what this means! We get to be moms together!"

The girls screamed and began talking excitedly, and I tore my eyes from my wife and sister-in-law to look at my little brother. His eyes were bright, and with a choked sob, the tears began falling down his face.

Grabbing his shoulder, I pulled him in to hug him and watched as he wiped at his cheeks when we parted. Squeezing his shoulder once, I smiled and tried to control my own emotions. "I'm really happy for you, man. I know this is something you've been wanting for a long time now."

He just nodded hard and laughed when my very pregnant wife squeezed between us to hug him. I moved around them and grabbed Kinlee up in a bear hug, squeezing her tighter when her soft cries turned into sobs.

"You're going to be a great mom, Lee. You and Jace deserve this, and you'll be the best parents. Okay?" She nodded, and I kissed the top of her head. "Love you, Lee."

"Love you too, you big jerk," she said with a laugh and punched my arm.

She moved into Jace's arms, and he pulled her back a few feet as she tried to control her crying, and I wrapped my arms around Kamryn, bringing her back against my chest.

"What are you thinking?" I asked when I caught her staring up at me.

"That everything's perfect. And how so long ago, I didn't know how we would ever make it through the beginning. So many things seemed too hard to get past. Hiding our relationship, hiding from my family, trying to get your divorce finalized . . ." She drifted off. "I remember thinking that someday we would be done with all of that, and we would finally get to just live." Shrugging, she smiled up at me and placed my hands on her stomach. "I just realized we are."

Leaning down, I pressed my mouth against hers and whispered against her lips. "We're living our forever, Kamryn."

A Note from the Author

FOR SOME, THIS story touches on a very sensitive subject, and for others, I'm sure it's something that could be frustrating to read. But I wrote this story because I've witnessed it firsthand, and I knew others needed to hear the beauty of Brody and Kamryn's relationship. (I've changed their names here.) I won't lie to any of you. When I first found out about them—but before I had met them—I distinctly told my husband I didn't want to meet them. I couldn't believe people in their situation would even tell anyone, let alone would other people be okay with it.

And then I met them, and I got it.

Everything I'd thought about them changed in an instant. I said it that same night after meeting them, and I said it when I watched them finally get married almost two years later: I've never seen two people more perfect for each other than them.

I've heard their story countless times, I've cried with "Kamryn" over it, and I've watched them struggle just to be together and be happy. Do I support cheating? No. But I'll stand behind them and their relationship any day. I can honestly say, I've never been more genuinely happy to see two people finally start their forever together, and I hope you all can understand exactly why I wanted so badly to share their story.

Acknowledgments

THERE ARE SO many people I want to thank . . . my closest friends, the bloggers and readers who've helped me with promoting this book, my street team . . . but this book is very special to me, and there are a handful of people who definitely need recognition here.

My husband, Cory, thank you—always. But for this story? I have to thank you for introducing me to R & S. If it hadn't been for your incredible friendship/bromance with R, I would have never met them, and I would have never heard their story, and *Sharing You* would have never come about. Love you!

My agent, Kevan Lyon, thank you for actually allowing me to write this story. I will never forget our first conversations over this, but I'm *so so* glad you've fallen in love with their story as well! So much love to you for being the most amazing agent ever.

My editor, Tessa Woodward, thank you for being the one to push for this story and for being the biggest believer in their story. I love you! Thank you, a million times *thank you*!

AL Jackson, thank you for going through at least three different drafts of this story and understanding my need to write it and have it be a certain way. I love you, BB!

Last, but certainly not least, R & S. Thank you for letting me tell your story. Just . . . thank you! I've never met two people who were more meant for each other than you two. Hearing your story, and knowing what you went through to be together . . . I still get chills when I remember hearing your story for the very first time. I can honestly say that, other than my own, I have never been more moved by a wedding than by yours. If only for the fact that you two were finally starting your forever together and no two people deserved that more. Cory and I love you both!

About the Author

MOLLY MCADAMS grew up in California but now lives in the oh-so-amazing state of Texas with her husband and furry four-legged daughter. Her hobbies include hiking, snowboarding, traveling, and long walks on the beach . . . which roughly translates into being a homebody with her hubby and dishing out movie quotes. When she's not at work, she can be found hiding out in her bedroom surrounded by her laptop, cell phone, and Kindle and fighting over the TV remote. She has a weakness for crude-humored movies and fried pickles, and she loves curling up in a fluffy comforter during a thunderstorm . . . or under one in a bathtub if there are tornadoes. That way she can pretend they aren't really happening.

About the Author

Want more drama and romance?

Turn the page for a sneak peek at Molly McAdams's next book, *Letting Go*.

Prologue

Grey

"THEN OVER THERE is where the girls and I will be waiting before the ceremony starts," I said, pointing to the all-seasons tent just off to the side. "I think the coordinator said she'd get us in there when the photographer is taking pictures of Ben and the boys on the other side house, so he won't see me."

I glanced to my mom and soon-to-be mother-in-law talking about the gazebo behind me, and what it would look like with the greenery and flowers, and I smiled to myself. They'd been going back and forth on whether we should keep the gazebo as is, or decorate it, ever since Ben and I had decided on The Lake House as our wedding and reception site. And from the few words I was hearing now, they were still undecided. I honestly didn't care how it was decorated. I wanted to be married to Ben, and in three days, I would be.

"Grey, this place is freaking *gorgeous*. I can't believe you were able to get it on such short notice," my maid-of-honor and best friend, Janie, said in awe.

"I know, but it's perfect, right?"

"Absolutely perfect."

I grabbed her hand and rested my head on her shoulder as I stared at the part of the property where the reception would be. Ben and I had promised our families that we wouldn't get married until we'd graduated from college, but that had been a much harder promise to keep than we'd thought it would be. School let out for summer a few days ago, and we wanted to move off campus for our junior year . . . together. That hadn't exactly gone over well with my parents. They didn't want us living together until we were married. I think in my dad's mind, it helped him continue to believe I was his innocent little girl.

I'd been dating Ben since I was thirteen years old; the innocent part flew out the window over three years ago. Not that he needed to know that. After a long talk with both our parents, they agreed to let us get married now instead of two years from now.

That was seven weeks ago. Even though Ben had asked me to marry him last Christmas, we'd officially gotten engaged once we'd received the okay from our parents, and had started planning our wedding immediately. Seven weeks of being engaged. Seven years of being together. And in three days I would finally be Mrs. Benjamin Craft.

With how the last few weeks had dragged by, it felt like our day would never get here.

My phone rang and I pulled it out of my pocket. My lips tilted up when I saw Jagger's name and face on the screen, but I ignored the call. Putting my phone back in my pocket, I kept my other hand firmly wrapped around Janie's and walked over to where the rest of the bridesmaids were. My aunts and grandma had gathered around the gazebo-debating duo, and were helping them with the pros and cons.

"So what are we going to do tonight?" I asked, hoping to get some kind of information about the bachelorette party.

"Nice try." Janie snorted. She started saying something else, but my phone rang again.

Glancing down and seeing Jagger again, I thought about answering it for a few seconds before huffing out a soft laugh and ignoring the call a second time. I knew why he was calling. He was bored out of his mind and wanted me to save him from the golf day Ben and all the guys were having before the bachelor party. Normally I would have saved him from the torture of golfing, but today was about Ben. If he wanted to go golfing with all his guys, then Jagger just had to suck it up for his best friend.

Almost immediately after ignoring the call, I got a text from him.

Jagger: Answer the goddamn phone Grey!

My head jerked back when the phone in my hands began ringing just as soon as I'd read the message, and all I could do was stare at it for a few seconds. A feeling of dread and unease formed in my chest, quickly unfurling and spreading through my arms and stomach.

Some part of my mind registered two other ringtones, but I couldn't focus on them, or make myself look away from Jagger's lopsided smile on my screen. With a shaky finger, I pressed on the green button, and brought the phone up to my ear.

Before I could say anything, his panicked voice filled the phone.

"Grey? Grey! Are you there? Fuck, Grey, say something so I know you're there!"

There was a siren and yelling in the background, and the feeling that had spread through my body now felt like it was choking me. I didn't know what was happening, but somehow . . . somehow I knew my entire world was about to change. My legs started shaking and my breaths came out in hard rushes.

"I—what's happ—" I cut off quickly and turned to look at my mom and Ben's. Both had phones to their ears. Ben's mom was screaming with tears falling down her cheeks; my mom looked like the ground had just been ripped out from underneath her.

Jagger was talking, I knew his voice was loud and frantic, but I was having trouble focusing on the words. It sounded like he was yelling at me from miles away.

"What?" I whispered.

Everyone around me was freaking out, trying to figure out what was going on. One of my friends was asking who I was talking to, but I couldn't even turn to look at her, or be sure who it was that had asked. I couldn't take my eyes off the only other women currently talking on a phone.

"Grey! Tell me where you are, I'm coming to get you!"

I blinked a few times and looked down at my lap. I was sitting on the ground. When had I sat down?

Janie squatted in front of me and grabbed my shoulders to shake me before grabbing my cheeks so I would look at her instead of where my mom and Ben's were clinging to each other.

"What?" I repeated, my voice barely audible.

Just before Janie took the phone from me, I heard a noise that sounded weighted and pained. A choking sound I'd never heard from Jagger in the eleven years we'd been friends. The grief in it was enough to force a sharp cry from my own chest, and I didn't even struggle against Janie when she took the phone from me.

I didn't understand anything that was happening around me, but somehow I knew everything. A part of me had heard Jagger's words. A part of me understood what the horrified cries meant that quickly spread throughout every one of my friends. My family. Ben's family. A part of me acknowledged the sense of loss that had added to the dread, unease, and grief—and knew why it was there.

A part of me knew the wedding I'd just been envisioning would never happen.

Chapter 1

Two years later . . .

Grey

I DRESSED IN a fog and sat down on the side of my bed when I was done. Grabbing the hard top of the graduation cap, I looked down at it in my hands until the tears filling my eyes made it impossible to see anything other than blurred shapes. I knew I had to leave, but at that moment I didn't care.

I didn't care that I'd done my make up for the first time in two years and I was ruining it. I didn't care that I was graduating from college. I didn't care that I had already been running twenty minutes late before I'd sat down.

I just didn't care.

Falling to my side, I grabbed the necklace that hadn't left my neck once in the last couple years, and pulled it out from under my shirt until I was gripping the wedding band I'd bought for Ben. The one he should be wearing, but I hadn't been able to part with it—almost like I'd needed to keep some part of him with me.

The last year had been easier to get through than the one before it. I hadn't needed my friends constantly trying to get me to do my schoolwork. I hadn't needed Janie pulling me out of bed every morning, forcing me to shower and dress for the day. But exactly two years ago today, I'd been showing off the place where I was going to marry Ben. Completely oblivious to anything bad in the world. And Ben had died.

At twenty years old, his heart had failed and he'd died before he'd even dropped to the ground on the golf course. He'd always seemed so active and healthy; nothing had ever picked up on the rare heart condition that had taken him too early. Doctors said it wasn't something they could test for. I didn't believe them then, and even though I'd read news articles of similar deaths in young people, I wasn't sure if I did now. All I knew was that he was gone.

Heavy footsteps echoed through the hall of my apartment seconds before Jagger was standing in the doorway of my bedroom, a somber look on his face.

"How did I know you wouldn't have made it out of here?" One corner of his mouth twitched up before falling again.

"I can't do it," I choked out, and tightened my hold on the ring. "How am I supposed to celebrate anything on a day that brought so much pain?"

Jagger took in a deep breath through his nose before releasing it and pushing away from the doorframe. Taking the few steps over to the bed, he sat down by my feet and stared straight ahead as silence filled the room.

"I honestly don't know, Grey," he finally said with a small

shrug. "The only way I made it to my car and your apartment was because I knew Ben wanted this, and would still want it for us."

"He was supposed to be here," I mumbled.

"I know."

"Our two-year anniversary would have been in a few days."

There was a long pause before Jagger breathed, "I know."

I stopped myself before I could go on. Nothing I would say right now would help either of us, not when all I wanted to do was curl up in a ball on the bed that was supposed to be *our* bed, and give into the grief. I had to remember that today wasn't hard for only me. I hadn't been the only one to lose him. Ben and Jagger had grown up together; they'd been best friends since they were six. And two years ago they'd been in the middle of a conversation when Jagger had looked over at Ben because he hadn't answered, and watched as he fell.

"Jag?" I whispered.

"Yeah, Grey?"

"How do we do it?"

The bed shifted as he leaned forward to rest his forearms on his legs, turning his head so he could look at me. "Do what?"

"Keep moving on. I thought this year was easier, I thought I was doing better until this last week. And then today . . ." I drifted off, letting the words hang in the air for a few seconds before saying, "It's like no time has passed. It's like I'm right back where I was when you picked me up and took me to the hospital. I feel like my world has ended all over again. There are still some days where I don't want to get out of bed, but not like this."

"There isn't an answer to that. Even if there were, it would be different for you, for me, for anyone else who'd ever been in this situation. I get up and keep going because I know I have something to live for, and I know it's what he would want. I can't think about how I'll deal with the next day, I just take each day as it comes. There will always be hard days, Grey, always. We just need to take them with the good days, and keep living."

"I feel like it's cruel to his memory to move on," I admitted softly a few minutes later.

"No one ever said we had to move on, we just need to keep moving."

I met his gaze and held it as he stood up and turned, holding a hand out to me.

"You ready to move?" he asked, and the meaning in his question was clear.

"No," I replied, but still held my hand out. Slipping my hand into his, I let him pull me off the bed, and wrapped my arms around his waist, dropping my head onto his chest.

Jagger folded his arms around me, and brought his head down near mine to speak softly in my ear. "Don't think about next week, or tomorrow, or even tonight. Just focus on your *right now*. Right now we have to go to our graduation. Right now Ben would be flipping out because you would be making both of you late."

I choked out a laugh, and a deep laugh rumbled in his chest.

"And you would tell him?" His question drifted off, waiting for my response.

"To get over it and bet him twenty bucks that we would still beat you there."

This time his laugh was fuller, and he rubbed his hands over my back before stepping away from me. "Exactly. Then he would put an extra twenty on it, saying I would show up with fresh charcoal on my hands."

"And face," I added.

Jagger rolled his eyes. "That was one time."

"It was to your mom's wedding."

"I didn't like the guy anyway." I smiled and his eyes darted over my face before he held his hands up. "No fresh charcoal, and we'll show up at the same time. So no one wins today."

I took a deep breath in and out, and nodded my head. "I think I'm ready to move now."

"All right." He bent forward and grabbed my cap and gown off the bed before turning to leave the room.

I followed him down the hall and into the living room, pausing in the entryway only long enough to look in the mirror and wipe away the streaked make up. Once we were in his car, I touched his forearm and waited for him to look over at me.

"Thanks, Jagger. For coming for me, for talking to me—just . . . thank you."

He shook his head slowly once, and his green eyes stayed locked on mine. "Sometimes I need motivation to keep moving too. You don't need to thank me, just let me know when you have to talk about him, okay?"

"Yeah." Letting go of his arm, I sat back in the seat and grabbed the long chain holding Ben's wedding band on it. Taking comfort in the feel of it in my palm, and the knowledge that he would be proud of Jagger and me right now.

I MADE IT through the graduation without crying again, but I never felt like I was happy that it was happening. Even though Jagger had gotten me to a point where I'd been smiling and laughing, the second he'd left my side when we'd arrived, I'd fallen back into a state where I was constantly on the verge of crumbling from the grief of what today was. Only to be made worse when Janie had hugged me longer than normal, and then I'd seen my parents and older brother, and none of them had been able to force anything more than a strained smile and "congratulations."

Lunch afterward didn't prove to be much easier for anyone. One of my uncles mentioned the date and asked how I was dealing with it, and it had turned into some awkward hush-fest where everyone started kicking the other under the table, and giving them meaningful looks as if to say: shut the fuck up! For the next forty-five minutes, no one said a word. Not even a thank you to the waitress when she'd brought the food.

As much as I hated it, and as much as I loved my family, I was relieved when we'd said our goodbyes and my brother had driven me back to my apartment.

"You doing okay, kid?" he asked when he pulled into a parking space.

"Some days."

"But not today." It wasn't a question, he knew.

"Yeah . . . not today," I said softly.

"Do you want me to come up? I can hang out, crash here for the night, and head back tomorrow."

"No, it's fine. I didn't really sleep last night, so I'll probably go to bed when I get in there."

"Grey, it's four in the afternoon." He looked at me with either pity or sympathy, neither I wanted to see.

"Today was kind of rough, it felt like three smashed into one, and like I said, I didn't really sleep last night. I'm tired."

He was silent for a minute before he twisted in his seat to face me. "I'm worried about you."

I gritted my teeth and took calming breaths before saying, "You shouldn't be. It's been two years, I'm getting better."

"Are you?" he asked on a laugh, but there was no humor in his tone. "I knew today would be hard for you, there's no way for it not to be. But, shit, how much do you weigh?"

I jerked my head back. "What? I don't know."

"Do you look at yourself in the mirror? Do you see how you look in your clothes? You look like you're wearing someone else's clothes, and they're a size or two too big."

Glancing down at my shirt and skirt, I shook my head. "No they—well, I'm eating! You saw me at lunch, I ate half that burger."

"No, Grey. *I* ate half your burger. You picked it up and put it down at least a dozen times before cutting it in half, and then picking up one of the halves only to put it back down. I watched you. You ate two fries. Nothing else."

I tried to think back to the restaurant, but I couldn't even remember ordering the burger, let alone cutting it. I just remembered half of it was gone when the waitress asked if I wanted a box. I'd said no. As for the clothes, today was the first time I'd actually done my hair or make-up in years. I usually just put on clothes and left, not caring to see how I looked.

"Well, what do you want me to say, Graham? I'm *trying*. You have no idea how hard it is to lose someone who has been a huge part of your world for over half your life. Who has owned your heart for most of that. Who you were supposed to marry *days* before they passed! You don't understand what I've been through," I seethed, and wiped at my wet cheeks. "I finished school, I'm living, what more do you want?"

"I want you to live, Grey."

"I just said—"

"You're existing," he barked, cutting me off. "You're existing, *not* living. You're going through the motions you're supposed to without realizing that you're doing them, or why."

"That's not true!" I screamed. "You can't judge me based on what you've seen of half a day. A day that is a horrible reminder of what happened."

He grabbed my hand and squeezed, and when he spoke again, his voice was calm. "Kid, I'm not saying any of this *only* based off of what I've seen today. Janie's worried about you—"

"Janie? Janie?! You're having my friends keep tabs on me, Graham?"

"Grey—"

"How often do they check in with you? Huh? Do they only see me now so they can tell you how I'm doing? Because I don't see them very much, but, then again, who the hell would want to be around someone who is just *existing*."

"Grey!" he snapped when I opened the passenger door and jumped out of his truck.

"Screw you and your *existing* bullshit, Graham! I'm fine! I'm dealing the only way I know how, and I. Am. Fine."

I didn't care that I had tears streaming down my cheeks. I didn't care that I was overreacting. I was overreacting because I was terrified he was right, and I didn't want him to be. I was tired of everyone looking at me with sympathy or pity. I was tired of rooms getting quiet when I walked into them . . . *still*. I was tired of the way everyone seemed to walk on eggshells around me. And I was tired of feeling like I was giving them a reason to.

I took off for my building, ignoring Graham's voice as he followed me from his truck. Grabbing my keys from my purse as I ran toward my apartment, I fumbled to find the right key so I could get in there before he could catch up with me. The keys slipped from my hand, and I reached out for them at the same time I tripped out of my sandals and hit the concrete on my hands and knees.

Ignoring the spilled contents of my purse, I rocked back so I was sitting on my heels, and let my head hang as hard sobs worked their way through my body.

Two large hands grabbed at my upper arms to help me up, and I swatted at him. "Leave me alone, Graham!" I cried.

"Shh. It's okay," a deep voice crooned. I lifted my head enough to see Jagger before letting him pull me into his arms. "It's okay."

I pressed my forehead into his chest, and shook my head back and forth. "It's not. This day won't end, and the way everyone is looking at me or talking to me is making me feel like I'm failing."

"Failing?" he asked and tipped my head back, a soft smirk playing at his lips. "Hardly, Grey. I told you, you just gotta keep moving, and you are. You have been. You're strong, not everyone sees that because they're waiting for you to break. Just because they're expecting you to not be handling this doesn't mean you're failing."

"But they won't talk about him, they won't talk about what happened. Graham said I'm not eating, and I'm losing weight. He said Janie's telling him that she's worried about me. He said I'm just existing and going through the motions."

"Fuck Graham. He's wrong. He's not with you every day to see how you're improving." Jagger's green eyes bore into mine. "Your family hasn't seen you much this year while you've been getting better, so they don't know how to handle the situation— especially because of what today is and the fact that you are upset. He's your brother, he's going to be worried about you; but, Grey, don't let him make you feel like you're not doing better than you should be. Today is an exception. And he just happened to see you *on* an exception, all right?" His arms tightened around me, and he leaned back until he was pressed up against the wall. "You're doing fine, I promise."

He held me until I stopped crying, and released me when I pulled back.

"See? Fine."

Today was making me question everything; I didn't think I could agree with him on that. "What are you even doing here?"

"I thought you could use some company since it's an exception day, but I'm gonna go so you can spend time with your brother," he said, jerking his head at something behind me.

I looked over my shoulder to see Graham standing against the wall opposite us, his arms crossed over his chest, a strange look on his face. "How long has he been there?" I whispered to Jagger when I turned to face him again.

"The whole time."

"So he heard you . . ." I had the sudden urge to stand up for Jagger. Graham had hated him ever since we'd become friends when we were nine. But, then again, he hadn't really ever liked Ben until right before the wedding was supposed to happen, so it could have been an overprotective big brother thing.

"Yeah, but he knows I'm right." Jagger's eyes moved to look behind me, and one eyebrow rose in silent challenge, but Graham never said anything. "Go hang out with—"

"I don't want to," I said quickly, cutting him off. "I need to either be alone, or be with someone who knows what it's like to force yourself to keep moving."

He looked down at me for a few seconds before nodding. "Okay, let's go."

"We're not staying here?" I asked when he bent down and started shoving things back into my purse.

"No. You want to keep moving, Grey. We can't do that if we sit in that apartment all night."

I took my purse from his hand, and turned to follow him out of the breezeway, Graham behind us the whole time. Jagger opened the passenger door of his car, shutting it behind me after I'd slid in, and I met Graham's stare from where he stood a few feet from the front of the car.

Graham's hand shot out, gripping Jagger's arm as he went to pass him, and I opened the door—ready for who knows what. It's not like I could stop them if they went at it.

"Make sure she's okay," Graham demanded, his gaze hardened when Jagger ripped his arm free.

"What do you think I've been doing for the past two years?" he hissed. "She is okay, she's better than okay. Today sucks for her, but you can't treat her like she's made of porcelain because it's a bad fucking day. She needs to talk about him, she needs to talk about what happened. She doesn't need the way you all stood there at the graduation staring at her like you had no idea who she was."

"Do you see her?" Graham asked, getting closer. "Do you see how thin she is?"

"Yeah, I see her. I see her every day. She lost a lot of weight; she's also put on weight in the last few months. Give her some fucking credit, Graham. Don't just take Janie's word for it—Janie isn't around enough to give you updates on her. You want to know how your sister is doing, ask her yourself. Don't *tell* her how she is." Jagger didn't wait for him to say anything else; he stalked around the hood of the car and slid in to the driver's seat.

Graham looked like he couldn't decide if he wanted to stop me from leaving with Jagger, or if he was relieved I was leaving. When I shut my door, he put a hand over his chest in our silent *I love you*, and kept his eyes trained on mine until I put my hand over my chest as well; nodding once as Jagger backed out of the spot.

Jagger

I LET MY phone fall to the table, and sighed loudly as I rubbed my hands over my face. After driving around with the music blasting and windows down for a few hours, we'd come to one of the places we used to always go to before Ben died. They had live music on the weekends, and the best diner food in the area.

"Graham?" Grey guessed, and I grunted in confirmation.

"He just wanted to make sure you were okay."

"You haven't," she began, but paused for a few seconds. "Have you been giving him updates too?"

"Seriously, Grey? Your brother hates me; I didn't even know he had my number until a few minutes ago. Besides, if I had, he probably wouldn't have said all that shit to you, and your family wouldn't have acted like statues at the graduation."

"I heard you say something about that to him before we left. So you noticed it too, huh?"

"Wasn't hard to. My sister wanted to see you, but after we found you and saw the way they were all just staring at you, she was afraid to say anything."

"Charlie was there? I wish she had said something. I'll have to call her this summer, or something. I haven't seen her in forever." She frowned for a second before turning to look at the stage when everyone clapped.

I hadn't set foot in here in two years, and it felt strange, but good, to be in here again. Almost like I could see Ben sitting on the opposite side of the booth, right next to Grey. But just as soon as the memory hit me, it was gone. "Do you ever feel like he's disappearing?" I asked suddenly.

Grey's head shot up, her eyes wide as she took in my words. "What?"

"Ben. Do you feel like his memory is disappearing? Everywhere, all around us."

"All the time," she murmured and nodded absentmindedly for a few moments. "I forced myself to stop buying his cologne, and there are times I don't remember what he smelled like. When I realize that, I panic. I'm afraid I'll forget forever, and I want to go buy another bottle. But I know I can't, I know it'll just make it harder to move on. I don't—" She cut off on a quiet sob, and covered her mouth with her hand as tears filled her eyes. "I don't remember what his laugh sounded like. I don't remember the way it felt when he held me. I'm afraid to go back to Thatch, Jag."

"What? Why?"

"I don't want to see his parents' house and know that Ben's been completely erased from it."

I sagged into the booth and blew out a heavy breath. "Yeah, I'd forgotten about that."

Six months after Ben died, his parents had moved. Not just to another house, not just out of town. They'd moved across the country to get away. They hadn't been able to handle all the memories of Ben when their only child was now gone. And in a town the size of Thatch, there were memories everywhere.

I'd felt the same, but now I was in the same spot as Grey. I was terrified of forgetting him, and now I wondered if his parents regretted leaving.

"So what are you going to do?"

She blinked a few times, like I'd just pulled her from somewhere else, and after a few seconds she shrugged. "I'm still going back. The apartment here isn't much better. He's the one who picked it out, and all I ever think about when I'm in there is that he's supposed to be in there too. It'll be hard at first, but I need to go home. What about you?" Grey's lips curved up in a rare smile, and I felt myself smiling back at her until she spoke. "I always pictured you just taking off. No one has ever been able to hold onto you, and I feel like towns and cities are no different. I don't see you ever finding a place where you'll want to settle down forever."

Of course, you don't. My eyebrows pinched together, and I looked down so she wouldn't see anything she wasn't supposed to. There was truth to her words, and at the same time, she was so wrong. No one had ever been able to keep me because I'd only ever belonged to her. I'd dated a handful of girls in the first two years after leaving Thatch . . . if you could call it "dating," and had only ever had one girlfriend back home—and that had been in hopes that it would get a reaction out of Grey as much as it had been a distraction for me from the constant in-my-face relationship of Ben and Grey. If Ben hadn't died, and if they'd gotten married, leaving is exactly what I would've done. It was one thing to stay back, not saying anything to her, hoping one day she would see in me what I've seen in her since we were kids. It was another when I had to finally acknowledge she would never be mine.

But even though I wasn't sure she would ever get to a point in her life where she was ready to move on, there was no way I could leave her now. She wasn't mine, but she needed me. And I would be there for her as long as she did.

"So where do you think you'll go?" she asked, and I looked back up at her.

"Thatch," I said, my voice low and gravelly. "I belong in Thatch."

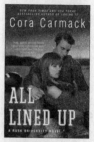

Available in eBook

Available in eBook

Available in eBook

Available in Paperback and eBook

Available in Paperback and eBook

Available in Paperback and eBook

Available in Paperback and eBook

Available in eBook

Available in Paperback and eBook

Available in Paperback and eBook

Available in eBook

Available in eBook

Available in eBook